The Imposter's Trail

J.C. FIELDS

~~~~

Any resemblance to actual people and events is purely coincidental.

This is a work of fiction.

Paperback-Press
an imprint of A & S Publishing
A & S Holmes, Inc.

ISBN 10: 1-945669-31-4
ISBN-13: 978-1-945669-31-6
~~~~

Dedication

This book is dedicated to the next generation:
Mikey, Chloe, Peyton and Alice.
Your presence gives me hope for the future.

# Acknowledgments

Everyone should have a passion. Mine is writing. My love of writing started in my teens, continuing through college. Lacking confidence in my abilities with a pen and graduating during a particularly difficult retrenching of the United States economy, I put my passion aside.

The passion was rekindled around the turn of the century when everyone thought Y2K would cause all life on earth to cease. It didn't.

During the years since I have made the acquaintance of numerous groups and individuals who helped accelerate my journey as a writer.

I tip my hat to the following:

The Springfield Writers' Guild. Before I joined, I was writing in a vacuum. No one was giving knowledgeable feedback on my prose. I remember the first piece I submitted to Mentor Hour, it was ripped to shreds. BUT, it helped me understand what I was doing wrong.

Wayne Groner, friend, mentor, and former newscast announcer, is a member of the Guild. He took me under his wing and assisted my growth as a novelist with the simple phrase, "It's over-written."

Kwen Griffeth is a fellow author, friend, and critique partner. His varied careers, including military and civilian police, have helped his development as a magnificent story-teller. He can read a chapter and tell me to move this part here and another part there. Suddenly the story flows.

To my editorial team: Emily Truscott and Norma Eaton. Emily handles the heavy lifting with developmental edits. Norma continues as my line editor and beta reader, tasks she has endured for all three novels. She fine tunes the manuscript and provides a first review.

Not sure I would have three books published without Sharon Kizziah-Holmes, owner of Paperback-Press. She believed in the project from the beginning and has been the publisher for all three novels. Thank you, Sharon.

Niki Fowler, a graphic artist extraordinaire, created all three covers and provided the *Trail* series with its unique look.

As with the previous two novels, I give thanks for my wife Connie. She keeps me grounded and reminds me there are other important events in our lives besides my books. She continues to be my best friend and partner in life.

Part 1

St. Louis, MO
Six Years Ago

Paul Bishop parked the rented Kia Rio next to the lake and stared across the water in the pale early light of dawn following another sleepless night. Geese swooped in, flared their wings, and one by one, gracefully settled on the calm water. On any other day, he would have marveled at the beauty of the sight.

He once again opened the white envelope addressed to his brother, unfolded his hand-written one page note, and read it for the twentieth time. A tear slid down his cheek as he folded the letter and returned it to the envelope. This time he sealed the envelope, then placed it on the passenger seat next to the Taurus Millennium G2 9mm and stared at the gun. Returning his gaze to the eastern sky, he watched as the sun peeked above the horizon.

Looking back at the pistol, Paul picked it up, placed the barrel under his chin, and without hesitation, pulled the trigger.

The sound echoed off the hills surrounding the lake,

startling several flocks of geese and ducks. Eventually, the clamor of their honking and quacking subsided and once again, the tranquility of early morning returned to the lake.

***

FBI Agent Sean Kruger stood in the middle of Paul Bishop's sparsely furnished living room. It was a small house located in the town of Wildwood, MO west of St. Louis. The house contained two bedrooms, a kitchen, laundry room, and one bathroom. Today the entire place was a beehive of activity, with members of an FBI forensics team and local detectives combing every room for clues about the owner. Referring to a small notebook, Kruger said, "Teri, can I ask you a question?"

Teri Monroe, lead technician for the FBI team, walked over. "Sure, what's up, Sean?"

"We've worked more than a few cases together over the years, haven't we?"

"More years than I care to think about." She smiled.

"Do you notice anything unusual about this place?"

She looked around and shook her head. "Nope. Looks like a man's house to me."

She looked back at Kruger. "Why?"

"It's unnaturally neat."

"We've seen it before." She shrugged. "The guy was a compulsive cleaner. Everything has its place, and everything's in its place."

Kruger shook his head. "The guy lived here twenty years. I don't see any pictures of family, friends, or pets. There's nothing personal in this house, absolutely nothing."

Monroe looked around the room and frowned. "Now that you mention it..."

Kruger checked his notes and continued, looking back at Monroe.

"There's nothing in this house identifying who the envelope is for. Just the name Randy. No last name. Who's

Randy?"

He frowned and paced the small room. "Did Paul Bishop strip this place clean before he took his life, or did this Randy person do it?"

He stopped moving and focused on Monroe. "I need answers, Teri."

"Shit." Monroe shook her head. "Okay, everyone gather in the living room. We have a problem."

Of the four technicians gathering evidence, three were women from the St. Louis FBI office, and the fourth was a young skinny man who arrived at the scene with Monroe. Monroe waited until everyone was in the living room. "Agent Kruger just made an observation, and I tend to agree with him. Before we arrived, someone may have been in this house and taken evidence. We need to step up our game and determine if anything is missing. You know the drill. Let's get to it."

They all nodded and returned to their tasks.

"Charlie, would you stay here for a second?" Monroe pointed at the tall skinny kid. "Agent Kruger, this is Charlie Craft. He's young and inexperienced, but someday will make an excellent forensic technician for the FBI."

Kruger smiled and shook the young man's hand. "Nice to meet you, Charlie."

The young man stared at Kruger while he shook his hand. "Uh… Oh my… I mean… Uh, nice to meet you, Mr. Kruger."

"The name is Sean." Kruger chuckled. "My dad was Mr. Kruger."

Monroe grinned, "Mr. Kruger, please show Charlie how you would look at a crime scene." She winked at Kruger and walked away.

"Charlie," Kruger looked around the room, "what do we know about the man who owned this house?"

"He committed suicide and left a note confessing to the four killings known as the Quarry Murders. That was your case, wasn't it?"

Kruger nodded. "The reason we're here. What else, Charlie?"

Charlie shook his head. "That's all I've been told."

"Exactly. We know very little about this man, except he owned this house free and clear. No mortgage. We know his name: Paul Bishop. We know he had one credit card with a zero balance. We know he had a cell phone because of a bill found in his mailbox. We also know he owned a computer because the house has a Wi-Fi router. But we haven't found a cell phone or a computer, have we?"

Kruger remained silent as Charlie looked around the room. "Maybe he hid them off-site, or possibly they were stolen."

Kruger nodded. "I prefer to think the former."

"Why?"

"Good question. I'll answer it in a minute. One other fact we know about our Mr. Bishop: he has a clean background. Never been arrested, not even a traffic ticket, nothing. He didn't exist in the criminal system until they found his body with the note. It's rare. Most people get a speeding ticket at some point in their lives, but he didn't."

Charlie's eyes didn't waver as he watched Kruger.

"So here we are in his home of twenty years. It should reveal something about Mr. Bishop, wouldn't you agree, Charlie?"

Charlie nodded.

"So why is this house not telling us anything about Mr. Paul Bishop?"

Charlie shook his head. "I don't know?"

Kruger smiled.

"I think our Mr. Bishop has a secret. A secret someone doesn't want us to know."

While the forensics team systematically searched Paul Bishop's house, local detective Barry Winslow tapped Kruger on the shoulder. "Sean, we found someone at home who says she knows Bishop. I think you need to talk to her."

Kruger nodded and followed the detective out of the

house. It was a picturesque neighborhood: a shady canopy of mature trees drooped over the street, with sidewalks on both sides of the road, nicely manicured lawns, and well-kept older homes. They turned to the south and walked diagonally across the street toward a house obscured by shrubs, flowers, and hanging baskets on the front porch. Alfonzo Cordero, another local detective, opened the door and introduced Kruger to the elderly owner.

"Mrs. Sellers, this is FBI Agent Sean Kruger. Agent, this is Norma Sellers."

Kruger smiled and offered his identification, which the petite woman examined with care. Though slightly stooped over, she stood barely as tall as Kruger's chest. He smiled. She probably didn't weigh as much as the German shepherd his parents used to own. Her silver hair was nicely done, and she wore a patterned dress accented with an open solid blue sweater. She handed his ID back. "I've never met anyone from the FBI."

"It just means I travel more than these detectives." Kruger smiled. "I'm basically here to assist them."

She returned the smile. "Can I offer you coffee, Mr. FBI Agent?"

"No thank you, ma'am."

"I offered these gentlemen coffee, but they turned it down too. You know, you remind me of my late husband. He was tall and slender just like you and a runner. Do you run, Mr. FBI Agent? Sorry, I've forgotten you name."

"It's Sean, ma'am. Yes, I run. What can you tell me about your neighbor, Paul Bishop?"

"Nice man. Friendly and always waved, a rarity in this neighborhood. After my husband passed, Paul always shoveled my driveway and sidewalk when it snowed. Never asked. He just did it. Wouldn't take a penny for his labors. He'd tell me he was already shoveling and got carried away. Then he'd laugh and continue shoveling."

Kruger nodded. "Do you know if he had any family?"

She frowned. "There was a woman living there when my

husband and I moved into the neighborhood, but she disappeared several years later."

"Did he ever mention someone named Randy to you?"

She shook her head "Not that I recall."

Kruger nodded and smiled. "Okay. What can you tell me about the woman?"

She was silent, tapping her right index finger on her lips.

"When we moved into the neighborhood, oh, I guess it was nineteen years ago, we would see her on rare occasions. She wasn't very friendly—kind of snooty, actually. She never waved or spoke. One day she disappeared, and we never saw her again. I thought it odd and was going to ask Paul about her. But my husband told me to mind my own business."

"Do you know if they were married?"

"Oh yes. Paul introduced her as his wife when we first met them."

Kruger looked up at the two detectives. Winslow nodded and left the house. Kruger returned his attention to Norma Sellers. "Did you ever see him with another woman?"

She shook her head. "No. Can't say I did. Bob, that's my late husband, always said he thought Paul was queer. You know, uh, didn't like women."

Kruger nodded. Cordero jotted something down in a small notebook, and Kruger asked, "Did he ever mention a brother or sister?"

"No. Now that you mention it, he never talked about himself. He would ask about our health and was concerned when Bob got the cancer." She paused. "I will never forget, he stayed at our house during the funeral—kept the burglars away, you know. They wait for people to die and then steal from them during the funeral."

"I've heard that." Kruger paused for just a few seconds. "What else can you tell me about Paul Bishop?"

After a long silence, she shook her head. "Don't you believe a word they're saying about him. He was a gentleman, respectful and considerate. Not many men left like that anymore."

Kruger talked to Norma Sellers for another twenty minutes but failed to learn anything else of importance. He thanked her and left the house with Cordero. Once they were off the front porch, Kruger said, "Let's see if Winslow's found anything about the mysterious Mrs. Bishop."

They found Winslow sitting in the passenger seat of a dark green unmarked Chevy Impala police car. The door was open, and Winslow was hunched over, holding his cell phone to his ear with his shoulder as he rapidly made notes on a yellow five-by-eight notepad. When they approached, he held one finger up. Finally, he spoke into the phone, "No, that's what I needed. Thanks, Sharon. I owe you."

He smiled as he looked up at Kruger and Cordero. "We didn't think to look at divorce records. Bishop wasn't married here. They were married out of state. The divorce papers were filed here."

Kruger titled his head slightly. "And?"

"Timeline doesn't jive with the story Miss Sellers told."

"How so?" Cordero asked.

"She indicated the woman disappeared a few years after they moved in. The divorce wasn't finalized until six years ago. That's a ten or more year gap."

"Maybe she was confused," said Cordero. "Got her times wrong."

Kruger shook his head. "No. Her husband died six years ago. She mentioned a long period without Bishop being seen with a woman. Her husband thought Bishop was gay."

Cordero nodded. "Yeah," he paused. "There is that."

"What was her name?" Kruger asked.

Referring to his notes, Winslow flipped back a few pages. "Court papers state her name was Brenda Parker Bishop. Petition states reason for divorce was abandonment. It was filed by Paul Bishop, and her maiden name of Parker was restored. He got the house, and she got cash."

Kruger frowned. "I don't suppose there is any mention of her current address."

Winslow shook his head.

"I didn't think there would be. Dammit. How many Brenda Parkers can there be? Six or seven million?" Kruger slapped the roof of the police car.

All three men were quiet. Kruger rubbed the back of his neck. "Where were they married? Does the petition say anything about that?"

Winslow referred to his notes and nodded. "Illinois."

"She might have gone back to Illinois. Or, she could still be here in St. Louis. I'll have one of the techs start searching for her there. Why don't you two see if you can locate her here?"

Cordero nodded and headed toward the driver's side.

Just before they drove off, Kruger bent down to look into the car. "Have we been able to determine where this guy worked?"

Winslow shook his head. "Not yet. None of the neighbors at home knew him. Apparently he kept to himself. He'd wave, but they never spoke to him. The neighbors on both sides of the house aren't home from work yet. Maybe we'll get lucky with them."

Kruger nodded and looked back at the house. Yellow crime-scene tape was stretched around the yard. A white forensic van was parked in the driveway, along with several black-and-white police cars. The crowd on both sides of the house was growing. Curious onlookers were scattered in various yards on both sides of the street.

Cordero leaned over from the driver seat and remarked, "How many of your neighbors do you two know?"

Winslow looked over at him. "Not many."

Kruger smiled slightly. "I know one."

CHAPTER 2

Wildwood, MO

An hour after the two local detectives left, Charlie Craft waved at Kruger. Kruger walked over to the kitchen table where Charlie worked. "Did you find something?"

Charlie nodded and pointed at the laptop. "I believe that's her."

Kruger looked at the screen; it showed a profile of Brenda Parker of Rockford, Illinois. Charlie pointed at the screen. "I hacked into her Facebook page. A week ago, Paul Bishop sent a friend request; so far, she's ignored it."

Kruger put his hand on Charlie's shoulder. "Nicely done. Have you ever been to Rockford, Illinois?"

Charlie shook his head.

"Me neither."

***

Brenda Parker lived in a quiet neighborhood in the southeast section of Rockford. The homes were small and older, with the occasional car parked on the street. Her ranch-style home sat at the end of a cul-de-sac and featured a triangular-shaped yard. A ten-year-old Oldsmobile Cutlass was parked in front of the detached garage, and Kruger parked the rental car behind it. He turned to Charlie. "Let's go meet the ex-Mrs. Paul Bishop."

As they approached the front door, it opened, and a woman in her mid-forties stepped out. "Are you the FBI agent that called earlier?"

"Yes, ma'am. Special Agent Sean Kruger, and this is Forensic Specialist Charlie Craft."

He opened his ID wallet, showed his badge and identification card. "May we come in?"

She nodded, and Charlie entered the house first. Her height barely reached his shoulders. She had medium-length brown hair with gray peeking out at the roots. The square glasses seemed an odd addition to her round face. They walked into the house while she held the door open. He noticed her eyes were red; Kruger guessed from crying.

Kruger's first impression of Brenda Parker's home was the stark contrast of her organized clutter to the minimalist furnishings of Paul Bishop's house. As he stood in the entryway, he noticed several cats scurrying for cover.

"I hate to be rude, but why do you want to talk to me about Paul? We were married for a very short time, a very long time ago."

Kruger stood in the living room and turned to look at the woman, who remained by the front door. Her hand still on the knob, as if anticipating she would be escorting them right back out.

"When was the last time you spoke to Paul?"

"As I told you on the phone, it's been at least six years. Not since he finally filed for divorce."

Kruger smiled. "Yes, I'm aware of what you told me." He looked around and continued, "Why don't we sit down? We have a lot of questions."

She took a deep breath, sighed, and walked over to a wooden rocking chair. After taking a stack of magazines off of the seat, she sat down and pointed at the sofa for Kruger and Charlie. Finally she spoke, "I'm not sure I can help you." She paused and sighed. "But since you're here, go ahead."

"Are you aware of what's happened to Paul?" Kruger paused, searching for anything noteworthy in her response.

"My sister called. She still lives in Wildwood. But I can tell you right now, he didn't kill those women. I assume that was the reason for your visit."

Kruger was silent. He looked at the woman for several moments. "Well, it was going to be one of my questions. What makes you so sure, Ms. Parker?"

"Paul Bishop was a gentle and kind man. He never physically hurt me during our time together. That was a little over eight years. We started dating our freshman year in college and married a year after graduation."

Even though his predetermined role in the interview was to take notes, Charlie looked up. "What changed, Miss Parker?"

She turned her head and focused on something outside the picture window next to her rocking chair. She wiped a tear from her eye. "I changed."

Kruger asked gently, "How so?"

She was quiet for a moment, continuing to gaze out the window. "A lot of things. Paul was a very shy man—brilliant, but shy. After we married, he struggled to find new clients." She sighed. "He only worked for one company, his brother's. He said it made him feel closer to Randy. But that wasn't the real reason."

Kruger raised an eyebrow, looked at Charlie, and then returned his attention to Brenda. "Randy? Who's Randy?"

She looked at Kruger with wide eyes. "You don't know?"

"No, we don't." Kruger shook his head. "A note we found was addressed to Randy, but it didn't specify who Randy was. All we found were a few tax records showing Paul as a self-employed independent computer consultant."

She stood suddenly. "That son of a bitch. Damn him. I tried to tell Paul, but he wouldn't listen."

Kruger leaned forward on the sofa. "What did you try to

tell Paul?"

"About his brother. He's the one you should be talking to. The man's crazy." She closed her eyes. "And sick."

Kruger and Charlie glanced at each other. Kruger returned his attention to Brenda. "Why don't you sit down? This is all new information to us."

Sobbing, she excused herself and disappeared into the small kitchen off of the living room. Several moments later, she returned with a small square box of Puffs. She took a deep breath and exhaled. She sat down in the rocking chair and dabbed her eyes with a tissue. "I've tried to forget Paul, but I couldn't. Every day for the past sixteen years, I've thought about him. Wondering what our life would be like together." She wiped her eyes again. "His brother was the real reason I left. The man scared me. He pushed Paul around and treated him like dirt. But Paul idolized his brother. Randy—"

Charlie looked up from his notes. "Randy Bishop?"

She shook her head. "No. That's what Paul called him. He insisted on being called Randolph. This was after he graduated from high school and left for Yale. Paul went to the Missouri University of Science and Technology at Rolla. That's where we met. I was a chemical engineering student, and he was in computer science. We met at a freshman mixer the first week." She paused and stared at a stain on the carpet. "He never dated anyone else that I know of."

She raised her head and stared out the picture window again. Kruger and Charlie remained silent. A minute later, she sighed. "Those were good times. I dated a few other guys but always went back to Paul. He treated me like I was the only girl he would ever love. I guess I was."

Low and soft, Kruger said, "Brenda, tell us, what did Paul's brother do that scared you enough to leave?"

Once again, she stared silently out the window, tears rolling down her face.

"After college I found a job in St. Louis with a pharmaceutical company and Paul started a computer consulting business. At first he did well, using contacts from school and leads his professors sent. But for some reason, after a while, the contracts dried up. Paul was too shy to pursue new ones. I know his brother had something to do with it, but I could never prove it. Anyway, Randolph's company started using him as a computer consultant. He was never an employee. But it was the only company he did business with. His brother told him it needed to be that way. Because of company policies, they couldn't hire relatives. Randy was a vice president of sales at that time and always told Paul he would make him an employee as soon as possible. Because he was an independent contractor, he received no benefits. Just another way Randy abused his brother."

She stood and looked at both of them. "I need a glass of water. Can I get either of you anything?"

Kruger and Charlie shook their heads.

After being gone for several minutes, she returned with a glass of water and sat back down. "We were married a year after graduation. It was to be a small ceremony, his brother was to be the best man. Randolph never showed up. A day later, he called Paul and said he'd been too busy. Paul was heartbroken, but he didn't complain. He just took the crap his brother dished out." She paused. "Sorry. I still can't believe he did that to his brother."

She sipped more of the water and continued to stare out the front window. "My job was going well, and Paul developed a steady income from his business. Things were good. We bought the house in Wildwood and made plans to start a family. Then one day, Randy came by the house unannounced. I never knew the reason, he just showed up. Anyway, he walked into the house, looked around, and immediately started yelling at Paul. He was appalled by our messy house, screaming how ashamed he was to call Paul his brother. He stormed back out, never telling us why he was there. Paul was manic. He stripped the house of everything except what was essential—no pictures, no decorations, no clutter, nothing."

She shook her head but stayed silent.

She waved her arm around the room. "As you can see, I don't live that way. We fought constantly after Randy's visit. I tired. I tried so hard." She paused and brought her fist to her mouth. "I tried to make him see how his obsession with satisfying Randy was affecting our marriage. When I told him I was leaving, he still didn't get it. Randy was manipulating him. Finally, six months after the incident I gave up. After packing a suitcase, I walked out the door with the few possessions I still owned and left. Deep down inside, I prayed leaving Paul would help him realize what Randy was doing. But it never did."

She looked straight at Kruger. "I've never stopped loving him. I waited, but he wouldn't go against his brother."

She was silent for a few moments.

"It hurt because Paul seemed more interested in his relationship with his brother than with me," she continued as her eyes narrowed. "A brother who never gave a damn about Paul."

Kruger nodded. "Why did it take so long to get the divorce?"

She took a deep breath, sighed, and shook her head. "Paul wanted to give me everything. I told him I only wanted a little money to help buy a house. I think he always thought I would come back. But I didn't. Six years ago, a company here in Rockford recruited me and I moved. He finally realized I wasn't going to change my mind and filed for divorce."

Kruger titled is head slightly. "When we first got here, you told us he didn't kill those women. How can you be so sure?"

"I was with the man for eight years," she smiled grimly. "I just know."

***

Kruger waited until they were heading back to the

Rockford airport before speaking. "What do you think?"

Charlie looked at Kruger. "She believes Paul didn't kill the women."

"She's the second person we've interviewed who's told us the same thing. Paul Bishop couldn't have done it." He paused. "I got involved with the case after the third woman disappeared, and the chief of police suspected a serial killer might be responsible. So he contacted the Bureau. Since I live in Kansas City, I was the closest profiler. The first thing I noticed was the timing of the murders. It was odd. Every two or three years. Most serial killers have a fairly discernable time gap between killings; this guy didn't. However, the women were similar; highly educated and professional. All but one was married and had families."

Charlie glanced at Kruger. "I don't remember hearing about them."

"I'm not surprised. The killings took place over the course of a decade. With so much time involved, the news media lost interest. But the chief of police didn't forget." He paused, checking traffic before making a right turn. "I've profiled a lot of serial killers over the years. Normally, those profiles produce leads, and we catch the guy. If Paul Bishop is guilty, I missed the profile by a mile. He just doesn't fit."

Charlie was quiet as he stared out the car's front window. "How was it determined they were killed by the same person?"

"All the women were killed in the same manner, and their bodies found in the same location."

"That could just be a copycat killer?"

"Except the pattern of the bruises on their necks matched exactly. Same hand."

Charlie whistled softly. "Do we need to go back to each victim and dig a little deeper?"

Kruger nodded. "I think we have to, we're missing something. Why don't you go back through the murder books? Put a fresh eye on them. My bet is we'll find something they all have in common."

CHAPTER 3

Wildwood, MO

Kruger sat in the conference room of the St. Louis County Police Department's sixth precinct in Wildwood two days later. Detectives Winslow and Cordero, Captain George Kenneth, Charlie Craft, and Teri Monroe sat at the table waiting for Charlie's report.

Charlie placed four files and a sheet of paper summarizing each one in front of him. He read from the first summary: "Nina Watkins, twenty four, disappeared on June first 2003. Her body was found in a lime quarry off Bussen Road in St. Louis. She was last seen leaving a friend's house on the way to an interview at a local CPA firm. She never arrived for the interview.

"Debra Riley was vice president of sales at Nixdorf Computers. She was thirty and disappeared on September 29, 2006. Her body was found in the same location as the Watkins woman. Her husband knew she was interviewing with another company, but she kept the company's name confidential and never told him.

"Julie Martin was thirty-five, married, with two kids. She was a senior vice president with Harmon, Harmon, and

Kinslow in their computer services department."

Kruger stopped doodling on his notepad. He frowned and flipped through several pages of one of his notebooks and interrupted, "Randolph Bishop is the CEO of Harmon, Harmon, and Kinslow."

Charlie nodded.

"Go on Charlie, tell us more about Julie Martin."

Looking back at his notes, Charlie continued. "She was in line to become an executive vice president of the company when she disappeared one night after working late..."

Winslow looked at Charlie and asked, "When did Bishop get promoted?"

Charlie opened another file. "The company profile says Bishop was promoted to executive vice president on…" He stared at the page for several moments, then looked at Kruger. "November 2009. Two months after Julie Martin was killed."

Cordero whistled, and Captain Kenneth said, "That's thin. Real thin."

Kruger nodded. "It's beyond thin; it's anemic. But it's the first link we've found. Charlie, keep going."

Charlie continued, "Martin's car was found in the parking lot of a high-end restaurant. Her husband called the police after she failed to come home. Something she'd never done before. Her body was found in the same location as Watkins and Riley. This was the event that brought Agent Kruger into the case in the fall of 2009. It was established all three women were killed by the same assailant. Trace DNA was found on the Martin woman, but the FBI could not match it to any sample in their database.

"In April 2011, the body of Karla Gray was found at the same location two days after she was supposed to have left on a business trip to New York City. Her itinerary indicated she was meeting with two of the managing partners of KKR, a private equity company."

Still looking at the notes in front of him, Kruger announced, "At the time of Gray's death, KKR was in negotiations to buy Harmon, Harmon, and Kinslow."

Charlie frantically started pulling papers out of the earlier files. After skimming each of them, he looked up. "Nina Watkins interviewed at Harmon, Harmon, and Kinslow two days before she disappeared. That's three of the women with a link to Harmon, Harmon, and Kinslow."

Kruger stared at Charlie. "I hate coincidences." He paused and looked at Kenneth. "Guess it's time I had a little face-to-face visit with Randolph Bishop."

Efforts to interview Bishop were met with resistance by his gatekeepers. After several days of stalling, Kruger contacted the Missouri Department of Revenue and was told the make, model, and license plate number of Bishop's car. That evening, he sat in his Ford Mustang in the parking lot of Harmon, Harmon, and Kinslow. A jet-black Cadillac CTS-V coupe was the object of his surveillance. At ten minutes after seven, a tall man wearing a dark-blue suit and a tieless shirt approached the parked Cadillac. Kruger started the Mustang. He waited until Bishop was in the car before driving and parking directly behind the Cadillac. Bishop was pinned in his parking slot. Kruger got out and walked to the driver's side window with his credentials in hand.

The window silently slid down and Randolph Bishop screamed, "What's the meaning of this? Who are you?"

Kruger held his credentials so that Bishop could clearly see. When Bishop reached for them, he pulled them back. "FBI Agent Sean Kruger. Mr. Bishop, I've been trying to arrange an interview with you for the last two days, but you're a hard man to reach."

"I've been out of town."

Bishop was clearly lying. Kruger's eyes narrowed. "Your staff wouldn't even let me schedule an appointment. Why is that, Mr. Bishop?"

"I make my own appointments. They don't know my itinerary."

"Ahhhh, no one knew your itinerary." Kruger's voice

dripped with sarcasm. "Okay, I'm making an appointment with you right now. I'll be in your office at precisely eight o'clock in the morning. If you're not, I'll hold you in contempt. Then I'll issue a warrant for your arrest. Does that spell out the seriousness of this, Mr. Bishop?" He turned to walk back to his car.

"I'll have my lawyer present."

"Good." Kruger looked back without breaking stride. "A wise decision on your part."

***

At 8:00 a.m. the next morning, Kruger and Teri Monroe were escorted to Randolph Bishop's office. Three men were in the room besides Bishop. An older man with silver hair sat in a guest chair in front of Bishop's desk. The other two men stood off to the side. They were younger, and Kruger assumed corporate security. The older man in the chair stood and offered his hand, saying, "I'm Tyson Ernst, Mr. Bishop's lawyer. May I examine you credentials?"

Kruger shook the man's hand. "You may look at them, but you will not examine them. If you need proof of my credentials, here's the number of Assistant Deputy Director Alan Seltzer. I report directly to him." Kruger handed the lawyer a business card, which the lawyer took and examined.

He nodded. "Very well."

Kruger continued, "This is Senior Forensic Technician Doctor Teri Monroe. She is the head of our forensics team looking into the death of Paul Bishop."

Teri nodded, but no one responded.

Ernst spoke first. "What can we do for you, Agent Kruger?"

"You can't do anything for me." Kruger turned and looked directly at Bishop. "I need to ask Mr. Bishop about his brother."

Ernst shook his head. "I speak for Mr. Bishop. I have advised him not to become involved with this matter."

Kruger looked back at the lawyer. "Really, that's not very good advice, counselor. In my world, silence is an indication of guilt." Kruger looked back at Bishop. "Is Mr. Bishop guilty of something?"

"Of course not," Ernst snorted with indignation.

"Then he won't mind answering a few questions about his brother."

Randolph Bishop removed his stare from Kruger and looked at the lawyer. Ernst nodded and sat down. "What do you want to know?"

"When was the last time you saw your brother, Mr. Bishop?"

Bishop glared at Kruger. "I haven't seen my brother for over six years."

"Have you spoken to him recently?"

Bishop shook his head. "The last time I spoke to him was on the phone over a year ago. He invited me to his home for Christmas. I declined due to a prior commitment."

"Did you have a strained relationship with your brother?"

"I'm a busy individual, agent. Time gets away from me. Our relationship was fine."

"But you haven't seen him in six years."

Bishop shrugged.

"A letter was found next to his body."

Bishop was silent. He continued to stare at Kruger.

"In the letter, he confessed to all four of the so-called Quarry Murders which occurred over the past ten years. The letter was addressed to you. Do you have any idea of why he would do that, Mr. Bishop?"

"Not a clue."

Kruger nodded. "I heard from the coroner that no one has inquired about the body. Aren't you his next of kin?"

Again, Bishop did not answer right away. He just glared at Kruger. "I will have someone in our legal department take care of those details. Does that satisfy you, agent?"

Kruger shrugged. "It makes no difference to me. I just

found it odd that his only brother did not inquire about the body."

Bishop looked at the lawyer. Ernst immediately stood. "I believe those are all the questions we will be answering today. Mr. Bishop has a busy schedule."

Kruger stared at Bishop, who in turn stared back. Neither man averted his gaze. After several long moments, Kruger gave the man a lopped sided smile, but did not divert his eyes. "Yes, I'm sure he does. Very well. I'll get back to you if I need more information."

Ernst escorted Kruger and Monroe to the office door. "Please direct all inquiries to my office, Agent."

***

Kruger was silent until he and Teri Monroe were back in his Mustang. She still looked at the building containing Harmon, Harmon, and Kinslow. "That was odd."

Kruger nodded. "Yes it was. He knows something or he wouldn't have lawyered up. I'm driving back to Kansas City today to do some research on our Mr. Randolph Bishop. What about you?"

She glanced at him as he drove. "I'm flying out on a 6 p.m. flight. Charlie will stay here and finish up. What do you think of him, Sean?"

Kruger smiled. "I'll be keeping my eye on him. He's going to be good."

She smiled and nodded. "I thought you might like him."

***

Kruger sat on a sofa in his condo on the second floor of a newly remodeled building west of the Kansas City Plaza. He was reviewing several reports sent to him by Charlie Craft concerning Randolph Bishop. He heard a key in the lock and looked up. When the front door opened, Stephanie Harris, his next-door neighbor and girlfriend, walked in. "Hi."

Kruger smiled and stood. "Hi, back. You hungry?"

"Starved." She walked over to him and they embraced. "Where do you want to go?"

After a nice dinner and a lot of conversation centered on catching up with each other's lives, they were back on the sofa in Kruger's condo. When a case puzzled Kruger, he would sometimes bounce ideas off Stephanie. "Maybe you can make sense of this. We found connections with Harmon, Harmon, and Kinslow to all four of the murdered women. Nina Watkins interviewed with the company two days before she disappeared. Debra Riley confided in a close friend that she was in line to be offered a position at Harmon, Harmon, and Kinslow—a position Bishop accepted a year later."

He paused and put his arm around Stephanie and she snugged against him. He smiled and continued, "Bishop was promoted to the position Julie Martin was given two months after her death. Karla Gray was going to KKR to discuss the CEO position at Harmon, Harmon, and Kinslow. She would be named to the position once they executed the buyout. The death of Gray caused KKR to withdraw their offer."

Stephanie looked up at him. "Do you think Paul Bishop killed them to help his brother?"

Kruger shook his head. "I think he might have done it after his brother told him to, but not on his own."

"What if Paul is completely innocent? What if Randolph killed those women?"

Kruger frowned. He stared ahead and was silent for several moments. "I've thought of that, but I can't get past why Paul Bishop would kill himself and confess with the note?"

She shrugged. "Maybe his brother told him to."

Kruger tilted his head to the side. He grinned and kissed the top of her head. "I knew there was a reason I liked you so well. You might have something there."

***

The next evening, Kruger's Mustang was parked next to Bishop's black Cadillac CTS in the parking lot of Harmon, Harmon, and Kinslow. Kruger was leaning against the trunk when Randolph Bishop walked to his car. At first, the man hesitated. Then he moved quickly to get around Kruger to enter his car. As he walked past, Kruger spoke. "Tell me something, Bishop. Was it your idea, or was it Paul's? My guess is it was yours."

Bishop stopped and glared at Kruger. "I've no idea of what you're talking about."

"Sure you do. You know exactly what I'm talking about. Was it Paul's idea to kill those women after you whined to him about them, or did you tell him to do it?"

Bishop glared at Kruger and, for a fraction of a second, Bishop's face showed the pure raw rage Kruger knew was inside him. Then just as fast, a mask of complete indifference was displayed. He turned to the door of the Cadillac and opened it. Just before he sat down, he turned to Kruger and in a very controlled voice said, "I'm going to call my lawyer and have a restraining order filed against you for harassment."

Kruger smiled. "Go ahead. You see, I'm not here. You're making this up." Bishop frowned and Kruger continued, "There are ten FBI agents in downtown St. Louis who will swear in a court of law I'm with them in a meeting."

Bishop glared at Kruger as he sat down in the car. His face crimson and his jaw locked tight. Kruger grabbed the door just before Bishop tried to shut it. "Here's the deal, I know who and what you are. I've dealt with scumbags like you for over twenty years. I'll find the truth, Bishop, and when I do, your world will become the worst nightmare you could ever image."

Kruger let go of the door and Bishop slammed it shut. He continued to stare at Kruger as he started the engine and backed out of the parking space. Kruger smiled as he watched him drive off. "I just saw behind your mask, Bishop."

***

At 8:30 the next morning, two St. Louis County Police Department patrol cars, one detective's car with Winslow and Cordero, and Kruger's Mustang were parked in front of Harmon, Harmon, and Kinslow. At 6:30 that morning, Charlie Craft received an email with the results of Paul Bishop's DNA analysis. Paul Bishop's DNA did not match the DNA found on Julie Martin. It was genetically similar, just not a match.

However, the analysis showed the DNA found on Julie Martin was close enough to be Paul Bishop's brother.

With that evidence, Kruger prepared a federal arrest warrant for Randolph Bishop properly signed by 7:45.

When the group entered the front lobby, Kruger could tell something was wrong. The reception desk was empty. Men with their sleeves rolled up scurried from office to office. Finally, a tall elderly man looking slightly disheveled approached the group. "Are you Agent Kruger?"

Kruger nodded.

"I'm Frank Netters, chairman of the board. If you're looking for Bishop, you're too late."

Kruger frowned, "How so?"

"He's gone. I just heard from one of our board members who went to find him. He told me the house is empty. Plus, there's more than five million dollars missing from the firm's four bank accounts. We think more is missing, but in the short time we've had to look, that's all we can find."

Kruger stared at the man. "I'll call our financial sector and have a team of FBI accountants here by afternoon."

Netters gave Kruger a grim smile. "Thanks. I'll tell everyone. Do you want us to stop looking?"

Kruger nodded as he pulled his cell phone out. He walked out the front door and made a call to the St. Louis field office. He ended the call and immediately dialed another number. His boss, Alan Seltzer at the FBI headquarters in Washington, answered on the second ring.

"Alan, it's Sean."

"How did the arrest go?"

"It didn't. He's in the wind."

Seltzer was quiet for a long time. "When did he leave?"

"Not sure. Sometime after 7 p.m. yesterday. I've got the St. Louis team checking the airports. We might know something later. I blew it, Alan."

"I doubt it. What did you do?"

"I was here last night when he left the office. I wanted to see his reaction when I asked him about his brother."

"And…"

"The tell, it was there, as plain as it could be. The uncontrollable rage before he could get it under control."

"What can we do at this end?"

"I want a national BOLO issued."

"Send me the details."

After the call, Kruger leaned against the trunk of his car. He pressed his palms against his eyes. "Shit."

***

Kruger met Brenda Parker at the St. Louis County Coroner's office. She arrived thirty minutes prior and was signing papers when he walked into the office. He waited silently while she completed the paperwork and thanked the clerk. She turned to him and offered her hand. As he shook it, she tucked her purse under her arm. "Thank you, Agent Kruger, for calling me."

"I thought you would want to know the truth."

She smiled. "I always knew the truth. Paul didn't kill those women."

Kruger nodded. "At first I believed he did, until I spoke with you in Rockford. Plus, we found Paul's computer and cell phone at Randolph's house."

"Oh, what did I say that changed your mind?"

"When you told me about Paul's reaction to his brother's visit to your home, I realized the control Randolph had over him."

A small tear formed in the corner of her eye. "Was there something on Paul's computer?"

"Yes."

She waited, but Kruger did not explain further. "Why did his brother treat Paul so badly? I don't understand."

Kruger half smiled. "The same reason he killed those women and looted his company. I can stand here and lecture about the psychiatric diagnosis for hours. But simply put, he doesn't have the ability to feel any guilt or empathy. All he cares about are his own needs. Randolph will do anything to satisfy those desires."

"Sad. So sad for Paul."

"Yes ma'am." He was quiet while he watched her wipe tears from her eyes. "What are your plans?"

She took a deep breath, sighed, "I'll take him home with me. After you called the other day, I contacted a funeral home in Rockford. I bought a double plot with a headstone. I'll be able to visit him often. When it's time, I'll be next to him."

Kruger nodded and remained silent, not knowing what to say.

Brenda Parker looked up at him. "I still love him, Agent Kruger. Always have."

Kruger suddenly realized Randolph Bishop claimed his first victim a long time ago. His brother's marriage. Finally, he gave her a sad smile. "We'll probably never know why Paul took the blame for his brother."

She smiled back at Kruger. "I know. All Paul ever wanted in life was for his brother to love him. All Randolph did was to constantly forget about Paul. It's that simple, Agent Kruger."

Kruger was silent for several moments and then just nodded.

Part 2

Present Day
Bangkok, Thailand

The Glock's barrel pressed hard against the Vietnamese man's forehead, leaving a discernible impression on the skin.

"Are you lying to me?"

"No, no, no, device inside suitcase, I place in plane like you say." He stared at the taller man, eyes blinking rapidly, his back to the wall of the tiny apartment's living area. The room was sparsely furnished and smelled of body odor, spoiled seafood, and urine.

"Why is the plane still flying?

The smaller man eyes widened. "I not know."

"You're lying."

"Not lying, earn money."

Randolph Bishop lowered the gun and stepped back. The man in front of him relaxed slightly, but kept his eyes on the Glock. Bishop asked, "Okay, exactly what did you do?"

"Like you told me, I wait until last minute to put bag on board. I shut baggage department door. Plane taxied away from terminal fifteen minutes later. No problems, all good."

He smiled slightly, still nervous.

Bishop looked at the man. "It's been almost four hours and there's no reports about the plane disappearing. Can you explain that?"

The smaller man shrugged, still staring at the Glock. "Maybe device not work."

"You'd better hope it worked."

"You pay rest of money now?" The baggage handler raised his eyebrows and grinned, displaying numerous missing teeth.

"No, not until I hear the plane went down. Then you'll get your money."

"I did what you ask. Not my fault device not work."

Bishop shook his head, raised the Glock, and shot the man in the chest. The Vietnamese man's eyes grew wide as he stared down at the blossom of red on his right breast. Eyes still wide, he looked up at Bishop as he slid down the wall to the floor. Bishop walked over to where the man sat and looked down with no emotion. The man on the floor stared up at Bishop.

"No, I don't suppose it would be your fault the device didn't work. But I don't want you discussing it with the authorities."

He raised the Glock again and aimed it at the now sobbing man's forehead. He shook his head and pulled the trigger. The sobbing stopped.

Looking around, Bishop found the two ejected brass casings and put them in his pant pocket. The dingy apartment only contained two rooms; it took only a few minutes to find what he was looking for. Hidden in a metal box buried under folded clothes in a foot locker, Bishop found the money. Thumbing the stack of bills, he determined it was all there except for a few hundred dollars.

Bishop glanced around to make sure nothing incriminating was left. Satisfied, he walked out of the apartment and shut the door behind him. No one opened their door as he walked down the hall. Neighbors knew not to be curious or react to gunshots in their building.

Outside in front of the baggage handler's apartment building, he looked up and down the crowded street. It was a shabby part of a modern, but ancient city. A part seen by few of the city's visitors. Private conversations were held in shadowy corners as street vendors hustled their wares and money exchanged hands for illicit goods or services. The din of activity made it hard to concentrate as Bishop walked west away from the baggage handler's apartment.

Several blocks later, the side street ended. He stood on the corner of a busy thoroughfare, looking for one of the thousands of taxis populating the city. He flagged one down. As he shut the door, he said in Thai, "No meter," and handed the driver a crisp United States hundred dollar bill. The driver's eyes widened and he smiled as the taxi pulled away from the curb.

"Destination?" asked the driver in heavily accented English.

Bishop gave him an address, then sat back as the driver negotiated the incessant Bangkok traffic. As the taxi crawled along, Bishop took a passport out of his inside jacket pocket. He opened it and stared at the name and picture: Everett Stewart from Sydney, Australia. The man was in his fifties, heavy set, with gray hair.

***

"How much to make changes to the passport?"

Arane, the only name Bishop knew for the forger, looked up from the magnifying glass. The passport, given to him by Bishop, was in his hand directly under the glass. The man's English was clipped with a heavy accent. "Ten thousand, US dollars." He smiled and stared at Bishop.

Bishop shook his head. "Too much, six."

Still smiling, Arane shrugged and handed the passport back to Bishop. "No can do. Take elsewhere."

Bishop folded his arms across his chest. "Seven."

Arane still held the passport, but pulled it back closer to his body. "Maybe eight, no less."

Bishop nodded. "How long before it's done?"

"I take picture now, you come back tomorrow."

Shaking his head, Bishop's eyes narrowed. "I'll wait."

The artist shrugged. "Could take hours."

"I'll wait."

"You steal passport?"

"The man's dead, Arane. Don't ask questions."

"I not care, just curious."

"It's not healthy to be curious."

Arane nodded, turned, and disappeared behind a curtain covering a door frame. A moment later he reappeared with a digital camera on a tripod, which he placed in front of a blue sheet hanging on a wall.

"Step over there, smile big." He pointed toward the sheet and Bishop complied, but did not smile. When the picture was taken, Arane connected the camera to a laptop on a cluttered desk. He opened the laptop and started.

As Bishop sat down in a chair and watched the man, his thoughts wandered back to how he obtained the passport.

Everett Stewart was waiting outside the gate for Malaysia Airline Flight 24, destination Sydney. At Stewart's feet sat a backpack with the man's passport and boarding pass half exposed in one of the pockets. Handy to get when his flight was called, but also easy to steal. Bishop nonchalantly sat next to the snoozing man and waited several minutes to make sure the man did not wake. He then bent over and pretended to tie his shoe. With one swift move, he switched his own passport and boarding pass for Stewart's.

Twenty minutes later, as Bishop watched the boarding of the doomed flight, he saw Stewart hand the boarding pass to the agent at the gate, never once looking at it. As the man disappeared into the jet bridge, Bishop smiled, turned and left the airport.

Four hours later Malaysia Airline Flight 24 disappeared over the Indian Ocean.

Three hours passed before Arane stepped out of the back room and handed the passport to Bishop. After flipping through the document he smiled. "Very good, Arane. Very good."

"You owe eight thousand US dollars." Arane held his hand out and grinned. "You pay big bonus for quick job, right?"

"Yes, Arane, I will pay you a bonus for your excellent work."

Bishop reached behind his back and withdrew the Glock. He pointed it at the forger and fired. The hollow point 9mm bullet pierced the skull just above Arane's left eye. His life ended before he realized there would be no more forging jobs to perform.

Bishop stepped over the body. "No good deed shall go unpunished."

He retrieved the laptop and digital camera, placing them in a black canvas bag he found next to the desk. After wiping down all the surfaces he remembered touching, he retrieved the brass casing ejected by the gun.

Looking around the room, he felt satisfied nothing remained to incriminate him. Walking to the door of the dingy office, he opened it and glanced up and down the dimly lit hallway. Seeing no one, he locked the door, pulled it shut, and casually left the building. Gunshots were common in this part of Bangkok. As with the baggage handlers neighbors, everyone knew not to be too inquisitive.

CHAPTER 5

Springfield, MO

Sean Kruger, Ph.D. and recent retiree from the FBI, read the paragraph for the third time, still not comprehending what the undergraduate writer was trying to convey. His six-foot frame leaned back in a squeaky desk chair with his scuffed brown loafers propped on an ancient gray metal desk. Grading the essay portion of the semester's final exams was challenging his alertness as his eyelids kept spontaneously closing. Taking his feet down, he concluded the one he held was hopeless. Giving up on trying to understand the student's logic, he placed the paper on his desk and circled the opening paragraph with red ink. As a final note of his frustration, he made several big question marks at the top of the page.

Putting down the pen, he removed his reading glasses, placed his elbows on the desk and leaned forward to press the palms of his hands against his eyes.

There was a knock on his closed office door.

"Come in, it's open."

Opening the door was a tall slender man in his late sixties. He wore a navy blazer, white button down oxford shirt, khaki cotton pants, shiny loafers, and boldly colored socks. He bore an uncanny resemblance to the actor Morgan Freeman.

The man smiled. "You look bored."

"I am. Grading final exam essays isn't exactly my favorite thing to do. Necessary, but that doesn't make it fun."

"Just give multiple choice questions. Easier and faster to grade than essays."

Kruger chuckled and nodded. "True, but you can't truly test a student's knowledge that way."

The visitor sat down in a straight-backed metal chair in front of Kruger's desk. "I remember a post-grad student, many years ago, who used to blow the minds of his professors with his essays."

"Urban legend."

"It's true. I read them before I started recruiting you."

Kruger gave his visitor a weak grin. "What brings you to campus, Joseph?"

Looking around the small gloomy basement office, the visitor chuckled. "Quaint."

"I don't need a large fancy office. I'm only here a few hours a day for students. Most of my work is done at home." Leaning toward the man sitting across from him, his eyes narrowed. "Again, Joseph, why are you here?"

"Should I call you Dr. Kruger?"

"You do, and I'll shoot you."

"Does that mean you still carry a weapon?"

Kruger smiled. "Only during class."

Joseph grinned at the comment, then his expression darkened. "We need to talk. But not here."

Looking at the small clock on his desk, Kruger started placing final exams in his backpack. "My office hours were up a half hour ago. Let's go grab a beer somewhere."

Twenty minutes later, the two friends sat in the back corner of a sports bar a few blocks from Kruger's house on the south side of town.

"So what's the big mystery we couldn't discuss in my office, Joseph?"

Casually looking around before he spoke, Joseph leaned toward Kruger. "Do you remember Roy Griffin?"

Kruger nodded. Roy Griffin was a member of the United States House of Representatives from a district south of San Francisco. Kruger and his team saved the congressman and his wife a year earlier from an assassin's bullet.

"Did you know he was drafted as a Senate candidate last fall and elected in November?"

"I remember reading something about it. Why?"

"His party is now in the majority, and he was named Chairman of the Homeland Security and Government Affairs Committee."

"Good for him."

"He's a rising star in Washington, Sean."

Kruger shook his head. "Too bad, I thought he was a good guy."

"He still is. The president likes him."

"Joseph, what are you dancing around? Get to the point."

They both stopped talking as a young waitress placed two beers on the table. Joseph thanked her and watched as she walked away. He turned back to Kruger. "I am. Stay with me. Do you know we found the Imam from San Francisco?"

Kruger's eyes narrowed, and his head shook slightly.

"He was found in Paris four months after you stopped the vans."

As he listened to Joseph, Kruger's thoughts returned to the last investigation of his FBI career. A year ago, almost to the day, he started searching for a group of individuals targeting rich businessmen. As it turned out, their actions were a diversion for a well-planned and highly sophisticated terrorist attack planned on the Walmart Annual Shareholders meeting in Fayetteville, Arkansas. Three vans loaded with explosives were sent to the Bud Walton Arena where the meeting was taking place.

"I didn't stop them, Joseph. I had a good team; they

deserve the credit."

"Everyone knows that, Sean. Your team is why two of the vans didn't reach their destination. But guess who stopped the last one before it could explode inside Bud Walton Arena and saving thousands of lives?" He paused for a few seconds waiting for his friend's response. When there was none, he leaned forward in his chair. "You."

The explosion almost killed him. With a new wife and adopted baby girl now part of his life, he retired to teach Psychology at a large university in Southwest Missouri.

"Where's the Imam now?"

"No longer a problem." Joseph raised his beer to his lips, but before taking a drink, said, "He had an unfortunate accident on a busy street in Paris. Seems he stumbled into the path of an oncoming delivery truck." He drank, then placed the beer mug back on the table. "I was told it was messy."

Kruger smiled grimly. "I take it he's the only one they've found."

"A correct assessment."

"Joseph, you and I both know more individuals were involved."

Taking another sip from his beer, Joseph nodded.

Raising his glass for the first time and taking a sip, Kruger looked over the rim of the glass. "I know I'm going to regret asking, but why are you telling me all of this?"

"Senator Griffin has been holding closed door inquiries about the incidents. No press. He would like for you to testify. No pressure, but the first time you can be in Washington, he would like for you to meet with his committee."

Kruger was about to take another sip of beer, but stopped. He sat up straight, frowned and stared at Joseph. "I've been retired from the FBI for a year now, Joseph. I wouldn't know anything new, therefore, there's no need for me to testify."

"Did you know Ryan Clark stayed with the Bureau?"

"Yes, we've kept in touch."

"Ryan testified about the two Washington, D.C., assassinations he investigated with the Alexandria PD. Your name came up."

"I was there as a consultant, nothing more."

"Clark gave details about how you two tracked Norman Ortega from St. Louis to San Francisco."

Kruger frowned. "Did he mention JR during his testimony?"

"No, I had a word with him before. Since Charlie Craft was working with JR at the time, he got the credit."

"Good."

"Do you know how many individual careers you helped advance with your investigation of that one incident?"

Staring out one of the plate glass windows, Kruger slowly shook his head.

"Paul Stumpf is now the director of the FBI, Alan Seltzer is the deputy director, Roy Griffin is a senator, Ryan Clark is an up-and-coming investigator with the Bureau, and Charlie Craft is now over the Cyber Branch of the agency. All of these advances came because of you."

Kruger smiled. "I didn't know about Charlie. Good for him."

"The only person who didn't benefit from your hard work was you."

"I did benefit. I retired."

"Why?"

"You know my reasons."

"They were the wrong reasons, Sean."

A dark mood swept over Kruger. He set his beer down hard and glared at Joseph. "You of all people know the sacrifices of devotion to career, so don't lecture me about my reasons. I never questioned doing the Bureau's bidding while my son grew up. During those years, I missed key events in his life a father shouldn't miss. Most people don't get second chances. I get one with Stephanie and our daughter Kristin. So if you don't mind, I'll not be repeating my mistakes."

Joseph put his hands up, palms toward Kruger. "Wrong

choice of words. Sorry."

Kruger gripped his beer with both hands and watched the tiny bubbles ascended to the surface.

"There were other options. Retirement wasn't the best one."

"I've been in facility meetings more enjoyable than this conversation, Joseph. What's on your mind? I've never heard you this vague, and we've known each other for thirty years."

Taking a deep breath, Joseph slowly let it out. "They want to expand my responsibilities, Sean. Your investigation last year uncovered a simmering problem the FBI, CIA, NSA and all the other agencies ignored for years."

"What's that?"

"Domestic terrorism. Not immigrants who come here to cause havoc. Terrorists who are born and bred here. Hell, they're US citizens. Congress is wringing its collective hands about changing gun laws, but that won't stop anything. We have to identify these people before they commit atrocities."

Kruger tilted his head to the side. "You've never told me what your real responsibilities are, Joseph. What responsibilities does the president want to expand?"

It was now Joseph's turn to stare out the plate glass window. "I've been a talent scout for the government for years."

Kruger nodded. "You're the reason I joined the Bureau. I know that part, what else?"

Hesitating, Joseph took a sip of his now warm beer. "The problem the United States has fighting terrorism is the separate functions of each agency. The FBI is for domestic problems, the CIA is for foreign ones, and the NSA can only listen. It's more complicated than that, but it summarizes the issue. The president asked me to take on a project last year after the Imam had his accident."

Not taking the bait, Kruger remained silent.

"Here's the part where you're supposed to ask me what the project is."

Kruger chuckled. "You're dancing again, Joseph. What

the hell are you trying to say?"

"The President of the United States wants an audience with you and me tomorrow at 4 p.m."

"Why?"

"He didn't go into detail. Roy Griffin will be there as well."

"JR is getting married this weekend, I'm not going to miss it."

Nodding, Joseph gave Kruger a slight grin.

"Trust me, we won't. I'm the best man."

CHAPTER 6

Washington, D.C.

It was two minutes before noon when Kruger, followed by Joseph, exited the plane at Reagan National Airport. It was the first time he had flown to Washington, D.C., in over a year. He was not sure what he felt, but knew it was not excitement. The summons to Washington was confirmed when the President's Chief of Staff called with an itinerary and hotel accommodations. It was Tuesday, and he was scheduled to be here until Thursday.

Joseph caught up to him as they made their way to the passenger pick-up area of the airport. "We have a ride waiting."

Kruger remained quiet.

"I'm glad you decided to attend."

Kruger shot Joseph an angry glare. "Just make sure we're out of here Thursday."

"We will be."

Staring ahead as they walked, Kruger nodded.

Joseph gave Kruger a grin. "You were bored and restless. Stephanie saw it, I saw it, even JR saw it. You've got to admit, JR doesn't normally notice those types of subtleties."

Kruger remained silent.

As they walked out of the terminal, Joseph spotted their ride, a black GMC Yukon Denali with dark tinted windows. He pointed toward it, and Kruger followed. Both put their overnight bags in the back, and Joseph slipped into the front passenger seat. Kruger got in the back. The vehicle started moving just as Kruger shut the door.

Joseph turned to the driver, a large man with bulging biceps, blond hair cut short, a deep tan from too much time outdoors, and mirrored Ray-Ban sunglasses. He was dressed in a dark gray business suit and when Joseph sat down, a small grin appeared on his face.

"Good to see you, Major. Thanks for the lift."

Major Benedict "Sandy" Knoll nodded. "My pleasure sir. It's always good to see you." He looked in the rearview mirror at Kruger. "Welcome back, Agent, glad to hear you're joining our little party."

Smiling from the back, Kruger ignored the implications of the last statement. "I haven't seen you since you left the hospital. How are you doing?"

"Wouldn't even know I got shot, except when it gets cold out, damn thing aches like a mother." Joseph brought Knoll in four years earlier, along with several other experts, to protect JR and his then-girlfriend Mia. During an altercation with one of the individuals searching for JR, Knoll was shot twice, and another man was killed. "I understand JR and Mia are getting married."

"This weekend."

"Good. Great couple. Glad we kept them out of the shit."

Smiling, Kruger nodded and stared out the window as they exited Reagan National Airport. Ignoring the conversation in the front seat of the Denali, his thoughts drifted back to his conversation with Stephanie just before leaving for the airport.

"Are you two going to be okay?"

"Sean, stop worrying. It's only for two nights. Kristin

and I will be fine. Besides, I'm already seeing a change in your demeanor."

Kruger stopped packing his overnight bag, turned and stared at her. "What do you mean?"

She chuckled. "After you decided to attend this meeting, you've had a spring in your step. Your old self is starting to come back out, don't you see it?"

He shook his head. "No, I don't."

"Well, you are acting different. Last night you slept all night for the first time in months. You walk just a little straighter and faster, like you have somewhere to go now. You're the guy with the PhD in psychology, and you don't see it. Amazing." Her smile lit up the room. He had not seen her smile that way for a long time. Or was it, like she told him, his perception was sharper, not dulled by the lack of anything mentally challenging?

His attention was drawn back to the present when Joseph spoke, "There's been a change in meeting locations."

"Where now?"

Joseph turned in his seat so he could look at Kruger as he answered, "First floor conference room at the White House, not the Oval Office."

"Thought there was only going to be the four of us."

"I know, but I just got a text from Senator Griffin. Apparently the President feels this is an important meeting, so he's called more advisors."

"Wonderful," Kruger's voice dripped with sarcasm. "How many people know we're meeting with the President?"

Joseph shrugged. "You know as much as I do."

***

For the second time in his life, Kruger walked into the White House for a meeting. After being dropped off by Sandy, he and Joseph were escorted to a conference room. Standing around the table were Senator Roy Griffin, FBI Director Paul Stumpf, CIA Director Dwight King, Director of the NSA Admiral Leland Berry, Secretary of Homeland Security Joanne Black, and the President's Chief of Staff, Bob Short. Pointing to two chairs next to Stumpf, Short said, "He's running about five minutes late. Not bad for a Tuesday."

Kruger stood next to Stumpf and shook his hand. Stumpf leaned close to Kruger's ear and whispered, "The President was glad you agreed to attend."

Before he could respond, Bob Short started introducing Kruger to everyone. Joseph was not introduced and called everyone by their first name as they shook hands. Another interesting factoid about Joseph, the man seemed to know everyone. With introductions out of the way, a door opened on the other side of the room and President of the United States Lawrence Osborne entered the room. Everyone remained standing.

With a disarming smile, the President sat down. "Thank you for coming everyone; please be seated."

The sound of scooting chairs and paper rustling permeated the room. While Kruger knew he should be nervous sitting in the halls of power, he was surprisingly relaxed. He sat back, anxious to see how the President handled all the egos gathered in the room.

The President looked over his glasses. "It's good to see you again, Joseph."

"Thank you, Mr. President."

The President cleared his throat. "I've asked all of you here to discuss a particularly troubling problem that has just recently been exposed. As we all know, Agent Kruger helped prevent an attack last year that could have been more devastating than 9/11. Your nation is grateful, Sean." The President nodded in Kruger's direction. "Since then, Director Stumpf and his agency, along with the help of Admiral Berry's group, have uncovered numerous plots by groups who seem determined to continue this mission. Most of these groups claim affiliation with overseas terrorists. ISIS has been mentioned, as has the various cells of Al Qaeda.

"With the assistance of Director King's CIA and Secretary Black's Homeland Security, we have prevented several smaller attacks from occurring. You are all to be congratulated."

Kruger smiled. Egos had been stroked. Well done, Mr. President.

The President continued, "However, I did not call you all together to break our arms patting each other on the back. We need to do more. It's the lone wolf, so to speak, that keeps me awake at night. The individuals who continue to defy detection. The man who showed up at a church prayer meeting and gunned down nine innocent citizens, and the five police officers killed in Dallas a while back come to mind. Not one of these individuals were affiliated with any known group. How do we stop them?"

The following discussion lasted more than forty minutes. The President listened, made notes, nodded his head occasionally, but remained quiet. Paul Stumpf spoke first. "Mr. President, it is my personal opinion we, as a collective group, need to step back and divorce ourselves from this task."

Everyone looked at Stumpf with a quizzical stare, but the President smiled slightly. Paul continued, "By no means do I mean abandon the task, but to put fresh eyes on it. We all know that if one agency is assigned this duty, it will become encumbered with our normal bureaucratic mentality. We can't afford that. The mission is too critical. Each of our respective agencies struggle to work together, even though we say we do. Assigning a joint task force won't solve anything either."

Everyone in the room shot fugitive glances at their counterparts and then nodded slightly. The President nodded. "I agree, go on."

"Therefore, I would propose the following: Assign this task to a new entity created specifically for the purpose of seeking out and monitoring individuals contemplating atrocities within our borders."

The President smiled. "Who do you propose this group

answer to?"

"You, sir."

Silence permeated the room, all eyes turned to the President as he doodled on the notes in front of him. Finally after several minutes of quiet, the President looked up and surveyed the room. "The idea has merit. However, the mechanics and funding would need to be ironed out before I give my consent. Do you have it figured out, Paul?"

Stumpf opened a tan nine-by-thirteen envelope and extracted a manila folder. He slid it across the table toward the President.

"This document outlines our proposal. Details on structure and funding are included. Each of the groups in this room will have a support role, but the new group will need total autonomy to function properly."

Osborne opened the file, scanned the documents briefly and nodded. "I like this. Work out the details and present them to Bob." He rose from the chair and everyone stood. "Would Senator Griffin, Joseph, and Agent Kruger follow me?"

Kruger frowned as he looked at Joseph and Griffin. Both shrugged. They followed the President out of the room through a door leading to the Oval Office. As soon as the door was shut, Osborne said, "Gentlemen, please have a seat."

Everyone found seats, and the President sat behind his desk. He placed his elbows on the surface and made a steeple with his hands and fingers. He pressed them against his lips and took a deep breath. "As you probably guessed, this meeting was more for show than anything else. Paul and I worked the plan out months ago. We just need the others on board." He paused for several seconds. "Which we do. Now comes the hard part. Senator, I need you to sponsor a bill that funds this group. It needs to be properly funded, but hidden. We can't have questions being asked at this time."

Griffin nodded.

The President looked at Joseph. "My old friend, Joseph,

has had a team of rapid response professionals assembled for several years. Not too many people are aware of it, but they have been dispatched to several hot spots around the globe over the years and have been quite successful. They will be the arms and legs of this new group."

He turned his attention to Kruger. "Agent Kruger."

"Yes, sir."

"I'm sure you're wondering why I keep referring to you as an agent."

"The thought crossed my mind several times."

Chuckling, Osborne continued, "Because you were never classified as retired. A slight of hand on my part and Director Stumpf. You were classified as taking a leave of absence. Your tenure is still in place, as are your benefits. I appreciate your assistance over the past year on the various projects I've sent your way. You've been most helpful."

"It was my pleasure, sir."

"You will be the head of this new group. Joseph has told me he would prefer to assist."

Joseph nodded.

Kruger stared at the President. "With all due respect, sir, I haven't agreed to come back at this point."

President Osborne nodded slightly, but retained his friendly demeanor. "True, but don't turn it down until you learn the details. I have a feeling you will find the position irresistible." The president changed the subject abruptly. "I understand you have a very competent asset in place that can assist with research."

Kruger shot a concerned look at Joseph.

"Relax, Sean," the President grinned. "Who do you think signed a pardon for his old identity? We'll start small and see how it goes." As he stood, everyone followed suit. "If you will excuse me, the ambassador from Spain has requested a meeting." He walked toward the door of the room and opened it. Before stepping out, he turned. "Make this work, gentlemen. I just hope we're not too late."

With this remark, he walked out of the room.

CHAPTER 7

West of Atlanta, GA

The home invasion occurred on the sixth day. Over the course of the first three days, the intruder tracked the comings and goings of the rural mansion intently, making note of who arrived and when. The structure was located in an upscale community on five wooded acres. Security was both electronic and structural. Cameras were spaced every hundred feet of the eight-foot wrought iron fence topped with electrified razor wire. The fence surrounded the property. A locked gate controlled by a keypad kept unwanted vehicles from entering the compound. The owner never left, and there were few visitors. A housekeeper arrived at exactly 7:30 in the morning and left before 5 each evening. UPS and FedEx trucks made regular stops, but they were required to wait at the gate for the housekeeper.

The only other activity was a contract landscaping crew that arrived on the fourth day of the intruder's observation. They arrived, punched in a code, and did their work. Afterward they left with no interaction with the occupants of the house.

On the afternoon of the fourth day, Bishop observed the

reclusive Stephen Blair walking in his back yard. Using a digital camera with a long telephoto lens, he snapped several pictures of the self-imposed hermit. The pictures allowed Bishop to make his final preparations for the next part of his plan.

The housekeeper was a middle-aged woman of Hispanic descent. She gained access each morning by touching the key pad at the gate and driving through after it opened. A five-car garage was attached to the west side of the mansion. As she drove up, the space next to the house would open, and once she parked inside, the door immediately closed.

Gaining access to the property from the surrounding land would be difficult, with the security cameras providing forewarning. The housekeeper seemed the best possibility for gaining entrance. On the evening of the fifth day, Randolph Bishop followed her home.

***

Stephen Blair was brilliant. His parents knew this, but also knew he had challenges. As a teenager and college student, the challenges were controlled with medication. During those years, the meds actually worked for Stephen. They allowed him to graduate with a master's degree before his twenty-first birthday and start a highly successful e-commerce company by his twenty-third. However, the pressures of running a multimillion-dollar corporation and the publicity of being a successful entrepreneur drove him back into seclusion. The meds could not overcome Stephen's new level of fear. He quietly turned the company over to his father and disappeared behind the walls of a newly purchased estate. Fifteen years later, he was still there.

Stephen was in the kitchen making coffee when Camila burst clumsily into the room. Not quite five feet tall and weighing less than a hundred pounds, she was no match for the six-foot tall Bishop, who shoved her roughly through the doorway. Her head snapped back as his hand pulled her braided ponytail, stopping her forward motion. Stephen saw terror in her dark brown eyes, but she remained quiet.

His gaze turned toward the tall man behind her. Stephen did not know much about handguns, but he knew one when he saw it. A large black pistol was pointed straight at the back of Camila's head.

With his fear of being seen temporarily overcome by his concern for Camila, he said, "What the hell's the meaning of this?" Looking at the man as he spoke, there was a sudden sense of familiarity. The man was several inches taller than Stephen. But the hair was the same dark brown and cut exactly the same. The man's green eyes were the same as the ones Stephen saw every morning in the mirror.

The man kept the pistol pointed at Camila. "Shut up and do what I tell you, or the woman dies."

"There's no money in the house, if that's what you're after."

The man shook his head and chuckled. "No, that's not what I'm after."

Camila stared at Stephen. "I'm sorry, Mr. Stephen, he followed me home…"

"Shut up," the intruder yelled. "Don't say another word."

As the gun pressed harder against the petite woman's head, she grimaced, her eyes shut tight.

Stephen wasn't crazy, but his disabling fear of anyone looking or staring at him caused people to think he was. To overcome this fear, he ran the company from the seclusion of his five acre estate in rural Georgia, just outside the western edge of Atlanta. Meetings with the management team were held via a secure video link, with Stephen's image blurred for everyone in the meeting. This system worked remarkably well, considering the challenges of dealing with a CEO no one ever saw. It worked well until the day Randolph Bishop pushed Stephen's housekeeper through the door connecting the laundry room and the kitchen.

With the initial shock of the confrontation wearing off,

Stephen Blair realized someone was staring at him. Perspiration appeared on his forehead, and he felt faint. He steadied himself by putting both hands on the kitchen countertop and took a deep breath.

Bishop smiled. "Still have scopophobia, don't you, Blair? Perfect."

Stephen let out a long breath and took another deep one. He didn't look at Bishop, but stared at a spot on the wall. "Who are you?"

Bishop laughed. "I'm you, Stephen. Can't you tell?"

Stephen forced himself to look closer at the man with the gun. There was a slight resemblance, not exact, but close. The man's facial features resembled a cross between his own and his father's. He stammered, "How?"

"The miracle of the internet and a remarkable, but now dead, plastic surgeon in Hong Kong. Isn't it amazing? The man did a better job than I realized. I thought I would look too old, but I can see you've aged."

Stephen's face contoured in comprehension. "You can't. No one will believe you're me."

"On the contrary, you're the ideal candidate. I'll make the perfect impostor. No one has seen you in almost fifteen years. Both of your parents are dead, and you have no brothers or sisters. The only people who know about me are you and Camila here." The man pressed the gun harder against the woman's temple. She cringed and let out a gasp.

"No. Leave Camila alone. She's done nothing to harm you."

"I have no intentions of hurting her. But from now on, she will be a permanent resident. Insurance, let's say, to keep you quiet while I learn about your company."

Stephen started shaking and his legs felt like they were anchored to the floor. He whispered again, "Who are you?"

"Stephen, it's not important for you to know who I am." The man's slightly jovial demeanor changed abruptly. His eyes narrowed and his tone lowered, "Stop asking."

Just as quickly, the smile returned. He lowered the gun.

"I need coffee." Looking at Camila, he pointed at a coffee pot. "If you're smart, señorita, you will stop crying and get me a cup of coffee."

Bishop leaned against the breakfast bar separating the kitchen and breakfast nook. He sipped his coffee and gazed at the two individuals sitting at a small dining table. Camila was still whimpering, and Stephen Blair studied the wood grain of the table top, perspiration beading on his forehead. Bishop set the coffee cup down.

"When do you talk to your management team, Stephen?"

"Not today."

Bishop leaned forward and slapped Camila aside the head. She screamed and cried harder. "Not the correct answer, Stephen. You have a video conference daily. When is it?"

Stephen shook his head, tears formed in the corners of his eyes. He closed his eyes as tears ran down his cheeks. He took a deep breath. "Ten this morning. It's 10 every morning Eastern Time, 9 for the Dallas office and 8 for the Denver office."

"That's more like it," Bishop nodded. "Now you will attend the meeting as usual this morning, and I will make sure you do not blurt out anything inappropriate."

"What are you going to do?" Stephen could not look at Bishop. He continued to stare at the top of the table.

"The señorita and I will be in the same room, listening. If you say anything at all about your current situation, she will die and so will you. It would be unfortunate for me, two years of planning down the drain. But if it's necessary, I will not hesitate to kill both of you. Do you understand the seriousness of your situation, Stephen?"

Stephen closed his eyes and nodded.

"Good." Bishop looked at his watch. "It's 8:30, we have some time to get to know each other better."

***

Forty five minutes after starting, the teleconference concluded. Stephen Blair had listened and offered few comments and no directions. The sight of Bishop holding a gun to Camila's head just out of view of the camera on Stephen's laptop, kept him subdued. As Stephen watched, the members of his management team gathered their papers and prepared to leave the conference room. The company's senior vice president, Thomas Zimmerman returned his attention to the camera. "Stephen, you've been unusually quiet this morning. Is everything okay?"

"Everything is fine, Tom. I'm just a little under the weather this morning."

"Very well," Zimmerman nodded. "Have you considered my proposal yet?"

Stephen shook his head. "No, Tom, I don't believe we have the funds to expand to the West Coast at this time. I don't wish to discuss it again." Instead of waiting for an answer or comment, Stephen ended his side of the conference by closing the lid of the laptop.

Bishop smiled. "Very good, Stephen. Both of you get to live another day."

***

Thomas Zimmerman was in his mid-fifties, with receding silver hair revealing more of his forehead than he liked. He was one of the original members of the management team put together by Stephen's father ten years ago. Now he was the number two man, answering only to Stephen.

He stared at the blank computer screen. "What that hell was that all about?"

Wendy Morgan, Vice President of Sales, stopped gathering her files and looked at him. "What did you say, Tom?"

Zimmerman shook his head. "I hope that wasn't a sign Stephen is getting worse. His last comment didn't make any sense."

She smiled. "You know Stephen…"

"I know, but this was way out in left field."

She frowned. "Okay, I'm not following you."

"I just asked Stephen if he had considered my proposal."

"Which one?"

"The one about bringing in a new therapist. She's had lots of success treating individuals with Stephen's condition. He was excited about it when we discussed it last week, but he wanted to think about it some more."

She remained quiet and continued to look at Zimmerman.

"His comment wasn't remotely related to the idea. He just told me we wouldn't be expanding to the West Coast. I've never discussed an expansion, because it's not necessary. Then he breaks the connection before I can correct him? That's not like Stephen at all."

Morgan sat back down at the table and asked, "Is he losing it, Tom?"

Zimmerman shook his head. "God, I hope not."

CHAPTER 8

Springfield, MO

Sean Kruger held Stephanie's hand as they walked into the hotel ballroom. The wedding was a small, private affair; a minister, the bride and groom, the best man, maid of honor, Stephanie, Kruger, and an elderly lady playing the organ in the small chapel. The reception was another matter entirely.

The din of hundreds of conversations met them as they entered. A band was setting up on the far wall, and two open bars were busy serving thirsty guests on opposite sides of the expansive room. Stephanie tugged on his arm. "Who are all of these people?"

Kruger smiled and shrugged. "Not sure. Joseph was the best man, he put this together. Let's find him and ask."

It took several minutes of maneuvering through the various groups of well-wishers, shaking hands with people they didn't know, exchanging hello's and how-are-you's. Eventually they found him. Tonight, Joseph was dressed in a tuxedo, instead of his normal khaki slacks, white button-down and navy blazer.

Kruger remarked, "I didn't think JR knew this many people?"

Joseph smiled. "You'd be surprised. JR's company is bigger than I realized. All I did was contact a few of his clients." He swept his hand across the air, adding, "This is the result."

"Speaking of JR, have the newlyweds arrived yet?" Stephanie asked.

Joseph shook his head and glanced at his watch. "They'll be here in a few minutes, just before the band starts playing. In the meantime, there are a few individuals I want Stephanie to meet."

He offered his arm. Stephanie smiled at the formal gesture, placed her hand on Joseph's elbow, and looked up at Kruger. "Don't wait up."

Kruger laughed and looked around the room as Joseph led Stephanie off into the gathering. Just as they disappeared into the crowd an old friend appeared at his side. "Let's go get a drink and step out into the hall. I need to talk to you."

Kruger nodded and followed. Alan Seltzer was a year younger than Kruger, although he looked ten years older. His short black hair was speckled with gray, and the lines around his brown eyes were more pronounced than Kruger remembered. Seltzer was the nephew of the man who just escorted Stephanie off to mingle with the guests. Joseph had been the person responsible for both men joining the FBI. They joined the Bureau at the same time and graduated in the same class at the academy. Seltzer moved into management, and Kruger remained in the field. During the last seven years with the Bureau, Kruger worked for Seltzer. Now as the first African-American Deputy Director of the FBI, Seltzer was in a position of power.

"So, what brings you to town, Alan?" Kruger sipped his glass of beer as he looked at his friend.

"I'm visiting my uncle."

Kruger grinned. "BS. Joseph goes to Washington on a monthly basis to see Mary. You two always have dinner when he's there."

Seltzer smiled and sipped his beer. "Busted. Okay, I

came to see you. I need to discuss something with you."

Kruger frowned, "What?"

"The director knows you have a special arrangement with the President of the United States."

"Not sure what you're talking about, Alan."

"I understand the confidentiality agreement. But I also know you've performed several tasks for the President, and he's been pleased with the results."

Kruger was quiet for several seconds as he scrutinized his old friend. "What did you need to discuss, Alan?"

"Do you remember Randolph Bishop?"

Kruger's eyes narrowed. "Yeah, what about him?"

"His brother's ex-wife was found murdered a week ago."

Kruger closed his eyes and took a deep breath. "Oh, no… What happened?"

"Good question. Local police were out of their league on this one. They asked the Chicago Bureau for assistance. She didn't show up for work one day, so her supervisor became worried. She'd never failed to call in when she was ill. Police were called and found her in her bed. I'm told it was bad."

"Raped?"

Seltzer nodded. "And more. I spoke to one of our techs who helped out. He's a twenty-year veteran, someone who's seen a lot. This one bothered him."

Kruger stared past Seltzer with a faraway look. "Her name was Brenda. Randolph had a hypnotic hold over his younger brother, Paul. The hold eventually broke up the marriage and Brenda moved to Rockford, Illinois, to get away from Randolph. After Paul killed himself, she took the body back to Rockford with her. Last time I spoke to her, she'd bought a double plot and planned on being buried next to her ex-husband—when the time came. Guess the time came sooner than she expected."

"I remember reading your report." Seltzer took a sip of his beer and continued, "Randolph embezzled how much money?"

"Somewhere around six million."

"That's right, six million. The guy just disappeared. He's still on the most wanted list."

Kruger nodded, his thoughts miles away. "Do they think Randolph killed her?"

"The prevailing theory is yes, but there's a slight problem."

Kruger refocused on Seltzer. "A slight problem?"

"Yeah, do you remember hearing about the Malaysia Airline jumbo jet that went down in the Indian Ocean?"

"Yeah."

"It's still missing, after months of searching."

Kruger nodded.

Seltzer sipped his beer. "When a plane goes down for suspicious reasons, like this one, our anti-terrorist division pours over the passenger manifest, looking for any known terrorist names or aliases. The passenger manifest listed a Randolph Bishop as a passenger. Since Bishop is still on the most wanted list, the name raised a red flag and was checked out further."

Kruger was now staring at Seltzer. "And…"

"One of the passports used to buy a ticket was for the Randolph Bishop who disappeared over six years ago."

"When did you find all of this out, Alan?"

"I got the report on my desk last Tuesday. I debated about calling you, but decided the right thing to do was fly out here and talk to you in person."

"I was in Washington, D.C. this week. You could have spoken to me then. You're not telling me the whole story, Alan. What else is wrong?"

"There were ten other Americans on the flight, the family of a State Department employee and a film crew for CNN. The plane had flown out of the Bangkok International Airport. Since it disappeared under suspicious circumstances, the Bureau also sent a team to investigate. They found something that's been kept out of the media coverage." Seltzer paused and drained the last of his beer. "I need another, how about you?"

Frustrated at the pause in the conversation, Kruger shook his head. "Dammit, Alan, finish the story."

Seltzer hesitated. "One of the baggage handlers for that particular flight was found executed in his apartment. Not murdered. Executed. One shot in the chest and another to the head from point blank range. The apartment was ransacked. Someone was looking for something. The agents believe whoever killed the baggage handler was looking for money, possibly money he'd paid the baggage handler for putting something on the plane."

"Sounds like a lot of speculation and few facts."

"The murdered man was seen placing a small suitcase in the baggage hold just seconds before it was closed. A long time after the other bags were loaded."

Taking a deep breath, Kruger stared at Seltzer. "Okay, you have my attention. What else?"

"Another passenger, an Australian named Everett Stewart, was returning to Sydney after a business trip in Thailand. He was issued a boarding pass, but never used it to get on the plane."

"People miss flights for lots of reasons."

"Mr. Stewart has never returned home."

Kruger said nothing keeping his attention on Seltzer.

"His passport was used to enter San Francisco two weeks ago. Brenda Parker was killed a week later."

Kruger stared at Seltzer for a few moments, and then turned his attention back to the door of the noisy reception. "What's the bureau's official stance?"

"Officially, we have no comment. We're still investigating."

"Unofficially, what does it believe?"

"The flight was brought down by something placed on the plane by the now-dead baggage handler. We also think someone traded places with Mr. Everett Stewart and used his passport to enter the U.S."

"Did anyone bother to check if Bishop's passport has been used since he left the country six years ago?"

"Yes."

Kruger chuckled, "Alan, are you going to make me reach over and shake the information out of you?"

"You're asking the right questions, Sean. His passport hadn't been used since he left the country. Then all of a sudden it was used to book a flight from Bangkok to Sydney. A flight that mysteriously disappears over the deepest water on the planet."

Kruger smiled grimly. "Bishop's back."

Seltzer nodded. "It would appear so." He paused for a few moments. "The Director feels the type of person who would deliberately kill over three hundred innocent passengers and crew members just to fake his own death is…"

"Sick? Psychopathic? Yeah, Bishop's all that and more." Kruger paused. "I'll have to clear any time away with the head of the Psychology Department."

"The Director told me about your new status."

"Great, who else did he tell?"

"Not too many, just me. We need you to fly to Rockford and review the crime scene."

Kruger shook his head. "Did anyone bother to discuss this with my wife?"

"Uh…" Seltzer paused for a moment. "No, the Director felt it was your responsibility to discuss it with Stephanie."

***

Stephanie Harris-Kruger was a petite woman, five-foot-five in her bare feet. She wore her naturally curly light brown hair down to her shoulders and resisted the urge to cut it. Their daughter would soon be older and hopefully not pull on it when she held her. Normally she wore her hair in a bushy ponytail, but tonight it fell gently down on her shoulders. At the moment, she was staring at her husband with her arms crossed tight against her chest.

"I vaguely remember the name. What's so important

about Randolph Bishop?"

Kruger stared out the glass wall opposite the ballroom entrance. "He's only fugitive to ever elude me during my twenty-five years with the Bureau."

"So, you want to run off and look into his return. Am I hearing you correctly?" She was unconsciously tapping her right foot.

He smiled and nodded. "Yeah, I guess you are."

She relaxed slightly. "How long will you be gone?"

"One night, maybe. No more than two."

She turned and stared out the glass wall, just like Kruger. Closing her eyes, she took a deep breath and sighed. "We'll be fine."

He turned to look at her. "Steph, I won't go if you feel strongly about it."

She shook her head. "No, I'm just being silly."

"You're not being silly. Besides, Alan offered to have some agents keep an eye on the house while I'm gone."

"No." She shook her head rapidly. "I don't need babysitters. We'll be fine. I'm not scared about you leaving, Sean. I'm worried about you getting hurt…again."

"All I'm going to do is look at the crime scene and talk to a few of the agents assigned to the case. That's all. There's nothing dangerous about viewing a crime scene."

"It is if this Bishop character is using it as bait. What if he killed this woman just to bring you back into the game? You just said he's a psychopath."

"He's also a sociopath." Kruger was silent for a few moments. "I hadn't thought of that."

"See, that's my point. You've closed your eyes and jumped into the lake without knowing how deep the water is."

"We don't have any positive proof that Bishop even killed her. It's all speculation."

"Now it's 'we.' Have you decided to accept the President's offer?"

"Figure of speech."

She smiled and put her arms around his waist. "You miss it don't you?"

He was silent for a long time and then hugged her back. "Yes, I do. I didn't realize how much until I went to Washington, D.C."

"Then go save the world. Kristin and I will be fine."

"I'll talk to Joseph before I go."

She nodded. "Thank you."

CHAPTER 9

Rockford, IL

Standing outside the yellow crime scene tape, Sean Kruger stared at the house. Little had changed in the six years since he stood in this exact same spot. The quiet neighborhood in southeast Rockford, Illinois, seemed stuck in time. Built in the sixties and seventies, the houses still looked comfortable and well-maintained. Brenda's fifteen-year-old Oldsmobile was parked in front of the detached garage, just like six years ago. The paint seemed a bit more faded, but the car looked well-kept and serviceable.

He ducked under the yellow tape and approached the front door of the bungalow. An old friend stepped out of the front door to greet him. Charlie Craft, with a broad smile and excited eyes, stuck out his hand. "Sean, damn, it's good to see you."

Kruger smiled while shaking it enthusiastically. "Good to see you too, Charlie. How've you been?"

Charlie raised his left hand and showed the slender gold band on his finger. "Married and happy."

"That's wonderful. How is Michelle?"

His face reddened, and he smiled mischievously.

"Pregnant."

"Congratulations." Kruger paused for a few seconds and continued, "Charlie Craft finally domesticated—I love it. I understand you're over the Cyber Division now."

Charlie nodded slightly. "Yeah, thanks to you."

"Your talent and knowledge got you there, Charlie. Never forget that."

Blushing, Charlie remained quiet.

Kruger's smile disappeared and he took a deep breath. "What's it like inside?"

Charlie shook his head. "Bad. One of the worst crime scenes I've ever seen, Sean. I'm here because you and I interviewed Brenda six years ago. We're hoping you can put fresh eyes on it."

Kruger nodded and put the cloth booties over his shoes Charlie handed him. He followed his old friend into the house. As he stood in the doorway, Kruger surveyed the living room. He remembered the organized clutter of the home. Piles of magazines neatly stacked in the corners of the room, clothes and towels folded on the sofa, storage boxes stacked against the walls. It was all still here, but now a chaotic mess, not the organized clutter he saw six years earlier. Stacks of magazines were scattered, books pulled off shelves, sofa cushions cut and ripped apart, and finally, the writing on the walls.

Charlie saw Kruger staring at the walls. "Yeah, it's written in her blood."

Kruger shook his head. "Let's see the bedroom."

"It's worse in there."

Kruger stood at the open door of Brenda Parker's bedroom. The body was no longer present, having been removed a week earlier. But the sheer violence of her death was still apparent. Photographs of the crime scene were pinned to the wall. They depicted the horror of Brenda's last hours of life. Writings on the wall remained, and Kruger scrutinized them. Systematically, he studied a photograph, then stared at the same location in the room. He repeated this process for each photograph, sometimes reviewing the physical room twice.

Finally after thirty minutes, Kruger spoke, "He's matured."

Charlie glanced at him. "Beg your pardon?"

Kruger stared at the empty room. "His needs have grown. His methods have evolved while he was overseas. My guess would be from experience."

"What do you mean?"

"He's not content to just strangle his victims anymore. The women in St. Louis were killed by strangulation. While he was overseas, victims may have been more plentiful and easy to find. He's become more violent." Kruger was silent, staring at the room. He closed his eyes. "He's studied anatomy somewhere. His temper is harder to control and what I am seeing in these photographs is pure blind fury. Also, what few inhibitions he may have had six years ago have completely disappeared."

Charlie stared at Kruger. "How can you tell, Sean?"

Kruger pointed to a particularly gruesome photograph. "He's made an incision similar to a coroner, although she was probably still alive when he started." Staring at the photograph, Kruger continued, "He's barely able to control himself when he kills."

Silence followed for a few minutes as Kruger studied the photographs again. Charlie finally broke it. "We were puzzled by the word Jezebel written on the walls. Any thoughts?"

His attention turned to the writings. Kruger gazed at each wall and sighed.

"In the Old Testament, Jezebel convinced her husband, King Ahab, to worship deities besides God. She was thrown out of a window and killed as punishment."

"We knew that, Sean. What we haven't been able to determine is how it relates to Brenda Parker?"

Nodding, Kruger turned to Charlie. "I saw the word in the living room as well. I'm guessing here, but it makes sense. This…" he swept his hand in the air toward the pictures, "was Brenda's punishment for trying to keep Paul from worshipping his brother."

Charlie's eyes grew wide, and he became more animated as he paced the floor. "Of course, now the word makes sense. But Brenda left Paul and moved here. I still don't see it."

Kruger smiled grimly. "Remember when she told us that Randolph came to their home one time and saw the clutter?"

Charlie nodded.

"Randolph threw a fit and screamed at his brother. He disowned Paul and shut him out of his life because of the way he lived. After that incident, Paul started pulling away from Brenda. Finally they separated. Randolph was avenging her attempt to corrupt his brother."

"So Randolph is back?"

"It would appear so," Kruger nodded. "Did you see the chess set in the living room?"

Charlie nodded again.

"Notice anything unusual about the set, other than all the pieces knocked over?"

"Not really, why?"

"All of the bishops are missing."

Charlie closed his eyes and shook his head.

***

The cemetery was huge. His first stop was at a small building just inside the entrance. An elderly lady in her mid-to-late seventies sat at a small desk with a computer screen. She looked up when Kruger entered and smiled.

"May I help you?"

"I'm looking for the grave of Paul Bishop."

She smiled and nodded. "How's it spelled?"

Kruger spelled the name and watched as her fingers typed on the computer's keyboard.

"It's in section H, third row." She pointed toward a large map of the cemetery hanging on the wall. "If you count twenty graves left of the driveway, that's his location." She smiled.

Kruger studied the map, thanked her, and walked back to his rental car. Five minutes later, he was staring at a headstone. The grass on the left looked undisturbed, normal for a six-year-old grave. The ground on the right side of the stone was bare dirt. Remnants of flowers, now withered and dry, lay scattered on top of the freshly closed grave. Brenda's date of death did not appear on the headstone.

He stared at the grave for a long time. "I'm sorry, Brenda. If I hadn't screwed up and let Randolph get away, you'd still be alive."

After several more minutes, he walked back to his rental car and drove to the airport.

Kruger sat in a chair outside the gate for his flight back to Springfield. O'Hare was busy as usual, and the flight was delayed. He sat fiddling with his smartphone, not really reading the emails, his mind racing.

Bishop disappeared over a week ago. Finding him would be, at best, difficult. He closed his eyes and rubbed his forehead with his left hand, the start of a headache making its presence known. As he sat there, his cell phone vibrated. He looked at the ID and quickly accepted the call.

"Hi, I was just thinking about you."

"I was thinking about you, too. When will you be home?"

Kruger looked at the display above the gate and sighed. "Looks like about an hour delay, probably somewhere between 8 and 9."

"How did it go?" Stephanie's voice was cautious.

"Pretty much like I anticipated. Gruesome and depressing."

There was silence on the other end of the phone for several moments. "What are you going to do, Sean?"

Kruger paused briefly. "I don't know, Steph. Guess I'm getting old, the lust for the hunt isn't there anymore. But I do owe something to Brenda Parker."

There was a momentary silence on the phone. "What do

you owe her, Sean?"

"I let the man get away six years ago. If I hadn't screwed up, she'd still be alive. I need to correct that somehow."

"You can't do anything about her death, Sean. You don't ever know if it was Randolph."

"Yeah, I do. It was him."

He heard a sigh on the phone. "Okay, sweetie, I'll have something for you to eat when you get home. We can talk then."

"I love you."

Stephanie replied in a cheery voice, "I love you, too." The phone went silent and Kruger stared at the blank screen. He smiled, his headache suddenly dissipating.

***

The plane landed at two minutes after 8. Exactly one hour late. Kruger grabbed his carry-on and headed toward the terminal exit. His car was in short-term parking, and he was out of the airport heading home before most of the other passengers received their checked bags. Halfway there, his cell phone rang. He glanced at the caller ID and accepted the call.

"Good evening, Alan."

"How'd it go?"

"I would agree with the Bureau's assessment. Bishop is back."

"Where is he, Sean?"

"How the hell should I know, Alan?" Kruger's voice conveyed his contempt for the ridiculous question.

"Sorry, wrong choice of words. Will you help us?"

Kruger kept silent for a few moments. "I don't know yet. Stephanie's not happy I went to Rockford. Right now the most important aspect of my life is her and Kristin. I'm really not sure I want to delve into the dark side of the human spirit again."

"Right, Sean. I know you. It's the hunt. Pure and simple, it's the hunt. You don't care about the dark side; you care about catching the fugitive. I spoke to Charlie Craft this afternoon after you left for the airport. He said you were in the zone, focused, you felt Randolph Bishop in the room. You need this, Sean. It's who you are. We, us, the FBI, need you to help with this one."

Kruger chuckled. "If I do this for you, you'll pull the same shit in a few months. Then it will be another monster you've found somewhere. No, Alan, I've sacrificed enough over the years for the Bureau. It's time to put my family and myself first for a change. Besides, I have other obligations I need to focus on."

"But you'll think about it, right?"

"I will think about thinking about it."

"Okay, Sean. I'll respect your decision, regardless if you decide to help on this one or not."

"Good night, Alan." Kruger ended the call before Seltzer could say another word.

As he turned into his neighborhood, he was overwhelmed by a sensation not felt in a long time. Pulling into the driveway, Kruger knew he would be involved in the hunt for Randolph Bishop.

CHAPTER 10

West of Atlanta, GA

Stephen Blair revealed the passwords for his computer and bank accounts just after midnight on the second day. Bishop felt generous; it only required cutting off two fingers from Blair's left hand to get the information. Armed with the correct letters and numbers, Bishop signed onto the morning Skype conference call with Blair's company. Doing the same as Blair, Bishop covered the computer camera, keeping his image unseen in the conference room.

Thomas Zimmerman started the meeting. "How are you feeling this morning, Stephen?"

Bishop responded in a low, hoarse voice, "Not well, I've a bit of a cold. I'll just listen this morning."

"Uh…" Zimmerman paused. Another unusual comment from Stephen. He shook it off. "Very well, we will proceed with the meeting."

Thirty minutes later, with all current issues discussed, Zimmerman said, "That's all for this morning, everyone. Do you have anything to add, Stephen?"

"No."

"Very good, thank you everyone. Uh… Stephen, could

you stay on line for a few more moments?"

"Yes."

"Good." Zimmerman waited until the room was empty and turned to the camera. "At our last meeting, Stephen, you responded to my question about the new therapist with a comment about expanding to the West Coast. Did I miss a memo from you?"

"No, I misspoke. Sorry."

"Ah, well, what do you think? She's had tremendous success treating individuals with challenges such as yours."

Bishop was intrigued. This could possibly change his short-term plans. "Tell me more, Tom."

"Excellent. She has agreed to meet you at your home at your convenience. If she's successful, maybe you'd be able to leave the house once in a while."

"When could she start?"

"Tomorrow, if you want."

"Good, set it up and email me the time." Bishop ended the Skype connection and sat back in his chair. His mind raced at the possibilities this presented. He stood and headed toward the stairs leading to the basement.

Bishop stood in the doorway staring at Stephen Blair. Blair was chained to a bed in one of the spare bedrooms located in the basement of the large estate. He was holding his heavily bandaged left hand in his right.

"I had my first solo conference call today. No one suspected it wasn't you."

Blair stared at him, his fear of being seen overshadowed by his situation. "Why should I care?"

"You'd better." Bishop smiled ominously. "Or the lovely Señorita Camila will be hurt."

"Goddamn you, she has done nothing to you."

Bishop's half smile evolved into a sneer, then with a snarl, he said in a low voice, "Yes, she has."

"What, for gawd sakes?"

"She's seen me."

Stephen stared at Bishop, speechless, the realization of

the finality of his situation dawning on him. He lay back down and stared at the ceiling. A small tear formed in the corner of his eye.

Bishop smiled again. "A therapist will be here tomorrow. She's going to start my road to recovery. Don't you just love happy endings, Stephen? I do, I just love them."

He chuckled, turned, closed the door to the room, and walked back upstairs.

***

Wendy Morgan walked back into the conference room and found Zimmerman staring at the blank conference room computer screen. "What's wrong, Tom?"

"I know Stephen has issues. We all do." He paused and turned his attention to the woman. "When his father was alive, we used to stop after work and have a few beers. Bill would tell me of the challenges presented by being the parent of someone like Stephen. The mood swings, the sometimes irrationality of his thought process, the moments of clarity when Stephen's brilliances shined through. But something has changed in the last few days. Did you notice it this morning?"

Wendy shook her head. "No, but you talk to him more than I do."

"I heard a very different Stephen today. His answers were short and cryptic. He's never spoken in short statements before. He either doesn't talk at all, or he doesn't stop talking."

"Maybe his meds aren't working again."

Zimmerman shook his head. "No…" Returning his gaze to the blank screen, "I'm sure everything is fine, I'm probably overanalyzing the situation."

She nodded and laid a quarter-inch thick file folder in front of him. "This is the proposal you requested. Go over it and let me know when you have time to discuss."

Zimmerman watched her leave the conference room. As

soon as the door closed, he stood and walked over to the door leading to his office. After sitting down at his desk, he dialed a number on his cell phone. It was answered on the third ring.

"Thomas, how nice of you to call. Have you heard from Stephen?"

"Yes, he's decided to see you."

Judith Day chuckled. "Excellent."

"How many visits will it take for you to declare him incompetent?"

"Several, I'm sure, but what's the rush?"

"He's changing again. Something isn't right. His meds may be losing their effectiveness again. I want to get this done before he's too far gone."

She laughed. "Well, I guess I'll have to rush my analysis. Why don't we discuss it over dinner tonight?"

Zimmerman smiled. "Yes, let's discuss it over dinner. My place or yours?"

***

Judith Day swirled the deep red merlot in her glass and watched the wine legs slide down the inside of the goblet. Her long black hair hung to the middle of her back, highlighting her oval face and crystal blue eyes. Well into her forties, she still possessed the body of a twenty-year-old, and she made sure men noticed.

"How long have you been planning this, Thomas?"

Zimmerman smiled. "It was actually his father's idea. Bill thought Stephen's condition would continue to deteriorate, and we would eventually have to have him declared incompetent. But before we could accomplish it, Bill had the heart attack and…" His smile disappeared, he frowned and looked at Judith. "If you think my intentions are less than honorable, you could be right. They're mostly aimed at self-preservation. Stephen controls the majority of our company's stock. He could get a wild idea someday and sell to the highest bidder, or he could decide to replace everyone in management. He has the power to do it. So far, I've seen no inclination he would go in this direction, but you never know."

Judith nodded and took a sip of her wine. "Having someone committed or declared incompetent takes more than the word of a psychiatrist; it takes a judge and a court order. My evaluation might be considered, or it might not be, depends on the judge."

"I know. The company's lawyer explained the process."

"What about the board?"

Zimmerman took a sip of his scotch and shook his head. "The board will follow my lead. I've already had conversations with several of them. They're also concerned about Stephen making a decision that could hurt the company."

Judith stood, picked up the small plates still on the table and walked them back into the kitchen. When she reappeared, two cups of coffee were in her hands. She placed one in front of Zimmerman and sat down. "Wouldn't it be easier to buy his shares?"

He looked at her and noticed two more buttons were open on her blouse. Staring at the exposed cleavage, he smiled. "It would be, but our lawyer says we can't buy them unless Stephen volunteers to sell them. The only alternative is to have him declared mentally incompetent and someone given power of attorney."

"And that would be you?"

Zimmerman nodded. "That's the plan, but a judge could appoint someone unaffiliated with the company. We were getting the paperwork ready, but Bill died before he could sign them. Now we have to go through the court system."

She leaned across the small table and placed her hand on his arm. "Maybe after I meet Stephen tomorrow, I'll have a better idea of his mental state."

"I hope so."

"Now, do you have to rush off or can you stay for a

while?" As she spoke, her left hand undid another button on her blouse.

Zimmerman watched and drained his last swallow of scotch. "I believe I'll stay."

***

Bishop stared at Camila's body. She expired too quickly for his tastes. Not like the women in Thailand. Those women were tough. Getting rid of the body would not be an issue. During his exile in Thailand, the process of ridding himself of a petite woman's body became routine. A newspaper story of the discovery of a missing man inspired him. The teen had been missing since 1976. His car was discovered in an Oklahoma lake, having failed to make a corner on a winding access road adjacent to the water. The perfect way to be rid of Camila.

He would drive Camila's car, with her in the trunk, to an estuary of the Chattahoochee River and roll it into the river. With luck, it might never be found, but if it was, he would be long gone. He would not tell Stephen about Camila until the final hours of the man's life. He smiled at the thought of seeing the look on Stephen's face when he learned about Camila.

CHAPTER 11

Springfield, MO

"I'm a little disappointed you didn't feel you could tell me I wasn't officially retired, Alan."

Alan Seltzer stared at the napkin he was folding and unfolding. He arrived in Springfield the night before to brief Kruger and Joseph on the details of the president's plan. Their location was the same sports bar where Kruger and Joseph met a week earlier. Their table was in a secluded part of the busy restaurant, and Joseph was in the men's restroom.

"We…" He shook his head. "I didn't want to have that conversation with you. I felt bad keeping it from you. But…" he sighed, "Paul thought it was the only way to keep you from losing your seniority when you came back."

"It was assumed I'd come back?"

Seltzer nodded. He continued to study the napkin in his hand.

Kruger smiled. "Thank you."

Seltzer looked up at his old friend. "I figured you'd be furious."

"I probably should be, but…" He chuckled. "I'm bored.

I like interacting with the students; it's the administrative work that bores me. Lately, it feels like that's all I do, admin stuff."

Joseph returned to the table. "Have you two figured out why you're not talking to each other?" He sat and crossed his arms, his brow pinched.

Kruger laughed. "Was it that obvious?"

Shaking his head, Joseph frowned. "The tension between you two has been on full display since Alan's arrival yesterday."

Both Kruger and Seltzer smiled. Kruger spoke first, "We're fine now, Dad."

Joseph chuckled. "Good, we need to get down to business."

The waiter appeared at the table and took their drink orders. They remained quiet while he was at their table side, except to order, and after he left, Joseph continued. He leaned slightly across the table and whispered. "NSA has agreed to allow JR access to their system. With conditions of course."

"How do they know about JR, Joseph?" Kruger's shoulders tensed and he stared at his old mentor. The humor of a few moments ago gone like mist in full sunlight.

Joseph raised his hand, palm toward Kruger. "Relax, Sean, they don't know who he is. They just know he's on my team. That's all I would tell them."

Taking a deep breath, Kruger let it out slowly, his shoulders slumped slightly. "Okay, what are the conditions?"

"He has to submit a report on everything he discovers."

Kruger's shoulders tensed again, and he sat up straight. "He won't agree to that."

"I know, I've already had this discussion with him. He did, however, propose a compromise."

"Not surprising."

"It was a typical JR solution. He'll use the access he's given to figure out how to circumvent their system, then create his own access. That way he can't be monitored. He'll use the access he's given with what he calls a zombie computer. They'll monitor the zombie. Since they won't be monitoring his real access, they'll never know what he's actually looking at. He tells me they won't be able to trace him either."

Seltzer shook his head. "Glad he's on our side. He can be scary sometimes."

The waiter brought their drinks and asked if they were ready to order. Joseph shook his head. "Please give us a few more minutes." The waiter smiled, nodded, and left to check on another table. "I agree, he can be scary. But he is ethical. He won't use anything he finds to his own advantage. No one in Washington understands that; they're afraid he'll use something he finds against them."

Kruger chuckled. "I have this funny feeling JR could bring the whole system down, and no one would know who did it."

Joseph half smiled. "Remember the four-hour interruption of trading on the New York Stock Exchange a few months back?"

Both Seltzer and Kruger nodded. Seltzer said, "Yeah, they blamed it on a software upgrade. Was that JR?"

"Yes. One of the companies JR consults for was working with the Exchange to upgrade their security. Someone in the company's IT department told him they succeeded in making the Exchange safe from hacking without his input. JR proved her wrong."

They ordered dinner, and the conversation turned to more mundane topics. After the waiter took the dishes away, Joseph swirled the ice cubes in his glass. "Sean, there's a reason you were named to head this new endeavor."

Kruger raised an eyebrow. "Oh?"

"I'm not getting any younger. I need someone available to take my place, should something happen."

Frowning, Kruger looked at his old mentor. "What exactly is that supposed to mean?"

"Just that someone needs to understand what I do and

be prepared to carry on. That's all."

"Does anyone, besides yourself, know what you do?"

"The President."

"Who besides the President?"

"No one, except maybe the Director of the CIA and Paul Stumpf. Lawrence Osborne will be the third chief executive I've served in my current capacity."

Neither Kruger nor Seltzer spoke.

"When the President asked you to do a few things for him while you thought you were retired, what do you think he was doing?"

Kruger shook his head.

"He was making sure you were the right person to take my place."

"What exactly do you do, Joseph?"

The older man smiled. "I help make problems go away. Actually I don't, but my team does."

"What type of problems?"

Joseph turned his drink tumbler clockwise, then he turned it counter-clockwise. "During the administrations prior to Osborne, my team was utilized mostly overseas. But since Afghanistan, the military has finally figured it out and increased the number of Special Forces personnel. Plus, they have improved their training. My team isn't needed as much anymore. However, Special Forces can't be used inside the United States. The Posse Comitatus Act prohibits the use of military force as a law enforcement agency. Since I was originally with the CIA, our, let's say, missions were always under their jurisdiction. We are and will remain independent. I answer only to the President. Because of the domestic aspect of our new mission, it was decided to bring in an agent with the FBI. You will officially remain an agent, but, like myself, you will only answer to the President."

Kruger stared at Joseph, his eyes blinking more rapidly than normal.

Joseph smiled. "That was why you were never officially classified as retired. It's also why all of the specialists with my team were transferred to the Coast Guard. Even though the Coast Guard is unaware of their status."

"Why the Coast Guard?" Seltzer spoke for the first time during this part of the conversation.

"Because the Coast Guard falls under the jurisdiction of Homeland Security and has domestic law enforcement capabilities within the United States."

"Very neat, Joseph, very neat." Kruger's frown increased. "Exactly what will this team do moving forward?"

Joseph looked Kruger in the eyes. "When JR finds a problem and local law enforcement is outmatched, or calling in the FBI would create a media circus, your new team will handle it. They will go in, take care of it and be gone. The team can be on the scene in less than four hours anywhere in the country. Usually a lot faster."

"What about the rights of the person we're concerned about?"

"That's one of the reasons you're being placed in this position. Your experience with psychotic criminals may help you determine if someone has the potential to walk into a crowded church and start spraying the faithful with an AR-15. You will be the individual who decides to send in the team. At that point, the situation will have deteriorated to where the individual or group of individuals has already forfeited their rights."

Kruger sat back in his chair. He looked at Seltzer and then at Joseph. He brought his hand up to cover his eyes. Shaking his head, all he could say was, "Ah… Geez."

***

Stephanie Harris-Kruger smiled. "I think you should do it."

Kruger was pacing. He stopped, shook his head slightly, and stared at her. "What?"

"I think you should do it. You'll be perfect."

"Do you realize what you're saying?" He paused briefly.

"I would have to determine if someone should be arrested or ignored. If I send in the team, someone could die." He stared at her and started pacing again. "Do you understand the consequences of that responsibility?"

She smiled. "I know you would agonize over the decision, and you wouldn't make it until you were certain." She stood, placed her hand on his chest to stop his pacing. She looked into his eyes. "I would rather see someone like you making those decisions than some faceless technician in a basement office somewhere in Washington, D.C."

He relaxed. "I guess…" He paused briefly, searching for the correct words. "Maybe I've lost confidence in myself."

She nodded. "Yes, you have. It's my fault. I've put a lot of pressure on you to not travel."

Shaking his head, Kruger hugged her. "No, that was my decision. I don't want to be away from you and Kristin." He grew quiet, turned his head, and stared out the window of their bedroom. "I missed eighty percent of Brian's childhood. Most fathers don't get a second chance. I'm not going to repeat the mistake with Kristin."

"Sean, I'm not going to let you repeat it either. But," she paused and smiled, "you are bored to tears with teaching. When you retired from the FBI last year, something changed. I can't put my finger on it, but you don't laugh as hard. You don't sleep well anymore and you don't jump out of bed with… I don't know, the enthusiasm you did when we first met. I've felt like a small part of you died when you retired. Does that make sense?"

Still staring out the window, he just nodded, but remained quiet.

"I've been a little selfish, too. I can deal with you traveling. I just don't like being away from you. When we both traveled so much those first years, I was miserable when we were apart. Even my friends at work noticed it." She stopped and hugged him tighter. "Don't worry, I'll remind you if the traveling gets out of hand. But I don't think you'll let it."

She fell silent and put her cheek against his chest. They stayed like that for several minutes.

He stopped staring out the window and kissed the top of her head. "Not sure what I would do without you."

CHAPTER 12

West of Atlanta, GA

Randolph Bishop stood at the library window and watched Judith Day get into her car parked in the circle drive of the mansion. His eyes were narrow, and his brow was furrowed. As the therapist's Audi moved forward and headed toward the gated entrance, he briefly thought about not allowing her to leave. The thought was quickly dismissed. Now was not the time to panic. When the car was out of sight, he headed down the stairs to the basement.

He opened the soundproof room where Stephen Blair lay dosing on a mattress. Bishop turned on the overhead lights and waited for Blair to stir. It took several minutes, but the groggy captive leaned up on one elbow and stared at Bishop.

"What do you want?"

"How long has Zimmerman been discussing having a therapist talk to you?"

"Don't know what you're talking about."

Bishop smiled grimly. "Are you sure you want to lie to me? Camila won't like it."

Taking a deep breath, Blair exhaled. "He started talking

about it several months ago."

Bishop ran toward the mattress and kicked Blair in the stomach. He screamed, "Why didn't you tell me? You fool, you've screwed everything up."

Gasping for air, Blair stared up at Bishop, but stayed quiet.

"She was here. She knows."

Blair shook his head and continued to gasp for air. In between labored breaths he said in a voice barely above a whisper, "Knows what?"

"I'm not you."

***

Judith Day nervously pulled out of the circle drive and drove to the front gate and waited anxiously for it to open. To her relief, it did. She drove straight to Zimmerman's luxury condominium in the Buckhead district and let herself in. After pouring two fingers of scotch into a glass, she downed it in one gulp. She sat at the kitchen table and pulled her cell phone out of her purse. She found the number she wanted and pressed the call icon. It was answered on the second ring.

"How did it go?"

She briefly hesitated. "I'm not sure. I've never had a therapy session quite like it."

Zimmerman was quiet for a few moments. "I'm not sure how to take that. What happened?"

"Well..." She didn't finish her sentence. "Let's say, he wasn't what I expected."

"How so?"

"He's on the edge. He's a volcano ready to explode. There's no way he has scopophobia. He's more psychotic than anything. He scared the hell out of me."

"Judith, you are a seasoned therapist. You've seen a lot of psychosis. What made this so different?"

"Not sure. His eyes got to me. They stare right through

you. I'm not sure how to describe them, but the word evil comes to mind."

"Judith, Stephen is a gentle soul, there is nothing evil about him. He has his challenges about being in public, but I've never heard him to say anything threatening or antagonistic."

"Tom, I did not detect one symptom of scopophobia. He looked straight at me the entire time, never sweated, wasn't short of breath and enunciated his words perfectly. He looks different from the picture you showed me. He looks ten years older and a lot heavier. It was…" She hesitated briefly. "Creepy."

"Should we be worried?"

"We should get the hell out of town, is what we should do."

Zimmerman was quiet for a long time. "You're exaggerating, Judith."

"No, I am not, Thomas. He has either lost it, or it was someone impersonating him, which I know sounds crazy."

"So you think we're too late?"

"I would say so. Thomas, I'm not going back. I will only see him in a professional setting with bodyguards."

"I doubt he will agree to that."

"Don't care. Those are my conditions."

"Very well, I'll see what he says in the morning during our call."

***

After the conference room emptied and Thomas was alone with the computer. "How did your therapy session go yesterday, Stephen?"

"You know exactly how it went, Thomas. You sent her to spy on me. She's no therapist. You're trying to have me declared incompetent, aren't you?"

Zimmerman took a quick breath, then calmed himself before he spoke. "Stephen, I'm not sure what you're talking about. She has over twenty years of experience."

"She's a charlatan, a fraud. I know what your plans are, Thomas. I'm way ahead of you. I've agreed to sell my shares to a private equity company. You'll be out of a job soon."

Zimmerman stared at the screen. Stephen's image was in shadows, but he could almost see the manic expression on the man's face.

"Stephen, the board of directors has to agree to any stock transfer, you know that."

"Not so, Thomas, I own fifty one percent of the outstanding shares. I can sell them without approval from anyone. It's a cash deal, and I'm not going to tell you when it will be finalized. For all you know, it might be tomorrow. What do you think about that?"

"I wish you would have consulted us. We might have found a way to buy your shares. You never mentioned an interest in selling."

Zimmerman heard a laugh that curled the hair on the back of his neck.

"No, Thomas, you would not have bought them. You were going to have me declared incompetent and stolen them. Your plan backfired."

The screen went blank as the connection ended. Sitting back in his chair, Thomas stared at the blank screen and put his hand on his forehead. Slowly, he pushed his hair back.

***

Bishop slammed the laptop closed. He stood and started pacing the mansion's library. His path took him from the desk to the picture window overlooking the circle drive and back. His breathing was rapid and uncontrolled. After several minutes, he stopped, placed his hands on the desk and leaned forward. After closing his eyes, the breathing slowed. It took several more minutes, but a calmness spread over him as he stood up straight.

He went back around the desk and opened the laptop. It

was time to finalize his transition to Stephen Blair and move on with his plan. Stephen would pay for his sin of forgetting to tell Bishop about the therapist.

***

"By the way, Stephen, I have some news for you."

Blair stared at the ceiling, and Bishop could not tell if he was cognizant or just ignoring him. The room smelled of unwashed male body, sour urine, and garbage. Plates with uneaten food lay strewn about

"Kind of stinks in here, Stephen. You should take better care of yourself." Bishop paused. No reaction from Blair. He continued, "It's amazing what one can do on the internet. Did you know with the right amount of money you can buy a car, have it delivered, and never leave the house? Amazing. Oh, by the way, you bought a Jeep Grand Cherokee this morning. They delivered it an hour ago."

Blair continued to stare at the ceiling.

"I have a few loose ends to tie up before I successfully take over your life, Stephen. Which means I need to be in and out for the next few days. Since there won't be anyone to take care of you..."

Blair turned his head slightly, his blank stare focused on Bishop.

"That got your attention, didn't it? You see, the lovely Ms. Camila isn't here anymore. She's at the bottom of Lake Lanier. Her car missed a turn and, well, she didn't make it.

A tear formed in Blair's eye and rolled down his face.

"I haven't decided what to do with your body yet. Would you rather be buried in the woods somewhere or join Camila in the lake?"

Blair returned to staring at the ceiling.

"You don't have to make the decision yet. We have a few days." He laughed, closed the door, and walked up the stairs.

***

Bishop parked the new Jeep Grand Cherokee in the Park Ride Lot A at Hartsfield-Jackson Airport. A shuttle bus delivered him, with his empty carry-on bag, to the north terminal. Without hesitation, he walked past the ticketing gates and headed toward the Sky Train. Ten minutes later he was showing his Everett Stewart passport and Australian driver's license to a young black female with mid-length tightly curled hair.

"How long will you be needing the rental car," she paused and looked at his passport, "Mr. Stewart?"

"At least two days, maybe three. Let's say three to be safe."

"Very well, I have a Toyota Camry available. Will that work?"

"Very nicely, thank you."

Twenty minutes later, Bishop left the airport property and headed north on I-85 toward the Buckhead district in northeast Atlanta.

CHAPTER 13

Springfield, MO

The nondescript three-story building near the resurgent downtown area was, at one time, an apartment building. Now, after being purchased by JR Diminski, it was a multipurpose building, housing his business and his residence. The first floor was utilized as reception, office space and storage. It was seldom used except for a receptionist who was only there during normal work hours Monday through Friday. She was JR's right hand and took care of everything businesswise, scheduling, billing, collections, and on the rare occasion when JR left town, his travel arrangements. Her name was Jodi Roberson. She was in her late-forties, round-faced, with nicely styled short brownish hair transitioning to gray, intense green eyes that missed nothing, and a perpetual smile.

The second story held the guts of JR's business; computers. The third floor was JR and Mia's home.

Kruger walked into the reception area from the parking lot. "Good morning, Jodi. How's the family?"

Jodi liked Kruger, and her smile intensified. "They're doing great, Sean. Grandson number one turns three this Saturday. How's that darling little angel of yours?"

"Growing and getting cuter by the day. Thanks for asking. Where's JR?"

She pointed up. "Second floor conference room. Joseph arrived a few minutes ago."

Kruger nodded and headed for the stairs. The second floor of the building was an open cubicle farm arranged around the numerous structural support posts for the building. On the opposite wall from the stairwell was a glass enclosed conference room. He could see Joseph with a coffee cup in his hand sitting across from JR. Stopping at one of the Keurig brewers JR kept outside the room, he chose a coffee pod and a mug. When the coffee was done, he stepped into the room.

JR was hunched over a paper file. Normally he would be hunched over a laptop or high-end computer keyboard, but not today. His laptop sat closed next to him. Kruger shook Joseph's hand and asked, "Is that the directive?"

Joseph nodded. "This is JR's first time to read it. He fussed about it being on paper." He grinned. "JR doesn't like real paper."

Without looking up, JR said, "Why kill a tree just so I can read something? That was the original concept for the computer. No paper."

"Who perpetuated that lie?" Kruger sat down next to Joseph.

JR looked up. "Do you see any paper scattered around the cubicles?" His hand swept the air toward the cubicle farm.

Kruger shook his head. "No." He took a sip of coffee as JR returned to his reading. Hearing a slight humming sound, Kruger looked around the room. "What's that noise?"

Joseph pointed toward several tiny speakers on the window ledges around the outside wall of the conference room. "Noise cancellation system. JR is using the same technology some luxury cars use to cancel outside noise. He claims it also prevents anyone from eavesdropping on conversations in this room."

Chuckling, Kruger said, "JR, no one is looking for you anymore."

Looking up again from his reading, JR removed his glasses. "So you say."

Shaking his head and turning to Joseph, Kruger took another sip of coffee. "How do we start this new endeavor you've gotten us into?"

"Good question."

JR closed the file he was reading and slid it over to Joseph. "As I told you before, I'm not comfortable using the porthole they're providing."

"I understand that." Joseph nodded. "Sean and I believe you should use the compromise you suggested. The only ones to know will be the three of us."

"Okay, then I'm good. I have an idea of how to start, if you're interested."

Both Kruger and Joseph nodded.

"I've been thinking we could start by canvasing Facebook and other social media sites."

"Won't that take a lot of resources, JR?" Kruger's expression was grim.

"No, not as much as you think. Since Joseph first approached me about this exercise, I've been thinking about writing a program to troll those sites. It's more complicated than it sounds, but that's basically what it does; troll."

"Troll for what?" Joseph asked.

"Keywords, pictures, hate speech, you name it. I would need guidance from Sean on the nuances for the program routine, but it could do it without monitoring."

Kruger pursed his lips. "I'd have to think about that for a while, but I can provide a start. What about the NSA data? It could be more beneficial."

"No problem there. I already have a computer sifting through it with a routine I wrote a couple of years ago."

The meeting lasted another hour as the three men finalized how to move forward. When it was over, JR said, "I know both of you think I'm too paranoid sometimes, but I just don't trust the motives of politicians. Are they setting both of you up for a fall?"

Joseph didn't reply. Kruger grinned slightly. "Maybe. But we have an ace up our sleeve."

Both JR and Joseph looked at Kruger. Joseph smiled and returned his gaze to JR. "You, JR. You're our hidden ace."

***

Joseph excused himself an hour later and left. Kruger made another cup of coffee and sat down next to JR at one of the cubicles. "Have you had a chance to look for Randolph Bishop?"

"Yeah, I haven't found anything since Everett Stewart went through customs at the San Francisco airport. He hasn't used a credit card or checked into a hotel. He just vanished."

"I was afraid he would. Bishop's smart and probably has plenty of funds available to him. He must have driven to Brenda Parker's house. Unless he has another alias, how did he get a car?"

"Fairly simple. When you buy a car from an individual, all you need from them is a bill-of-sale and the title. If there isn't a lien on the car, the title would be in the possession of the owner. It's the buyer's responsibility to register the car. In some states, the car's license plate stays with the car and other states with the owner. At this point, no one would know Bishop bought the car. He could have used Stewart's ID or another ID we don't know about. If he's paid cash for the car, gas, meals, and hotels, he'll be impossible to track. There are thousands of family owned motels across this country that love cash. They don't have to report it as income, so there is no record the individual renting the room was ever there. Very neat. I've done it myself."

Kruger furrowed his brow. "I know how it works. We know he was in Rockford at one time. I doubt he's still hanging around."

"I would agree. But from there he could have driven

anywhere."

Standing, Kruger started pacing. "Can you do the same thing on newspaper websites with this trolling routine as on Facebook?"

JR frowned. "Hmmm... Hadn't thought of that. What would we be looking for?"

"When Bishop kills, he does it viciously. He leaves a signature. In St. Louis, the four women were strangled and left nude in the same rock quarry. Brenda Parker's was a ritual killing. Bishop left biblical references written on the wall in Brenda's blood. I would think if you started the routine looking for vicious unsolved murders that occurred since his arrival, it might be a starting place."

"Hmmm…" JR stared at his computer screen for several moments. "Yeah, it's a start, Sean. I can set the routine to monitor all of the major news services and all of the newsprint groups."

Kruger was quiet for several minutes. "JR, he's back for a reason. I don't think it was to kill Brenda Parker, either. He has something else planned."

"Yeah, but what?"

Shaking his head slightly, Kruger sighed. "I wish I knew."

CHAPTER 14

Chicago, IL

Bassel Safar knelt on his prayer rug facing the east. An app on his cell phone reminded him of Fajr, morning prayers. Bassel was new to Islam, having been drawn to the faith while serving as a supply sergeant in Bagdad before the American withdrawal in 2011. He was 21 at the time.

His father, Ahmad Safar, and mother, Nona, were Coptic Orthodox Christians living in Egypt. Ahmad was a professor of religious studies at the American University in Cairo and Nona a legal secretary at a large legal office specializing in business consulting for importers. When Ahmad was offered a tenured position at the University of Chicago, they left their beloved Egypt in 1985 to escape the increasing violence toward Christians by Islamic fundamentalists.

Their dream of becoming naturalized citizens was realized in November of 1989. Bassel was born the following January. Growing up, he was known as Barry. Despite the cultural diversity surrounding his father's occupation, Barry felt isolated as he grew into his teenage years. Shy and withdrawn, he had few friends and made little effort to make new ones. During his freshman year at the University of Chicago, his parents were killed by a drunk driver one night on their way home from a reception for a new professor at the university.

His world collapsed. Without a family support system and resources, he withdrew from school and joined the Army.

On his return to the states, he started using the name Bassel again, finding it better suited his new-found pride in being from Egypt. The Army allowed him to understand who he was without the influence of his parents constantly reminding him he was an American citizen and to embrace their adopted country. He refused to ignore his heritage. He wanted to understand its culture and religion. Since Egypt was mostly Sunnis Muslims, he embraced their interpretation of Islam.

His experience in Iraq also gave him another gift: a seething hatred of American society.

On July 20, 2012 James Holmes, wearing a Blackhawk Urban Assault Vest and carrying a Smith & Wesson M&P 15 rifle, a Remington 870 Express Tactical shotgun and a Glock 22, entered a Century 16 movie theater. When he was done, twelve movie-goers were dead, and seventy others were wounded. Bassel absorbed every word he could find about James Holmes, studied where he made mistakes and followed his trial in detail.

On the day James Holmes was sentenced to twelve life sentences, plus 3,300 years, in prison, Bassel started making plans.

***

"The file you need to see is on this thumb drive."

JR handed the small storage unit to Kruger. He slipped it into a USB port on his laptop and clicked on the file when it appeared on his screen.

After fifteen minutes of study, Kruger looked at JR. "How did you find him?"

"YouTube. The trolling program works better than I anticipated. I got a bunch of hits, but this guy's rants are getting more aggressive. He's also an admirer of James Holmes."

Kruger nodded. "Has he bought any firearms yet?"

"Unfortunately, yes. Not the exact models, but similar to the types Holmes purchased. He doesn't have a criminal record, so all of his weapons were purchased legally."

"His military training suggests he might not be too familiar with assault weapons."

"Trust me, Sean, he'll know how to use them."

Staring at the driver's license picture of Bassel Safar on his laptop, Kruger remained quiet. After several minutes he asked, "Does he have an email account?"

"Several." JR nodded. "One he uses for his job, very benign. Boring, actually. He has a Gmail account he uses for personal business; it too is boring. But he has one well hidden from prying eyes that he uses to contact overseas jihadist. It—is not boring. He knows his way around computers, Sean."

Kruger looked away from the laptop and stared at JR. "Better than you?"

With a slight grin, JR shook his head.

"How did you find the hidden email account?"

"Well, let's say he clicked on a link in his personal email account he shouldn't have." JR gave Kruger a half smile.

Frowning, Kruger returned to staring at the picture of Sahar. "I probably shouldn't ask for more details, should I?"

"Probably best."

"How deep are you in his computer?"

"He can't sneeze without me knowing it."

Pointing to several items purchased by Safar, Kruger frowned. "Looks like he's getting ready for an urban assault with all of this tactical gear."

JR shrugged. "Not a crime to buy any of it. But the fact he's spread his purchases around to various suppliers denotes forethought and planning. Buying any one of these items by itself tells us nothing. Together they paint a dark picture."

Kruger withdrew the thumb drive from the USB port and put it in his jeans pocket. He closed his laptop and stood. "Keep monitoring him. We may have to send Sandy and his team to keep an eye on this guy."

JR nodded.

***

The opening of the new Star Wars movie was two weeks away. Bassel smiled when he discovered the number of screens on which the latest installment of the popular movie franchise would be showing. The internet was a wonderful place. Over the past six months, while Bassel was accumulating his arsenal, he also was acquiring a wardrobe for an appearance in the pre-movie parade at the movie theater.

He would attend as a Storm Trooper Commando.

He was confirmed after sending a picture of himself dressed in his outfit. All he would need to do was sign in at the movie theater three hours before the first showing, and he would be told where to assemble with the rest of the parade participants. His plan was simple: participate in the parade and once inside the theater, well, he would not make the mistakes James Holmes made.

***

Looking through half-readers, retired Special Forces Major Benedict "Sandy" Knoll scanned the file on the laptop in front of him.

Joseph sat next to Sandy in JR's conference room. Across from them were JR and Kruger. Sandy looked up over the half-glasses. "You found one, didn't you?"

JR and Kruger nodded.

"Damn. Are we too late to stop him?"

Kruger shook his head slightly. "Don't think so. But the

window of opportunity is closing. He fancies himself an improvement on James Holmes. So I believe he will follow Holmes's pattern of attacking a movie theater on an opening night of a major motion picture."

"Do we know which one?" Knoll looked back at the laptop.

JR said, "Click on the file marked 'Comparison.'"

Knoll moved the mouse and pressed the left side. A split image appeared with the left side showing a picture of a figure clad in black body armor holding an exotic looking rifle. On the right side was a photo of similarly clad figure also with an exotic looking rifle.

Looking up from the screen, Knoll looked at Kruger. "Guy on the right has a Beretta ARX 160 without a clip. Don't recognize the one on the left."

Kruger smiled. "That's because the guy on the left is from the fantasy world of Star Wars. His weapon doesn't exist. The guy on the right is our target."

"Shit."

Joseph nodded slightly. "That's an understatement. JR and I couldn't figure out what the one on the left had to do with Safar, but Kruger filled us in. It seems there's a new Star Wars movie opening in two weeks. Our friend Safar is an admirer of James Holmes, who killed twelve and wounded seventy in a Colorado Cinema 16 on the opening night of a Batman movie. Safar submitted the picture on the right to a theater management company as an audition for a Star Wars promotional parade they are planning opening night. He was accepted to march in the parade. We think he's going to use the parade as a ruse to get into the theater and then start firing his weapon."

Knoll continued to stare at Safar's picture on the laptop. "Huh."

"This is the first one we've been able to isolate, Sandy." Kruger pointed to the file. "It might be a false positive, but I don't think so."

"Neither do I." Knoll stood. "I can have three guys in

Chicago in less than six hours. I'll head that way tonight. What are my rules of engagement?"

Kruger gave Knoll a grim smile. "I would prefer an arrest, but don't let him harm anyone."

Knoll nodded and smiled. "We won't."

***

Sandy Knoll watched Bassel Safar enter the high-rise office tower in downtown Chicago. "What floor is his office on?"

Jimmy Gibbs looked up. "Thirty-second floor." Gibbs was in his late thirties, a recent retiree from the Seal Team Three and one of Sandy's newest recruits. Average in height, he was lean, tanned, black haired and dressed like a downtown Chicago commuter. "CPA firm named Chambers, Hall and Dvorjak."

Knoll frowned and looked at Gibbs.

Gibbs shrugged. "Sometimes you can't make this stuff up."

"What does he do?"

"He's a junior accountant. Working on his CPA. Not well liked, but they put up with him because he's fast, works long hours, and exceedingly good on a computer."

"I've heard that." Knoll looked up at the building. "Do we have surveillance on his house?"

Gibbs nodded. "Larry and Johnny are on it."

Knoll nodded. "You stay here; I need to take a look at his house. Call me if he leaves the office."

***

Dressed as an employee of the local utility company, Knoll casually walked to the rear of Bassel Safar's row house in southern Chicago. Using a slim tool from his wallet, Safar's back door yielded to Knoll in less than fifteen seconds. Inside he stood still, listening to the empty house. The place smelled of cumin and onions, but the only sound he heard was water filling the ice maker in the refrigerator. After it filled, he heard only silence. After clearing the ground floor, he cautiously climbed the stairs to the second floor. Ten minutes later, he determined there was nothing incriminating in Safar's bedrooms and bathroom. He headed down to the basement level and stood at the bottom of the stairs surveying the open space in front of him. Only a washer, dryer and a ping pong table met his gaze. Nothing on the three levels suggested Bassel Safar was planning a terrorist attack.

He walked the perimeter of the white-washed, wood-paneled basement and returned to the stairs. Nothing. Just as he was about to head back up, a mark on the floor next to the dryer caught his eye. Kneeling next to it, he placed his index finger on the mark and felt a slight indentation in the concrete. Standing up, he saw, between two planks of the paneling, a barely noticeable separation. On further examination, he saw the well-hidden outline of a door. He stood still as he stared at the well-concealed invisible entry. Not knowing what else to do, he pushed on the left side of the door closest to the dryer.

The door popped open.

Inside was pitch black. Using the flashlight app on his cell phone, Knoll pointed the bright light into the gloom of the newly discovered room. The hair on the back of his neck stood up.

CHAPTER 15

Buckhead District, Atlanta, GA

Judith Day's interview with Stephen Blair continued to unsettle her as she waited in Zimmerman's luxury apartment. She had been practicing more than twenty years, and this was the first time she walked out of a therapy session scared. Not just scared, but completely terrified about what the patient was capable of doing. She was on her second Glenlivet when Thomas Zimmerman entered.

"Judith, what the hell happened at Stephen's?"

She studied the empty glass and swirled the barely melted ice cubes. "I'm not sure, Tom. He scared the hell out of me."

"I gathered that from your phone call, but..." Zimmerman paused, struggling for words. "How could Stephen possibly scare you?"

"Well, he did."

"Judith, Stephen is not a violent man. You have to be mistaken."

"Thomas, I saw pure evil in his eyes. There was no gentle soul behind them. I really can't describe it any other way. Evil. Pure evil."

Thomas stared at her, unable to say anything. Finally he

cleared his throat. "Exactly what happened, Judith?"

She took a deep breath and let it out slowly. "The session started out fine, except he wouldn't look at me, which is normal for individuals afflicted as Stephen is. However, as we got further into the session, when he did look at me, his eyes would bore through me like I wasn't even there. I detected little emotion from him. People with Stephen's condition generally are afraid and reclusive. Not Stephen. He was more narcissistic than anything."

"What do you mean, narcissistic?"

She sighed loudly. "It means what it means. All he wanted to do was talk about how great he was and how he lifted his company up to be where it was, a global powerhouse."

Thomas frowned. "We're not a global powerhouse, we're a software company."

"Not according to Stephen. He was obsessed with your meddling in the day-to-day affairs of his company. He even accused me of being in collusion with you to take the company away from him."

Taking a deep breath, Thomas crossed his arms over his chest. "I spoke to him after you left. He was quite agitated. I've never heard him talk like that before."

Judith poured herself another Glenlivet. "He knows, Thomas. He knows."

"Apparently, but how? How the hell could he know?"

"He was impatient and not the least bit shy."

Remaining quiet, Thomas stared at the floor.

"Thomas, who told you he suffered from scopophobia?"

"His father. Stephen was diagnosed at the age of thirteen. Once he started meds, he got through high school and a master's degree in college, but managing a multimillion dollar company pushed him over the edge."

"He didn't look like the picture you showed me. He was more world-weary. He resembled a man ten years older than the person you described to me."

"I haven't seen him in several years, Judith. People age."

"That's not what I'm saying, Thomas. He didn't act like a man who has isolated himself for fifteen years."

"He isn't isolated. He meets with us every day on the internet."

"I don't know, it's hard to explain exactly how I felt. But he scared me."

Zimmerman was about to respond when the security intercom chimed. He walked to the unit. "This is Thomas."

"Sir, its Bill Harris at the gate. I have an FBI agent here who would like to speak with you. His name is Sean Kruger."

"Did he say what it was about?"

"No sir. His ID looks legit."

"Very well, give him directions."

He turned to Judith. "Wonder what this is all about. Could Stephen have called the FBI and told them we were trying to steal his company?"

Judith shook her head. "I don't know. I guess it's possible."

Five minutes later, there was a knock at Zimmerman's door. As he opened it, he was shoved back into the apartment and a man entered, shutting the door as he entered.

Zimmerman gained his composure and glared at the man. "What's the meaning of this intrusion? You can't barge your way into my home like this."

The man produced a small Ruger SR22 with a suppressor screwed into the barrel and pointed it at Zimmerman's head. "Shut up."

Staring at the gun pointed at him, Zimmerman heard a gasp from Judith. "Oh, my gawd, Stephen, what are you doing?"

Randolph Bishop, in the disguise of Stephen Blair, turned to Judith and said in a calm voice. "Nice to see you again, Judith. I trust our little session today stirred your desire to cure me of my psychological idiosyncrasies."

"You're not Stephen Blair." Zimmerman stared at the man holding the small gun.

"You are correct, Thomas. But I can't let you tell anyone." Bishop pulled the trigger and the 22LR hollow point struck Zimmerman above the left eye. His dead body slumped to the floor as Judith screamed.

***

FBI agent Tom Stark shook Kruger's hand as they stood outside Thomas Zimmerman's condo. "Thanks for flying in on such short notice, Sean."

"No problem. Bring me up to speed."

"Someone identifying themselves as you gained entry to this gated community last night. The guard saw the identification, thought it looked legitimate and called Thomas Zimmerman, who agreed to see the man. It's all in the log book. They even have a CCT picture of the man sitting in his car while the guard called Zimmerman. I knew it wasn't you; there's no resemblance. But using your name raised questions."

Three inches taller than Kruger's six-foot frame, Stark was high school skinny with an Ivy League haircut on top of an angular face. They worked several cases together after Stark graduated from the academy.

"I appreciate it, Tom."

"Zimmerman is an executive at a software company. Did you know him?"

Kruger shook his head. "Never heard of him."

Stark handed a print out of the CCT picture to Kruger. He studied it for a few moments and shook his head. "He doesn't look familiar, but his face is partially obscured by the fedora."

"I asked the guard about it, but he said lots of fashion-conscious men in this part of Atlanta wear them."

"Great. Okay, let's see what you've got."

"It's bad, Sean. Hope you can help us."

Kruger slipped the booties he was given over his shoes and inserted his hands into the latex gloves provided. When he entered the room, his eyes went to the outline of a body on the floor. "Is this where the male was shot?"

Stark nodded and handed Kruger an iPad with the digital pictures. After studying them for a few moments, he asked, "Where was the female found?"

"Back bedroom. This is where it gets gruesome."

As soon as he stepped into the room, Kruger stopped. The scene was all too familiar for him. "Shit."

Stark nodded. "Yeah, that was my reaction also."

Kruger shook his head slightly. "No, that's not what I meant, I've seen this before. Several weeks ago, I was in a house where a woman was murdered, and it looked exactly the same." Pulling out his cell phone, Kruger searched for a number. When he found it, he pressed the call icon. Three rings later, the call was answered.

"Charlie Craft."

"Charlie, it's Sean. I'm going to have an agent named Tom Stark send you a packet of pictures. I need your perspective. Call me when you get it."

***

"We haven't released any information to the media about what we found in Brenda Parker's home. There's no way this is a copy-cat murder."

Charlie Craft spoke to them via Skype. Kruger's laptop was pointed toward the wall Kruger was staring at. The words written in blood on the wall dominated his concentration. Kruger turned the laptop back, and he saw Charlie look back at the photos of the woman's body on his computer. "Same signature cuts and mutilation as Brenda Parker, Sean. It's him."

"I agree, Charlie. But what the hell did Thomas Zimmerman and Judith Day have in common with Brenda Parker?" Kruger continued to stare at the walls of the bedroom.

Charlie shook his head. "Apparently, Randolph Bishop."

Kruger turned to Tom Stark. "Tom, dig into Zimmerman's life. Maybe the answer is there. I have to catch the 6 p.m. flight back to Springfield."

CHAPTER 16

Springfield, MO

"I'm looking at two suicide vests, Sean. They're crude, but from what I can see, deadly. Plus there's an arsenal of assorted weapons: Remington shotgun, the Beretta ARX 160, two AR-15s, a Glock 17 and 19, a SIG Sauer .45 caliber, a couple of CZ 9mm's, and thousands of rounds of ammunition."

Kruger stood outside a departure gate at the Hartsfield-Jackson Atlanta International airport, his cell phone pressed to his ear as he waited for his flight back to Springfield.

"Are you sure about the suicide vests, Sandy?"

"Yeah, I've spent enough time in Iraq and Afghanistan to tell. Looks like he's packed them with ball bearings and small decking screws. If detonated in a crowded room, the result will be devastating."

Kruger was silent for a few moments. "Leave everything where you found it and get out. We need guidance from the Attorney General before we move forward."

"One more thing, Sean."

"What's that?"

"An ISIS flag is hanging on the wall."

"Don't let this guy out of your sight until I get back to you."

"Got it."

Kruger closed his eyes as he ended the call. His right hand rose to cover them. After several moments, he punched a number into his cell phone. The call was answered on the fourth ring.

"Alan Seltzer."

"Alan, we found one."

***

Kruger arrived at his home in southwest Springfield a little after 8 in the evening, fourteen hours after taking off earlier the same day.

After kissing his wife and his daughter, he took his backpack to his office and returned to the kitchen where Stephanie was feeding Kristin.

She stopped and looked at her husband. "What's wrong, Sean?"

It was several moments before Kruger could answer her. "Sandy found two suicide vests, guns and an ISIS flag in the basement of Safar's house."

Stephanie gasped as she raised her hand to her mouth. "Oh my gawd. What are you going to do?"

"Take him down. It's the only thing we can do. Possession of an explosive device is a felony, covered under Illinois Article 29D on possession of a terrorist weapon that can cause bodily injury. The only problem is we found everything during an illegal search of his residence."

She was quiet for a few moments, then smiled. "What did you do when you found the evidence about Norman Ortega?"

Kruger took a deep breath. "Used the ruse of a fire to enter his motel room?"

"Exactly. Why not now?"

He was quiet as he stared at Stephanie. Slowly, his stern

look relaxed, and he nodded slightly.

"Maybe. We're walking on egg shells, Stephanie. One false move, and his rights overshadow our attempt to stop him. We have to have everything by the book, or we lose the opportunity to get him off the street."

She nodded. "What was so urgent in Atlanta that made you leave before Kristin and I were up this morning?"

"One apartment, two murders, one a bullet in the head and the other…" He hesitated for several moments. "Randolph Bishop struck again."

Stephanie stood, walked to her husband and hugged him. "In Atlanta?"

Nodding, Kruger returned the hug. "Very upscale gated condo development. Bishop gained entry with a fake set of FBI credentials."

Lifting her head from his chest, she looked at him. "No…"

"Yeah, he used my name." He paused. "Because of that, they called in an agent from the Atlanta field office. He and I worked a few cases in the past, and he knew immediately from the security camera it wasn't me. But he knew I needed to be informed."

"Are you going to be involved in the case?"

Kruger remained quiet for several moments. "I already am."

***

It was after 10 when Stephanie joined him on the wooden deck attached to the back of their house. He was sipping on a cup of chamomile tea, finding it helped him sleep better than a glass of wine. Their home faced east, which made the back deck a perfect place to watch storms move in from the northwest. Above them, stars shined brightly, while off in the distance, they disappeared. While the storm was too far away to hear thunder, occasional flashes of lightning could be seen.

Their home was in a newer subdivision of the city. The terrain was hilly, which allowed for a walk-out basement configuration. The large deck was off the upper floor, accessed through the kitchen, supported by tall eight-by-eight posts. The only sounds to be heard were tree frogs and crickets. Kruger relished opportunities to watch a storm approach. Growing up in this part of the country, approaching storms fascinated him when he was young. They still did.

Stephanie was quiet as well. Her attitude about approaching storms diametrically opposite of her husband's. "How long before it gets here?"

Kruger consulted his cell phone and pulled up a local weather radar site. "The leading edge is just passing through Joplin, maybe an hour."

"You should have been a meteorologist."

Chuckling, he smiled. "I thought about it as an undergrad. But if I had, I never would've met you."

"Good point." She sipped her tea. "What are you going to do about Bishop?"

"Find him."

"How?"

"Don't know yet." He was quiet for a long time. "What I need to know first is how his last two victims knew him. Was it random? If it was, it will be almost impossible to get a lead on him. If he knew them, maybe, just maybe, we can get closer to where he is."

The first notes of thunder could faintly be heard as he watched the clouds grow closer, clearly visible with the constant flashing of lightning.

Their conversation changed as they watched the clouds grow closer. They discussed Kristin's upcoming year of pre-school and Stephanie's pending volunteer work at a nearby elementary school. When the first drops of rain fell to the deck, they stood and went inside.

***

Jimmy Gibbs stood in front of Bassel Safar's front door and pushed the button for the doorbell. He stood back, like most door-to-door salesmen and waited. Fifteen seconds later, Safar opened his front door, but not the glass storm door. "Yes."

"Are you Bassel Safar?" Gibbs asked with a large smile. He was dressed in an open collar blue oxford shirt, navy blazer, tan slacks and dress shoes.

Warily, Safar nodded.

Gibb's smile remained in place. "My name is Phillip Griffith. I'm with Mid-West Theaters." He held out a business card. "I was asked to come by and confirm your participation in our pre-opening gala event at the Metro Cinema 16."

Safar's concerned look faded, he smiled and opened the storm door. "Cool. Come on in."

Sandy Knoll was standing against the wall on the front porch, out of sight when Safar opened the door. As the glass storm door opened, he rushed in, followed by Gibbs. With the practiced ease of many years of subduing opponents, Safar was thrown to the floor on his stomach while both hands and feet were roughly secured with flex cuffs. Knoll dragged the bound man away from the front door as Gibb's closed it.

Safar spat blood and then demanded, "What the hell is this about? Let me go. I'll sue your ass off."

Knoll ignored the complaints and looked around. Seeing nothing, he walked back to the kitchen and found the Beretta ARX 160 in pieces on a table. Pages of a newspaper were spread out with gun oil, solvent and cleaning rods scattered next to the disassembled weapon. Next to the Beretta was an object he had not seen during his earlier search of Safar's secret room. Smiling, Knoll went back into the sitting area where Safar was cursing in Arabic. Knoll kicked him in the ribs. "Shut up."

Safar gasped, but shut up.

Knoll turned to Gibbs. "Beretta's on the kitchen table, and we got a bonus."

Gibbs smiled. "What?"

"Our friend here just screwed himself. Looks like a Russian-made grenade. Where'd you get it, Safar?"

"Who are you? I want a lawyer."

"We're not cops, Safar. Too bad for you."

Realizing his situation was not as it first appeared, Safar's eyes grew wide, and he put his head down on the floor.

"Yeah, I'd say a prayer or two, Safar. You're going to need them."

***

Kruger stood once again on the back deck. It was early morning, and his cell phone was pressed to his ear. Moisture from the previous night's storm still dripped from the trees.

"Where is he?"

Sandy Knoll had spent the night taking inventory in Safar's secret room. "He's in a hot-sheet hotel room near Joliet." He gave Kruger the address. "He's under sedation until we know what you want to do with him."

"How many people know he's there?"

"Just my team."

"Good."

"What have you found in his house?"

"Enough to classify him as a terrorist."

Kruger smiled. "Email the pictures to me, and I'll pass them on to a higher authority."

"Why can't we just make him disappear, Sean?"

"I wish it was that simple, Sandy." Kruger glanced at his wristwatch. "There'll be a van heading toward the hotel as soon as they have the address. There will be two very discreet and competent FBI agents who will take control of Safar. All your men need to do is check their ID's and walk out. Do not identify yourselves; they've been instructed not to ask."

"Wish we could follow it through."

"Not part of our job description. We're tasked to ascertain and prevent. We did both."

"What about his house?"

"Are you done?"

"Yeah."

"Go back to your car and wait. There will be an FBI swat team take it down at the same time they take control of Safar at the hotel. Once you're sure they've found the weapons, head to the airport."

"Got it."

"And, Sandy?"

"Yeah."

"Nicely done."

CHAPTER 17

West of Atlanta, GA

The passage of time was meaningless for Stephen Blair. Day and night were the same. Only the occasional visit by the intruder broke the monotony. His sleeping patterns were also unknown to him. He didn't know if he slept a minute or several days. His mental state continued to deteriorate, as he had no access to his normal medications. Meals remained untouched, and his weight declined. His only mental activity was writing computer code. Perception of the real world slowly slipped from Stephen's grasp.

Randolph Bishop observed Stephen's decline. On many visits he simply stood in the door of Stephen's prison and observed. Most of the time, Stephen would be curled into a fetal position on the mattress. Other times he would find him sitting on the toilet in the small bathroom off the room, his head down, his arms resting on his knees. Verbal communication stopped after Stephen learned of Camila's death.

During one of Stephen's more lucid moments, he heard the door to his room being unlocked. He was sitting on the mattress, his back against the wall. The intruder opened the door and smiled.

"Well, you're awake for a change. Good." The intruder used his foot to slide a box sitting on the floor just outside the door into Stephen's room.

"I'm going away for a few days. I went to a Costco this morning and bought food. It will have to last you while I'm gone. There's a bag of apples, two loafs of bread and a large jar of peanut butter. I was gracious and provided a spoon for your peanut butter. I didn't feel scooping it out with your fingers would be dignified." Bishop chuckled.

Blair stared at the intruder, but remained quiet.

"I forgot to tell you about this past week. It seems, if you have the right documents, you can get a legitimate driver's license in anyone's name." Bishop reached into his pocket and withdrew a laminated card. He held it so Stephen could see it. "It seems you haven't had a driver's license in a while. I had to take a test, but that wasn't too hard. Now I'm officially Stephen Blair. Not sure who that makes you." Bishop smiled, and his eyes bore into Blair.

"One other piece of news. A private equity company purchased your shares of the company. The funds were transferred to an account I set up specifically to receive them. Did you know your buddy Thomas Zimmerman was plotting to have you declared incompetent and steal your company?"

Blair did not respond.

"I didn't think so. Thomas has paid for his treachery with his life. Isn't that the punishment for treason, Stephen? Death. I find it a fitting punishment. Don't you, Stephen?"

Blair continued to stare blankly at Bishop. He heard the words, but their meaning eluded him. The coding didn't stop as he listened to the man standing in the door of his room.

Bishop walked over to look closer at Blair. He bent down, stared into the blank eyes of his captive.

"Are you in there Stephen? Knock, knock."

The man's expression didn't change. Bishop straightened, snorted and walked out of the room.

After the door closed and the lock engaged, Blair

continued to stare at it. After an hour, he slowly focused on the box containing the apples and bread. He made no effort to reach for an apple; he did not have the strength or desire to eat. After several hours, he lost the ability to focus. As his eyes remained on the food, the coding stopped in his head and his heart beat for the last time. His now lifeless body did not move, his unseeing eyes still pointed at the fruit.

***

Only Kruger and JR occupied the conference room on the second floor of JR's building. It was late morning, and Sandy Knoll and his team were now in the air, flying to their home base in Dallas. On the numerous flat screen TVs, in the computer room, various cable news stations were discussing the recent discovery, by an FBI swat team, of a trove of weaponry at a junior accountant's home. The talking heads were telling their audience a fictional account of how the young accountant's plans to attack a movie theater were discovered.

Kruger ignored the TV screens and concentrated on what JR was telling him.

JR studied his laptop, his fingers dancing over the keys like a maestro on a piano. He stopped typing and looked up at Kruger. "Found something."

"What?"

"Thomas Zimmerman was a vice president at a software company founded by an old college acquaintance of mine, Stephen Blair."

Kruger remained silent, knowing JR loved to stretch out his explanations.

"I met Stephen my sophomore year. We had numerous classes together but were never, what I would call, close friends."

"Why?"

"Stephen had an issue with being around people. I'm not even sure he knew who I was. He always sat in the back of the room and was never very vocal. I later found out he took meds to cope with the stress he was feeling. But he wrote eloquent code. I remember one routine he wrote for routers that was so concise and tight, it made me look like an amateur."

"Are you saying he was better than you?"

"Definitely better." JR nodded rapidly. "Coding was his passion. I was more interested in the practical side, concentrating on how to make code better and how to keep others out. Stephen didn't care about security; he just loved to write code. After college, he started a software company with his father. Last I knew, he had a mental breakdown and turned the day to day operations of the company over to his dad. I haven't heard anything about him since then."

Kruger frowned. "What does this have to do with Thomas Zimmerman?"

"According to the company website, Thomas Zimmerman took over the company as COO when Stephen's father passed away five years ago."

"Is this Stephen Blair active in the business?"

"Not sure, the website lists him as CEO and majority stock holder, but doesn't mention involvement." JR's fingers started typing again. He frowned. "Uh oh."

"What? What?"

"The day before Thomas Zimmerman's death, all of Blair's stock was sold to a private equity company. You know how I feel about those guys."

"I share your feelings," Kruger nodded. "What does the sale have to do with Zimmerman's death and Randolph Bishop?"

Shaking his head, JR remained quiet.

Kruger stood and started pacing. "We're missing something, JR. I spoke to Tom Stark earlier. Their investigation is leaning toward the attack being against Judith Day. Zimmerman may have been collateral damage. Sort of in the wrong place at the wrong time. She was a clinical psychologist, and they feel she ran into Bishop because of her occupation."

"At least that makes sense. But I can't get past the timing of the stock sale and Zimmerman's death."

"It bothers me too, JR. Can you find any references to Stephen's mental health?"

JR held up an index finger. "Hold on."

Several minutes pasted as Kruger paced and JR typed. Finally, JR stopped and sat back. "I found the Facebook page of a vice president at Blair's company. She references Stephen's sudden appearance at the firm after fifteen years of absence. He announced the sale of his shares to a hastily arranged meeting in a conference room and then promptly left. No explanation or reason. This woman described Stephen as cold and aloof, and he refused to even discuss the matter with them."

Kruger sat down and stared at JR. "I know Zimmerman and Judith Day were killed by Bishop. There are too many similarities. Stark said he doesn't have the results back from the DNA analysis and would call when they do. But, if it wasn't Bishop, we have to consider Blair a person of interest."

"I would agree with you."

"There is only one issue with it, Blair has an alibi."

JR looked up from the computer. "How so."

"Seems he flew to Miami the afternoon before the murders."

"Who told you that?"

"Stark. They wanted to question Blair, but no one was home at his estate. They found a ticket and boarding pass in his name on a 2 p.m. Delta flight into Miami."

JR frowned. "Convenient."

Kruger didn't say anything for a moment. "Is there a way to find Blair?"

"No. He doesn't have an internet presence. Hasn't for at least fifteen years."

"What do you mean, doesn't have an internet presence?

"I mean what I said. No email, no social media, no

website, nothing. He doesn't exist on the web and from what I can tell, he doesn't own a cell phone. At least not one I can find. But that's a meaningless statement since there are lots of ways to have a cell phone without using a major carrier."

Kruger sighed. "We aren't going to find him that way, are we?

JR shook his head. "Not at the moment."

"Keep looking. What else do you have?"

Sliding a thumb drive across the table, JR said, "Look these over."

Nodding, Kruger palmed the drive and placed it in his jeans pocket.

CHAPTER 18

Springfield, MO

Kruger's cell phone chirped. After glancing at the caller ID, he swiped the screen and answered the call. "Kruger."

"Sean, it's Tom Stark."

"Sorry about the phone tag. You called earlier."

"Yeah, I wanted give you an up-to-date on the Zimmerman and Day murders."

"Did you get the DNA back?"

"Yeah."

"Bishop?"

"Positive match with the DNA found at the St. Louis murders. The same guy did Judith Day." Kruger didn't respond. Currently at his desk in his home office, he stood and started pacing while listening. Tom Stark continued, "Before we knew it was Bishop, we were looking at Stephen Blair."

"Anything unusual?"

"We met him at the gate on his return flight from Miami. Funny thing, he didn't get indignant or seemed surprised to see us. After giving us a summary of his activities in Miami, we followed up."

"And?"

"He said he was meeting with investors."

"Was he?"

"Miami field office dispatched a couple of agents to interview several of the ones he told us about and confirmed he was there. But…"

"What?"

"Before we let him go, we checked with the hotel to confirm he there. There's a twelve-hour gap from when the plane landed and he checked into the hotel."

"Did he give you an explanation?"

"Kind of. Apparently, he was picked up at the airport and wined and dined until 3 in the morning. The hotel shows he checked in at 4 a.m."

"Huh."

"Now with the DNA confirming Bishop did the murders, we've cleared Blair."

"Only thing you can do, Tom. Good work on this. One other thing, how was Blair's demeanor?"

"What do you mean?"

"Oh, I don't know, was he nervous?"

"No, not really. Like I said earlier, he didn't seem surprised to see us. Almost like he was expecting something. He answered our questions, joked around a little, but he wasn't nervous. Why?"

"Nothing, just curious. Keep me up to speed, Tom."

"Will do, Sean."

Kruger ended the call and stopped pacing. There was nothing unusual about the twelve-hour gap and it wasn't a crime to check into a hotel at 4 a.m. But something about it gnawed at the back of Kruger's conscious. He sat down at his computer and pulled up Google Maps.

***

"It takes ten hours to drive from Atlanta to South Beach in Miami. Zimmerman and Day were killed between four and six in the afternoon. Blair checks into the hotel at 4 a.m. the next day. Bishop's DNA is found at the scene of the murders, clearing Blair of the crime. So, why does the ten-hour gap bother me, JR?" Kruger was standing on his back deck with the cell phone pressed to his ear and a beer in his other hand.

"It could be a coincidence." JR's reply was without enthusiasm.

"Right."

"Or, like he told the FBI in Atlanta, he was partying."

"I'm not buying it." Kruger shook his head. "You told me Blair had a mental breakdown and isolated himself from the world for almost fifteen years. Now, all of a sudden, he's making trips to South Beach to party and find investors. What's wrong with this picture, JR?"

Silence was his answer.

"You know the guy, JR. Was he the partying type?"

"No."

"If you take meds for a psychological problem, it's because there's a chemical imbalance within the brain. Most of those issues don't go away. As a rule, they're permanent."

"Maybe he's been in therapy and taking meds?"

"Judith Day was a therapist."

JR was quiet for a few moments. "So you've said. But was she Stephen's therapist?"

"How do we find out?"

"Not sure I want to hack into the records of a psychologist."

"Why?"

"I do have some scruples left. Not much, but some."

Kruger chuckled. "You have more ethics than you realize, my friend. I'll handle the Judith Day inquiry."

"Thanks."

The conversation lagged for several seconds. "Bishop's DNA at the murder scene and Blair's sudden change in behavior is an inconsistency I don't like. Something is askew."

JR took a deep breath. "Sean, you're talking about two

different men. We may never know how Bishop and Judith Day crossed paths. Zimmerman being there was purely by chance. Stephen may have been under therapy for years and decided to re-join the world. Who knows? Are you seeing relationships that don't exist?"

Lapsing into silence again, Kruger stared out across his back yard with the cell phone still pressed against his ear. "Maybe."

"You're not going to let it go are you?"

"Probably not. But I have to for now. Too many other projects need attention."

The call ended two minutes later. Kruger took a deep breath and looked up at the night sky as he returned his cell phone to his jeans pocket. He stood like that for several minutes until he heard the door to the deck open. He turned and saw Stephanie step out of the house.

"Saw you were off the phone. Kristin's asleep. Thought you might like some company."

He reached for her as she approached. He put his arms around her and kissed the top of her head. She smelled of jasmine. "You haven't worn that fragrance in a long time."

She looked up at him and smiled. "Nope." She wore one of his OU sweat shirts and no jeans. As he hugged her, he didn't feel the outline of a bra underneath the shirt.

"You're not wearing anything under there are you?"

"Nope." She reached up and pulled his head toward her. They kissed and went inside.

***

Kruger's arm was wrapped around Stephanie's shoulder as her head lay on his chest. He could feel her slow rhythmic breathing, a sign she was asleep. As he started to move his arm he heard. "Don't, I'm awake."

"Thought you were asleep."

"Just dozing." She snuggled closer as he hugged her tighter. They both were silent, enjoying the moment. "Are you going to Atlanta to follow up on Judith Day?"

"I'm thinking about it. Why?"

"I want to go with you."

Kruger was silent for several moments. "Any particular reason?"

He felt her head nod.

"Want to tell me?"

"You'll think it's silly."

"Probably not."

"I love being a mother. Having Kristin around has lifted my spirits more than I ever imagined…"

"Uh-oh. There's a 'however' in there somewhere."

She poked him in the rib with her index finger. "Hush, I was getting to the point. I miss being around adults."

"If you want to go back to work, I'm not stopping you."

"No, I don't miss my old job. Glad those days are behind me."

He stayed silent.

"I miss being around individuals with a shared purpose."

"Stephanie, I'm not sure how going to Atlanta to investigate a brutal murder is going to help you be around individuals with a shared purpose."

"I'm not either. But I want to go."

"No shopping."

"Wasn't planning on it."

Kruger chuckled and kissed her. "I'll book our flight tomorrow."

"Mia wants Kristin to stay with them while we're gone. She hasn't told JR yet, but she's pregnant."

"What?"

She nodded.

"Oh boy. Watching JR become a father is going to be interesting."

***

Randolph Bishop sat in a leather wing chair facing the

unlit fireplace that graced one wall of Stephen Blair's library. He sipped on the single malt scotch in the lowball glass in his hand. The presence of the FBI at the gate on his return to Atlanta from Miami had been expected. Satisfied with how he answered their questions, he once again went over the sequence of events after leaving Zimmerman's condo.

The drive to Miami in the rented Camry took ten hours. Everett Stewart rented the car, and since no one knew about Everett Stewart, he doubted it would be traced. After checking into a luxury motel room in South Beach as Stephen Blair, he spent the rest of his stay sampling the local cuisine and trendy nightclubs of the area.

Using his new found status as a multimillionaire, he visited several exclusive investment companies. The purpose was not to invest with them, but to learn how to approach rich investors and take their money.

After three days, he returned the Camry to the Hertz counter at Miami International Airport and used the return ticket to fly back to Atlanta. He had no idea where the man who used his boarding pass on the first leg of his Miami trip was, nor did he care.

The questioning by the fools from the FBI lasted longer than he anticipated, but he kept his cool and answered everything they asked.

When Randolph Bishop returned to Blair's home and walked into the house from the garage, he knew immediately his problem in the basement was resolved. He grabbed a towel from the kitchen, held it under the faucet until it was wet, and hurried toward the stair case leading down to the basement.

He took the steps two at a time to where the bedroom holding Stephen Blair was located. The stench of death grew stronger as he reached the room's door. Placing the wet towel over his nose and mouth, he unlocked the door and peered inside. The putrid odor washed over him. It was a smell he grew accustomed to in Thailand. Blair's body remained in the same position as the last time he saw him, but the eyes were dull and lifeless.

His last problem was solved. All the individuals who could possibly suspect he wasn't Stephen were dead. Dead men tell no tales.

Now three days later, the body was disposed of, the stench gone, and Randolph Bishop was the only person on the face of the earth who knew he wasn't Stephen Blair. Things were working out better than planned.

After another sip of the scotch, he smiled. Time to initiate the real purpose of his return to the United States.

CHAPTER 19

Atlanta, GA

Kruger showed his FBI credentials to Dr. Harold Northrup, the managing partner of The Northrup Clinic.

"Judith was a valued member of our staff, Agent Kruger. I'll help as much as I can."

"I appreciate it, Dr. Northrup." Kruger unbuttoned the jacket of his gray pinstripe suit and sat down in one of the chairs facing Northrup's desk. Stephanie sat next to him, dressed in a dark navy pantsuit with a white open-collar silk shirt.

"Agent Stark told me you hold a Ph.D. in psychology."

"Yes, sir. University of Oklahoma, Norman."

"Good school." Northrup was quiet for several moments. "Not sure I can offer more information than what I already have. But, I'll try. What did you want to ask me?"

"We know who killed Judith."

Northrup nodded. "I was told."

"What we're trying to determine is how she crossed paths with him. I understand the confidentiality of your profession, Dr. Northrup, but if she was treating Randolph Bishop, any notes from her therapy sessions might help us locate him. He's a dangerous individual and has murdered seven individuals that we know of. Probably more."

"I appreciate your understanding, but I can assure you, we have found nothing in Judith's files showing she was treating anyone by the name of Randolph Bishop."

Kruger nodded. "What about a person named Everett Stewart?"

Northrup stared at Kruger for a few moments, then turned to a keyboard sitting in front of a flat-screen monitor. "Just a second."

After typing and moving a mouse around, he stared at the screen and shook his head. "No, no one by that name, either. Who is Everett Stewart?"

"The name Bishop used to gain entry to the states. He became a fugitive after we found DNA evidence he was a serial killer in St. Louis. We believe he spent the last six years hiding in Thailand. Since he's on our Most Wanted list, entering under his real name would have raised red flags."

"I see."

"What about Stephen Blair? What was her relationship to him?"

"Judith specialized in phobia therapy. We were contacted a month ago by Tom Zimmerman in his attempt to help Stephen with his extreme case of scopophobia. Judith had the experience, so she was chosen to do the therapy."

"So it was Zimmerman who made the initial request? Not Blair."

"That is correct."

"And the initial contact was made just a month ago?"

Northrup nodded.

Kruger frowned. "This is the first time we've heard Zimmerman made the request. So, Stephen Blair had no contact with your clinic or Judith Day prior to her being assigned to treat him."

"Correct."

Stephanie asked the next question. "What was the relationship between Judith and Tom?"

"I beg your pardon?"

"Judith was killed in Tom Zimmerman's condo. Why was she there?"

Kruger smiled slightly; Stephanie's question was well timed. He looked at Northrup to see what his reaction would be.

Northrup cleared his throat. "Uh… This is uncomfortable, but you probably need to know. Judith was in a relationship with Tom. I was unaware of it until after the murder. Her assistant told me. It broke a number of our rules. We adhere to strict ethical guidelines concerning our therapists and their relationships with clients."

"I can appreciate your concern, Dr. Northrup. We're trying to establish a connection between Judith and Bishop, not raise ethical questions about your clinic."

With a single nod of his head, Northrup asked, "Could it have been random?"

Kruger shook his head. "Bishop's killings have never been random. He murders for a reason. In St. Louis, he killed four women who were in competition with him for a job. He butchered his brother's ex-wife as revenge for trying keep her husband from worshipping him. So, no, he does not kill randomly. There's a connection somewhere."

Northrup nodded thoughtfully. "Classical psychopathic behavior. I take it he hides his rage well?"

Kruger nodded, thinking back to the incident in the parking lot in St. Louis. "Yes, but I've seen it up-close and personal, Doctor. He's very intelligent and manipulative."

"Yes, it can be unnerving."

The conversation lagged for a few moments. Kruger used the pause to start another line of questioning. "Let me ask your opinion. In your experience, would someone who has isolated themselves from the public for fifteen years, without seeking therapy, suddenly get a driver's license and take a trip to Miami?"

Northrup stared at Kruger for a several moments, blinked several times, and slowly shook his head.

"I suppose it's possible, but I would highly doubt it."

"I concur. Thank you for your time, Dr. Northrup."

***

As they drove away from The Northrup Clinic, Stephanie looked at her husband and smiled slightly. "You suspect something, don't you?"

Kruger didn't respond right away, he stared ahead as he drove. Finally, he spoke, "I can't get past Blair having a miraculous recovery from his scopophobia, selling his company, and flying to Miami."

"It could happen."

"Yes, I agree, it could happen. I was under the impression Blair requested the therapy himself. Now we learn Zimmerman arranged for the therapy just recently. If Stephen was already being treated, why did Zimmerman contact the clinic for help?"

"Because Stephen wasn't being treated. Was he?"

Kruger shook his head. "No. Stark told me they interviewed most of the management team at Blair's company. Tom Zimmerman was as close to Stephen as his father used to be; he would have known about any previous or current therapy. In fact, Zimmerman's assistant told Stark the discussion had been going on for the last month about getting Stephen some help."

"What are you thinking, Sean?"

Kruger glanced at the clock on the rental's dashboard. "I'm thinking we need to find a nice place for lunch and then pay Stephen Blair a surprise visit."

***

Randolph Bishop raised the binoculars to his eyes as he watched from the library window. A white Ford Fusion was parked outside the security gate of the mansion. A woman he didn't recognize stepped out of the passenger door and looked around. When the driver stepped out, he recognized him immediately. It was the FBI agent whose name he used to gain access to Tom Zimmerman and Judith Day. The last time he saw the man was in the parking lot of Harmon, Harmon, and Kinslow on the day he fled the United States for a six-year exile. His stomach tightened, and he felt the rage boil up inside. Closing his eyes, he used the techniques learned in Thailand to calm the tidal wave of emotions. The FBI agent was pushing the call button on the security pad.

Remaining quiet, he did not move to respond. The buzzer sounded several more times, but he made no effort to answer it. He just watched the car. After several minutes, the man and woman returned to the Ford, got in and drove off. He stared out the window watching as the car receded into the surrounding neighborhood. When it was gone, he walked over to the telephone sitting on the desk in the library and dialed a number used the previous day.

The call was answered on the second ring. "Coldwell Banker Real Estate, this is Beverly. How may I help you?"

"Good afternoon, Beverly, this is Stephen Blair. We spoke yesterday about selling my house."

"Yes, Stephen. How are you?"

"I'm great. I've decided to list it. Could you bring over the paperwork so we can get started?"

"Wonderful, would five o'clock be convenient?"

"Excellent, I'll see you then."

***

"Now what?" Stephanie's question was met with silence.

After a long twenty seconds, Kruger shook his head. "I can't tell if I'm being paranoid about Blair, or if there's a legitimate reason to keep him as a person of interest in this case."

"Sean, you've always told me to follow logic with a touch of instinct when making decisions. What does logic tell you about Stephen Blair?"

"Hmmm… Logic tells me he's probably making a recovery. My instinct is telling me something is wrong."

"What's it telling you?"

"It's so crazy, I can't believe I'm actually thinking it."

She chuckled, "I won't tell anyone."

"Somehow, Stephen Blair and Randolph Bishop are the same person."

She frowned and looked out the front window of the car. "It would explain a lot."

"Yeah, but it's not possible."

"No, it's not."

"We could try again tomorrow morning to see him, but our flight home is at 9. Let's get to the hotel and relax tonight. I'll call Tom Stark and have him keep an eye on Blair. It'll be interesting to see what he does next."

As they drove toward the hotel, Kruger could not stop thinking about what a little voice in the back of his mind was telling him. Everything about Stephen Blair made zero sense. Something was wrong, but until he received more evidence to go on, he would have to drop it.

PART 3

Two Months Later
Springfield, MO

Mia Ling-Diminski stood behind her husband as they both stared at the computer screen.

"When did you meet him, JR?"

"College. He was a few years younger. The man was brilliant. Odd, but brilliant. The code he wrote was pure elegance. I'd never seen anything like it before. I considered myself pretty good, but he was light years ahead of me in college. This is the first time I've ever heard of him attending a conference. He sold his company, New Age Software, several months ago to a private equity company. Big mistake." JR sighed. "At one time, they produced top of the line networking software. I've used some of their protocols on several projects. But since the sale, I stopped. I've seen first-hand what private equity does to a company."

Mia put her hands on his shoulders. "If he doesn't own his company anymore, does it mention why he's attending?"

JR nodded. "He's in the process of developing a new artificial intelligence startup company, and he's looking for investors."

"Why don't we go to the conference and meet with him?"

JR turned around and stared at Mia. She was barely five foot tall, slender, and after three months of being pregnant, a small baby bump was starting to show. Today her long black hair was tied back in a ponytail that almost reached her waist. Her father was from China and her mother from Texas. The combination produced a round face, petite nose and brown almond-shaped eyes that sparkled with intelligence and mischief.

"I don't go to conferences, Mia. You know that."

She nodded. JR Diminski was not his given name. But it was now his legal name. His past was a mystery to everyone except her and a few close friends. She kissed him on the forehead.

"Yes, yes… That excuse is getting old. You don't even look like you did back then. You wear glasses, your hair is shorter and you've gained a few pounds. Just go as JR; you have an excellent reputation. You don't have to mention where you went to college."

He turned around and looked at the computer screen again. "I would like to talk to him, but I doubt he would remember who I am. Besides, I might run into someone else I don't want to run into."

"JR, when are you going to stop worrying? Sean's told you a thousand times, no one is searching for you."

"I know, but still…"

She shook her head, turned, and walked off toward the stairs leading to their third-floor living area. JR stayed on the second floor and stared at the screen for a few more minutes. He started typing, making their reservations for the conference. Except for a brief vacation in Colorado several years ago, it would be his first out of town trip since arriving in Springfield. As he finished making the arrangements for their flight to Las Vegas, he thought to himself, "I guess if you can venture out from your inner demons, I can venture out from mine as well. See you in a few weeks, Stephen Blair."

***

"Mia and I are going to Las Vegas next week for a few days."

Kruger smiled. "JR, are you finally accepting the fact no one is looking for you anymore?"

JR slowly nodded. "I guess. Old habits die hard, Sean. I still plan on being careful."

Chuckling, Kruger shook his head slowly. "You can be such an old man sometimes, JR. What's the occasion?"

"Black Hat USA."

"That tells me nothing."

"Black Hat's a global information security gathering. There are seminars on the latest information security research, development, tools and trends, without a bunch of salesmen trying to sell you something. It's perfect for Mia and me; they cater to security practitioners. Plus there will be venture capitalists attending. One of whom you know."

Kruger's eyebrows rose.

JR nodded. "Stephen Blair is attending."

"Really. This is the first I've heard about him for a couple of months. We kind of lost track of him after he sold the house in Atlanta."

"You never did tell me why?"

"Tom Stark put him under surveillance for a few weeks. With no results and manpower issues coming into play, he stopped. They never were able to determine a connection between Judith Day and Randolph Bishop. We may never know."

"Blair still doesn't have an internet presence. Which is kind of surprising." JR hesitated for a few seconds, thought about it and shrugged. "But then again, I don't either. My company does, but I don't."

"Are you going to meet with him?"

"No plans to at this point. If I get a chance, I'll say hello."

Kruger nodded, then added, "Oh, I forgot to tell you, the two files you gave us paid off. Sandy and his team stopped a couple of teenagers from entering their high school with AR-15s."

JR gave Kruger a grim smile. "How many does that make now?"

"Four."

Shaking his head, JR stood and placed his palms down on the conference table where he and Kruger were meeting. "I'm still not convinced this is the right way to search for them."

"JR, if you can think of a better system, I'm all ears."

"I just don't like the invasion of privacy. I've spent the last six years trying to keep the men in black from finding me. Now I'm one of them."

"I understand, but you weren't preparing to commit a mass shooting. The four we've found so far were prepared to take maximum lives with their attacks. We've had a few false alarms and false positives. But those individuals received a little scare and now don't pretend to be what they aren't. You're doing good work, JR. The powers that be are pleased."

"Do they know about me?"

Kruger shook his head. "Only Joseph, the President and myself."

"What happens when he serves his two terms? What about the next one?"

"Hopefully, he or she will understand the sensitivity of the matter. If not, we can shut down."

JR straightened from leaning over the table and gave his friend a grim smile.

"I'm getting a cup of coffee; do you want one?"

Kruger shook his head and returned to studying the screen of his laptop which showed a file JR gave him before starting their meeting. When JR returned, Kruger looked up.

"When did you find this?"

"It popped up this morning. I've had a new snooper program trolling police reports, news outlets, Twitter feeds, and Facebook postings for murders or series of murders similar to what Randolph Bishop commits."

"It's not his pattern, but…"

"I didn't think it was, but wanted you to see it."

"I don't like the proximity to Atlanta."

JR sipped his coffee. "Exactly why I included them in the file. Neither did I."

Kruger pointed to the screen. "This body was found in the trunk of a car submerged in the Chattahoochee River, a hundred miles from Atlanta, but…"

"The wounds on the body resemble Judith Day, don't they?"

"Similar. Not exact, according to the police report."

"Call them and get more details. Reading something on a police report is not the same thing as seeing the body, Sean."

Kruger nodded. "Yeah, I know."

"If it was Bishop, it establishes his presence in the area before Judith Day and Zimmerman were murdered."

"This report doesn't identify the body."

"Call them."

Kruger's brow furrowed and he gave JR a curt nod. "Not sure why I was hesitating. I'll patch through the Bureau."

***

"Troup County Sheriff's Department, can I help you?"

"My name is Sean Kruger, Special Agent with the FBI. Is the sheriff available?"

There was silence on the call, finally, "Uhhh… Please hold."

A tinny instrumental version of ZZ Top's song "LaGrange" was heard as Kruger waited for someone to answer.

"Sheriff Cooper's office, this is Nancy."

Repeating who he was, Kruger again asked for the sheriff.

"May I ask what this is about, Agent?"

"Official business, Nancy. Is the sheriff available or not?"

There was silence on the other end of the call. Taking a deep breath, Kruger closed his eyes as he calmed his aggravation about the lack of a response. Finally he heard, "I'm sorry, Agent Kruger, but he's in a departmental meeting at the moment. Is there someone else who could help you?"

Recognizing the stall tactic, he tried a different approach. "I'm inquiring about the body found in a tributary of the Chattahoochee River yesterday. It may be connected to a case we're investigating."

"I'm sorry, Agent Kruger, but the lead detective for the case is also in the meeting."

Although Nancy could not see it, Kruger smiled, knowing exactly what his next words would be. "That's fine. Please give the sheriff a message. There will be twenty FBI agents in route to his office within the next hour to investigate the discovery of the body. As I mentioned, it may be connected to a case we are working. But since he doesn't have time to discuss it with me, I'll just send the agents. I'm sure he won't mind dealing with them."

"Agent Kruger, please hold."

The same horrible rendition of the ZZ Top song came back on the phone line. Fifteen seconds later, he heard a gruff voice say, "This is Sheriff Cooper. What's this about twenty FBI agents coming here?"

"You have a very efficient gatekeeper, Sheriff. I need to talk to you, and she was not being very helpful."

Kruger heard a muffled curse, then, "Who am I speaking to?"

"FBI Special Agent Sean Kruger."

"How do I know you're a real FBI agent and not some reporter trying to get a story?"

"You are wise to be cautious. Have someone call the FBI

main number and ask for Deputy Director Alan Seltzer. Tell them you are confirming my identity. They'll connect you immediately."

An orchestral version of "Sweet Home Alabama" provided the only indication the call was still connected. As his wait time dragged on, he stared at his watch and observed the minute hand circle the dial four times.

"Okay, Agent Kruger, what do you want to know?"

The voice was still gruff, but there was a note of resignation at the same time.

Kruger smiled to himself. "A woman was murdered in the Buckhead District of Atlanta two months ago. The method of her death was similar to a woman in Rockford, Illinois, a month prior. From preliminary information we've received about the woman your department found in the Chattahoochee River, we believe there may be a connection with the other two."

"She'd been in the water about seventy days, according to the coroner. The water was warm, and the perch and crawdads were busy."

"I'm more concerned about the cuts."

"Oh, boy." The sheriff stayed quiet for a few moments. "Hard to describe."

"If I gave you an email address of a forensic technician with the Bureau, could you send pictures?"

"We can."

"It's important, Sheriff."

"How?"

"If this woman is one of his victims, it will be his eighth."

"Why am I just hearing about this?"

"Because they've occurred over the past fifteen years. He's smart, extremely disciplined, and dangerous as hell. I need to stop him."

"Give me the email address."

Kruger gave the sheriff the address and told him the tech's name. When they were done exchanging contact information, the sheriff asked, "Agent Kruger, did you really have twenty agents on their way to my county?"

"Well, Sheriff, I was able to turn them around just in time."

Kruger heard the man laugh as he hung up.

CHAPTER 21

Southlake, TX

Looking out the sliding glass door leading to his balcony, Randolph Bishop sipped a cup of coffee. His newly leased condominium was on the third floor of a residential complex in Southlake, TX. It was close to the Dallas-Fort Worth International Airport, and the surrounding restaurants provided a variety of eating experiences.

He watched the sun peek above the eastern horizon. Dallas and Fort Worth were growing financial centers, one of the reasons he chose the condo. The money from the sale of Blair's company was scattered across numerous accounts in the Cayman Islands and Zurich. The seven-figure sale of Blair's home provided plenty of funds for a lavish lifestyle.

Dallas was only five hundred miles from Mexico, far enough to be removed, but close enough to be able to get there in a timely manner. Mexico provided sanctuary if he was discovered and a supply of young women for his particular desires.

Today those particular desires were secondary. A meeting at 10 a.m. would draw the first of several well-to-do Texas investors into his web of falsehoods and empty promises. The success of Stephen Blair and his stellar reputation as a technology wizard made drawing these self-absorbed millionaires into his scheme easy.

He walked back to his desk where a laptop displayed the website of Black Hat USA. Moving the mouse over the Business Center icon, he clicked and rechecked his confirmed appointments for the convention. Smiling to himself, he closed the website and opened the file with his notes on the investor he would be meeting with later.

***

"I must say, Stephen, the prospectus you've presented is most intriguing. How long do you believe it will take to start generating profit?"

Marian Burke tilted his head slightly as he asked the question. He was a retired oil company executive with more money than he knew what to do with. Instead of playing golf, he enjoyed investing in longshot ventures. In his early seventies, his snow white hair was cut stylishly, but long. Forsaking suits when he retired, he wore expensive blue jeans, an oxford button-down light blue Joseph A. Banks dress shirt and a navy blazer. His permanently tanned face was wrinkled after decades in the Texas sun. Hazel eyes stared at the fake Stephen Blair behind rimless glasses.

They were meeting in an office suite close to his condominium. The temporary space contained a small office, a shared conference room for meetings and a part-time receptionist. Bishop was renting it for two months, with an option for additional months should it take longer to sucker investors into his scheme.

"As it says in the prospectus, once the research and development stages are completed, initial profit should occur, at minimum, in one year. Our preliminary research indicates not only a desire for the product, but a true need within the computer security segment."

Burke nodded as he looked back at the paperwork on

the conference table in front of him. "How many investors are you looking for?"

"Initial estimate is for ten with an outlay of three million each. These stakeholders will comprise the basis of the Board of Directors. Provisions are made for smaller investors without voting rights."

Nodding again, Burke removed his glasses and looked back at Blair. "What if a stakeholder wants to invest more than three million?"

Blair smiled. "At this point, we want to limit the liability of our partners. This is, after all, a new approach to AI. There are risks, and we would prefer to keep investor outlay at the three million level. However, once the project starts and we need additional funds..." He paused and smiled. "We can always open the door for more contributions."

"I appreciate your concern for my investment."

Blair nodded his head once.

"Okay, I'm in. When do you need the funds?"

"Before the end of the month. I will be attending Black Hat USA next week. After numerous conversations this past week, I see no problem filling the remaining slots for the board by then."

***

After Burke left, Bishop returned to his small office and closed the door. There was one more meeting scheduled later in the afternoon. Until then, he would work on scheduling appointments at Black Hat the following week. So far twenty were lined up over the course of the conference. He had lied to Marian Burke. His goal was to sign up as many investors as possible, take their three million dollars and return to Taiwan using the guise of Stewart Everett. Once the investments were received, they would be deposited, along with the proceeds from Blair's stock in New Age Software, in various accounts around the globe. If all went as planned, Bishop would disappear again, this time with enough money to pay off a debt and live the rest of his life in luxury. Once he was out of the reach of the FBI, the final element of his plan would be completed. An anonymous tip would be provided to CNN about the whereabouts of the real Stephen Blair's body. Once it was established the real Stephen Blair was dead before the investors made their contributions, the firestorm of a financial scandal would play itself out in the news media.

A slight smile appeared as he scrolled through the list of appointments for the next week.

CHAPTER 22

Mandalay Bay Resort and Casino, Las Vegas, NV

The line to check in was long, with what seemed like hundreds of conference attendees arriving at the same time. JR looked around nervously, scanning the room for someone he might recognize from his previous life. Mia's excitement was not quite contagious enough to calm JR's apprehensions. She held on to his arm as they stood in line, more for his sake than hers.

"JR, try to relax. This is the first time we've done anything like this as a couple. It will be fun, if you let it."

He sighed and nodded. "I know. You have to remember, I haven't been in a large crowd for a long time."

"What about our wedding reception?"

"Different circumstance. All of those people know me as JR. Not necessarily the case here."

"Have you seen anyone you recognize?" She asked with a conspiratorial smile.

"No."

"Didn't think so. Now, can we try to have fun?"

It took almost an hour to check in and find their way to their room on the 20th floor. The room featured a magnificent view of the mountains toward the west, one king-sized bed, Wi-Fi and a fully stocked mini-bar. As Mia stared at the mountains, JR unpacked his bag and set up his laptop on a desk. "Do you want to go to the mountains later?"

She nodded, but did not say anything right away. As JR looked inside the room's mini-bar, he heard. "I don't know why the mountains are so attractive to me. I'd like to live out here somewhere one day."

He shrugged. "Doesn't matter to me, we can live wherever you want. I can manage my business from anywhere." He stopped and looked at her. She was still staring out the window. "You've never mentioned anything about living in the mountains."

"I know. Just a fantasy I've always had. The week we spent in Colorado four years ago reinforced it. I'd never spent an extended amount of time on a mountain before. I loved the view and the crispness of the morning air."

JR heard her take a deep breath and then let it out slowly. He walked over to where she stood and put his arms around her. "Do you think it's because you grew up in a flat state like Texas?"

She shook her head. "Texas has mountains."

He chuckled, "Texas has hills, just like the so-called mountains of Missouri and Arkansas. They are nothing compared to the Rocky Mountains or even the ranges surrounding Vegas."

She turned around in his embrace and started pulling his polo shirt out of his jeans. As she did so, he backed up toward the bed.

***

Dinner was at the Border Grill. Mia ordered the vegetable quesadilla and JR the grilled fish tacos. After dinner, in deference to Mia's condition, they both sipped on virgin margaritas. She looked over her drink at JR. "What're our plans for tomorrow?"

"I have us signed up for a couple of hardware seminars in the morning, but in the afternoon, there wasn't anything I thought would interest you. If you want to go shopping, it might be a good time to do it, or you can lounge around the pool. Your choice."

"What are you going to do?"

"There's a seminar on cell phone security I'm attending. I've got a few clients expressing concern about their company phones being hacked. The seminar leader is someone I've been wanting to meet. We've exchanged emails. When he heard we were coming, he suggested the seminar."

"You're right, that doesn't interest me. Think I'll go to the pool."

***

Terence Craig was in his mid-thirties with short reddish brown hair and a closely trimmed beard. His black frame glasses sat on an unremarkable nose in front of green eyes. He didn't have the appearance of a tech geek, but was the owner of a very specialized security company catering to Fortune 500 companies.

After the seminar, as the attendees were shuffling out of the conference room, he walked up to JR and shook his hand. "I'm glad we finally got to meet in person, JR. I've followed your company's progress over the past few years. Impressive."

"Thank you. We've had several good years of growth."

"Did you learn anything this afternoon?"

JR nodded. "A lot. Thanks."

"Bullshit. You know more about his topic than most of the people here combined. Now why are you here?"

"Busted." JR gave Terence a sheepish grin "Sorry, I did enjoy your presentation."

"I'm glad."

JR took a deep breath and asked, "Do you know Stephen

Blair?"

Craig shook his head. "I've heard of him, but have never met him. I understand he's here looking for investors."

"That's what I heard."

"Are you wanting to invest in his AI research?"

"No, nothing like that. I just thought if you knew him, you could introduce me. I have a few questions for him."

"I know someone who can. There's a cocktail party before tonight's keynote speaker. Do you want me to arrange a meeting?"

JR shook his head. "Not necessary, I just need someone to point him out, I'll introduce myself."

Craig nodded. "Consider it done." He smiled and continued. "When are you going to merge your company with mine and come work with me, JR?"

With a half-smile, JR grinned. "Someday... Maybe."

***

Mia wore a tan sundress to the cocktail party, her shoulders displaying a slight sunburn from her afternoon in the sun.

"You look stunning in that dress."

She smiled. "I bought it this afternoon. Everything else I brought with me would have hurt my shoulders."

JR held her hand as they walked into the reception area. It took a few moments, but they found Terence Craig talking to several older gentlemen. When he saw JR, he excused himself and joined JR and Mia. JR introduced them. "Nice to meet you, Mia. Are you enjoying the conference?"

She pointed to her shoulders. "Probably too much."

They all chuckled. After a few more pleasantries, Craig turned toward the entrance of the banquet room they would soon be entering for the evening's dinner and keynote. He pointed toward a man talking to a group of Japanese businessmen.

"That's Stephen Blair. I've been told he's quite the

charmer. He's already secured twenty investors, and this is only the first day."

JR nodded, but said nothing as he stared at the figure of Stephen Blair.

"How much is he asking for?" Mia asked.

"Three million. I turned him down an hour ago. I was polite, but he didn't say anything that instilled confidence in his work."

JR turned back to Craig. "How so?"

"I asked him about a few protocols my company introduced into the AI mainstream several years ago. He acted like he'd never heard of them. After I turned him down, he excused himself to pursue others."

JR looked at Blair again. "Interesting."

"Well, good luck. Will I see you two after the speech?"

"Probably. We'll find you."

With this comment, Craig turned and returned to his previous conversation.

Mia looked up at JR. "Shall we meet the great Stephen Blair?"

JR smiled. "Don't be surprised if I say something you don't expect."

They walked over to Blair and waited until he was finished setting an appointment with the Japanese men. As soon as they walked off, JR quickly walked up to Blair with his hand out. As they shook hands, JR introduced himself using the name he had not used since becoming JR Diminski.

As he suspected, there was no recognition in the eyes of the man calling himself Stephen Blair. "I was surprised when I heard you sold New Age Software."

Blair smiled. "Time to move on. My interests have shifted lately and I wanted to do something spectacular with AI. Are you interested in the field?"

Nodding, JR crossed his arms over his chest. "Very much, I'm looking to integrate it into several security protocols I use with my clients."

Blair's eyes widened. "Really. If you invest in my new

venture, you'd have immediate access to our break-through technology."

"Interesting. Have you solved the problem of migrating algorithms?"

Blair hesitated before answering. He glanced around the room quickly and then answered. "No, but we have top people working on it. If you will excuse me, I have an appointment in a few minutes. It was nice to meet you."

He hurried off and was lost in the crowd within seconds.

"What the hell was that all about?" Mia chuckled. "Migrating algorithms and your old name?"

JR stared in the direction of Blair's retreat.

"That wasn't Stephen Blair."

"What are you talking about? Everyone here says it's Stephen Blair."

"I know. He may resemble Blair, but he's not Stephen Blair. Migrating algorithms was a joke we used in college. If someone expressed a crazy idea, we would compare it to migrating algorithms. Blair was the one who came up with the saying. While we weren't close, I did spend some time with him in college. His sense of humor was extremely dry when he took his meds correctly. He would crack us up with some of the things he said."

He paused and took a deep breath before pointing in the direction of where Blair disappeared. "The Stephen Blair I went to college with would have recognized my name. That Stephen Blair didn't."

"Do you think…?"

"Yeah, I do. We need to go back to our room and call Sean."

***

"Slow down, JR. Explain again why the man you met in Las Vegas is not Stephen Blair."

"I knew the minute I saw him it wasn't Stephen. There's a strong resemblance, but it's not him. I used to look slightly down at him in college. Now I looked up. The face is fuller, which is understandable, but the eyes are different. Stephen's eyes were always slightly droopy, with a faraway look most geniuses' exhibit. This guy's didn't. Plus he didn't have a clue about migrating algorithms. He acted like it was a real problem, and he had top people working on it. Give me a break."

Kruger was quiet for a long time. "Did you get a picture of him?"

"No, but we can tomorrow."

"Get one tomorrow and run it through your facial recognition routine."

"Who should I compare it to?"

"FBI facial database. You have access."

"Okay, who do you think he is?"

"I'll tell you after you run the comparison. I hope I'm wrong."

CHAPTER 23

Mandalay Bay Resort and Casino, Las Vegas, NV

JR did not want to spook the man calling himself Stephen Blair, so Mia was the one who followed him around during the lunch break taking clandestine pictures. Pretending to check her cell phone, she was able to obtain a number of profile and full frontal pictures. JR stayed in the background, noting the man's mannerisms and the amount of time spent talking to conference attendees.

It took thirty minutes for her to feel comfortable she possessed a good picture. She returned to JR. "I believe I've got a few good ones. But you better check to make sure,"

He took her cell phone and started paging through the various pictures. She watched him as he studied each picture. "He's up to thirty investors, JR. I heard him bragging to a group of men from India."

JR looked up from the phone. "At three mil each, that's ninety million dollars."

She nodded.

JR stared off into the distance and whistled softly. "What does he need ninety million for? He got eight figures for the stock in Blair's company."

Mia didn't answer. She knew JR was thinking out loud and did not expect a response.

Returning his attention to the cell phone, he paused on several pictures and stared at each for several moments. "You've got more than a few good pictures. I can use any of them. Let's get back to the room, and I'll send them to my system at the office."

***

Two hours later, JR was on the phone again with Kruger. "There's a seventy-nine percent match. Petty strong, Sean."

"It's not a hundred."

"The points not matching could be plastic surgery. Basic skull structure and eye width match perfectly. You can't change those indices."

Kruger sighed. "So your assessment is it's him?"

"The program says so. I can tell you he's not Stephen Blair. I ran the comparison to Stephen, and it only produced a thirty-five percent match."

"Damn."

"Is it who you suspected?"

"Yes."

"What about Blair's alibi in Florida?"

"You can drive from Atlanta to South Beach in the time gap. It also explains why Thomas Zimmerman and Judith Day were killed. They knew or at least suspected Blair was an impostor."

"Now what?"

"I'm thinking."

Kruger was silent for several minutes. "Can you keep an eye on him? I'll fly to Vegas for the arrest. The Vegas field office can send a few agents as well. Hopefully, they won't spook him until I can get there."

"Why not let them arrest him?"

"I want to make sure it's him. The only way to do that is stare him in the eyes."

"We'll do our best."

***

As JR and Mia watched from a distance, the Las Vegas FBI agents arrived with the subtly of British fans at a Manchester United game. When JR saw who was leading the three-man team, he turned to Mia. "Sean is not going to be happy."

"Why, JR?"

JR pointed to the agent demanding to see the hotel manager. "An old nemesis of Sean's. Last I heard, he was transferred to the field office in Fargo, North Dakota. That's Franklin Dollar."

***

Kruger stood on the tarmac outside the Springfield-Branson airport's General Aviation building. He was dressed in Docker khaki's, a light blue polo shirt with an FBI emblem on the left breast, and a navy blazer, his ever-present computer backpack slung over his right shoulder, and his FBI credentials attached to a lanyard hanging from his neck. He watched behind dark aviator sunglasses as the Gulfstream G280 taxied toward his position.

As the plane approached, he saw the front cabin door start to lower. As soon as the plane stopped and the door was down, he climbed the few steps up into the cabin. The co-pilot of the plane nodded as Kruger passed and raised the door.

Turning to his right and entering the cabin, he saw FBI Director Paul Stumpf sitting in the first seat on the right side of the cabin. An open file was in his lap. Stumpf nodded to the seat across from him, and Kruger sat down.

Paul Stumpf was in his mid-50s. At one time a dedicated marathon runner, he still maintained a lean body. But after having both knees replaced, he was starting to add a few pounds to his five-eleven frame. His hair was dark brown, perfectly styled, with no noticeable gray. Rimless glasses sat on an unremarkable nose in front of arctic blue eyes. Kruger knew Stumpf from his early career; he considered him a friend and was glad he helped propel the man into the directorship of the FBI.

Before Kruger could sit down, he felt the G280 start to taxi back to the runway. "Thanks for the ride, Paul."

"Are you sure it's him?"

After placing his backpack on the floor next to him and buckling his seatbelt, Kruger turned to look at the director. "Ninety-nine point nine percent sure."

Stumpf smiled. "You always leave room for an escape, don't you?"

Kruger returned the smile, but said nothing.

"Glad I was in St. Louis. We should have you on the ground in two and a half hours."

As the plane screamed down the runway, Kruger felt it lift and slide into the bright afternoon sky. "I called the Vegas field office. We should have several agents at Mandalay Bay by now. Hopefully, they can keep an eye on Bishop until we get there."

Looking up from the file, Stumpf removed his glasses and turned his attention to Kruger. "We might have a problem."

Kruger frowned and stared at his old friend. "How so?"

"For some reason, I haven't been able to find out why at this point, Franklin Dollar was transferred to the Vegas field office three months ago."

Taking a deep breath, Kruger put a hand over his now-closed eyes. "Don't tell me they sent him to the hotel."

"Wish I could."

"Shit."

"I would call that an accurate assessment."

"Thought you transferred him to the Fargo office?"

"I did. But since then I haven't been keeping tabs on him. Guess I should have. All I know is for some reason,

Personnel approved his request to be transferred out of Fargo. The Vegas office needed more agents and…"

Kruger finished the sentence. "He received the transfer. Hope he learned his lesson after the fiasco in Kansas City."

Stumpf was quiet for several moments. He put his glasses back on and returned his attention to the open file.

"We'll see."

***

With Las Vegas in the Pacific Time Zone, the G280 landed thirty minutes later than their departure time from Springfield in the Central Time Zone. An agency car met them on the tarmac and shuttled them to a back entrance of the Mandalay Bay complex.

They were met by Special Agent Franklin Dollar. He opened the door for Director Stumpf. "Glad you're here, sir. We have the suspect under surveillance."

Franklin "Mint" Dollar was slender and five-foot-ten inches tall, with close-cropped coal-black hair. Kruger considered the man an incompetent, uninspiring, lazy ass-kisser. The last time he and Kruger worked together, Dollar declared a case closed—a habit of his—before a proper investigation could be completed. He complained to Paul Stumpf's predecessor that Kruger was interfering with the investigation, resulting in Kruger being taken off the case, a case he solved not too long after Dollar was demoted and sent to Fargo.

Stumpf did not shake Dollar's proffered hand and instead stared him in the eyes.

"I hope you haven't compromised this investigation agent. Randolph Bishop has been on the agency's ten most wanted list for over six years. My sources tell me you haven't seen him in thirty minutes."

"He's behind closed doors in a meeting. We have the entrance secured waiting for your arrival."

Leaning closer to Dollar's ear, Stumpf lowered his voice

so no one else could hear. "So help me Franklin, if you've mucked this up, it will be your last act as an agent with the FBI."

Standing straight, he walked toward the door leading into the Casino.

Dollar stood still, his eyes wide as he stared into the distance at nothing. Kruger passed him heading toward the door and just shook his head.

***

JR and Mia sat at a wine bar across from the meeting rooms where Bishop was supposedly meeting with more investors. When Kruger walked up he gave Mia a hug and shook JR's hand. He sat in the only empty chair left at the small bistro table and stared at the door to the meeting room. "How long has he been in there?"

JR looked at his cell phone. "About forty-five minutes. He followed several men into the room and closed the door."

"Any other way in or out?"

"Don't know. Your buddy Dollar hasn't been the most discreet observer I've ever witnessed."

Kruger turned his attention to JR. "He's not my buddy. Tell me what happened."

"When Dollar arrived, he immediately went to the check-in counter demanding to see the hotel manager. He was flashing his credentials to anyone who would look at them. The other agents were rolling their eyes and staying as far away from him as possible. You could tell they weren't proud to be associated with him."

Kruger once again stared at the door to the room across from the wine bar. "Wonderful. Do you think Bishop saw him arrive?"

"Don't know," JR shook his head. "No way of telling. Everyone in the lobby and the casino area knew there were FBI agents looking for someone. If he was anywhere around..."

Nodding, Kruger closed his eyes. "Our surveillance is blown."

"Probably a good assumption."

After several moments of silence, Kruger changed the subject. "The director wants to meet you while he's here."

JR stiffened and sat straighter. "Why?"

"Because he's the Director of the FBI and wants to meet you."

"Again, why?"

Kruger smiled. "Don't know. You'll have to ask him."

Several men and Paul Stumpf approached the meeting room door. JR nodded in their direction. "Looks like they're going to force the issue."

Kruger stood and quickly walked toward the five men gathered at the door. One was the hotel manager, and the other three beside Stumpf were agents from the Las Vegas field office. Kruger did not know any of them. He pulled his lanyard with his credentials out of the inside breast pocket of his sport coat and hung it around his neck.

Stumpf acknowledged Kruger's arrival with a nod. "Glad you could join us, Agent Kruger." He glanced toward the hotel manager. "Please open the door, Mr. Mathews."

Using his pass card, the man unlocked the door and stood aside. One of the local agents, gun drawn, pushed the door open and the director of the FBI, along with two other agents, stormed into the room.

***

Paul Stumpf was furious. Kruger had known the man for twenty years and could not remember seeing him this agitated. The only occupants of the meeting room were three men from Dubai, waiting for the man they knew as Stephen Blair to return from the restroom.

Stumpf turned to Kruger and growled, "Find Franklin Dollar and get his butt in here."

Suppressing a smile, Kruger nodded and left the room.

Stumpf pointed at the tallest of the local agents. "Find out what you can from these gentlemen." To the other agent, "Bishop can't be too far. Find him."

The agent rushed out the door at the back of the meeting room just as Kruger followed Franklin Dollar through the front entrance.

Stumpf glared at Dollar. "Did you bother to check to see if the room contained a second exit?"

Dollar shook his head slightly.

Taking a deep breath, Stumpf let it out slowly. "My next question should seem obvious, but with your performance over the past couple of years, it might not. Why?"

Dollar stood straight, his shoulders back slightly. "The other agents should have checked. I was busy establishing rapport with hotel management."

Once again, Kruger suppressed a laugh, barely able to keep a smile off his face.

Leaning in, Stumpf was inches from Dollar's nose. "You were establishing rapport with hotel management? I've been told you were harassing them, flashing your credentials at anyone who would look your way. We've now lost track of a known serial killer because of your incompetence."

Dollar started to protest, but Stumpf cut him off. "You would be wise to keep quiet and seek counsel."

Now staring at his shoes, Dollar said nothing.

Stumpf stood straight and took a calming breath. He turned to Kruger. "Agent Kruger, please relieve Mr. Dollar of his credentials and weapon. As of this moment he is suspended, pending a review by the FBI's Office of Professional Responsibility."

CHAPTER 24

Mandalay Bay Resort and Casino, Las Vegas, NV

As the elevator door opened, Randolph Bishop observed the commotion at the casino check-in area. At the front desk, a man was berating a young woman and demanding to see someone from hotel management. When he started flashing his FBI credentials, Bishop bowed his head and hurried away from the bank of elevators in the opposite direction of the ruckus. Once he was at a safe distance he secured himself out of sight and watched the confrontation.

The realization hit him that his masquerade as Stephen Blair was probably at an end. Frowning and taking a deep breath, his thoughts turned to escape. He had achieved the commitment of more gullible millionaires than he originally anticipated. In fact, before coming down the elevator for his next meeting, a message from one of his banks in Zurich confirmed twenty of the thirty investors already transferred money to his account. He didn't realize how susceptible these individuals were to the prospects of doubling or tripling their initial investment. It had been child's play. Checking the time on his cell phone, he realized he was a few minutes late for his next meeting with several princes from Dubai. Once this meeting was concluded, he would leave the hotel and execute his escape plan. He smiled, turned, and walked toward their prearranged meeting location.

***

Forty minutes into his meeting with the Dubaian princes, Bishop struggled to mask his frustration and anger. The three men kept talking among themselves in Arabic. Their questions were becoming more technical as the meeting progressed. Questions he was finding more and more difficult to answer. Finally, Bishop excused himself to use the restroom and left through a rear entrance.

With the FBI in the building and lack of progress in his meeting, he decided it was time to return to his room, pack, and leave. Taking the back way toward the bank of elevators he stopped and from a distance, saw a familiar face walking across a common area of the hotel. FBI Agent Sean Kruger.

Bishop stopped and realized Kruger was joining a group of men preparing to enter the meeting room where the Dubai princes waited his return. Without hesitation and without waiting to see them enter the room, he hurried through the crowd near the check-in and casino area toward the front of the building. Once outside, he made a right turn and headed toward the parking valet for the hotel. Reaching into the front pocket of his suit pants, he made sure the flash drive with his files was there. His fingers felt the object. Satisfied, he withdrew his claim ticket from his suit coat breast pocket and handed it to a young male valet, who hurried off to retrieve his car.

***

JR and Mia watched as Kruger exited the room and hurried toward the two FBI agents posted near the lobby of the hotel. One of them was Franklin Dollar. Kruger pointed his finger at the man and motioned for him to return to the meeting room.

"Uh oh," JR sat straighter in his chair. "Something's wrong."

As Kruger walked behind Dollar, he glanced across toward JR and Mia still sitting in the wine bar. He frowned and shook his head slowly.

Mia looked over at JR. "Sean looks concerned and frustrated."

JR didn't respond immediately. "Something tells me Bishop wasn't in the room."

Five minutes after Dollar and Kruger disappeared into the room, Kruger was back out and motioned for the other FBI agent to join them in the room. The man hurried to where Kruger stood and listened for a few moments. Kruger handed him something, which the young agent slipped into his suitcoat breast pocket before sprinting toward the elevators.

"He's gone."

Mia looked at her husband. "What?"

"Bishop wasn't in the room. They've no idea where he is. This is going to get intense real fast."

***

Tim Gonzales, a recent graduate of the FBI Academy in his first assignment, barely made the height requirement. He made up for it with his strength. Broad shouldered with a thin waist, he could bench press three hundred pounds without straining. Born in Fort Worth, Texas, his proud parents were new citizens of the United States, having taken their oath the day after Tim's graduation. Clean shaven, with short, coal-black hair, his face was tanned and male model handsome. He spoke English like a Texan and Spanish like a native of Mexico City, one of the reasons his first posting was in Vegas.

As he hurried toward the elevator bank, his only thought was how not to screw up. Being around Franklin Dollar made him nervous. The man was a walking contradiction of a professional FBI agent. As the elevator door opened, he hoped the director did not judge the rest of the agents from the Vegas field office by Dollar's actions.

Watching the LED readout of the floors, he withdrew his agency-issued Glock 19 Gen 5 and held it at ready as he approached the thirty-first floor. When the door opened, he turned to his right and hurried down the hallway toward room 31141. Slowing as he approached the room, he continued to hold his weapon with both hands pointed at the floor.

He stood beside the door, reached over and knocked. In a heavy Spanish accent, he said, "Room Service." After several moments without a response, he repeated the knock and the announcement. Still no response. With his right hand still holding his weapon, he reached into his suitcoat pocket for the object Kruger handed to him. A pass key for the building. Sliding into the door's locking mechanism, he heard the click and saw the green light on the door. As quickly as possible, he opened the door and slid inside at the same time yelling, "FBI! FBI! Hands where I can see them."

With his weapon again in both hands, he swept the room, then the bathroom and closet. Next he checked under the bed. Nothing. Satisfied, he holstered his weapon and made a call on his secure agency radio. "All clear, suspect is not in his room."

He heard Kruger's response. "What do you see?"

Looking around the room, he saw a laptop, suitcase, assorted personal care items in the bathroom, and clothes hanging in the closet. "His personal items are still here."

"Do you see a computer?"

"Yes."

"Car keys?"

Gonzales did not see any on his survey of the room. He looked again and in several of the desk drawers.

"No, not at the moment. I'll keep looking."

"Don't worry about it. Seal the room and do not let

anyone in until we get there. Good work, Tim."

A board smile appeared on the young agent's face. Praise from an agency legend like Sean Kruger helped dissipate his concern about being around Dollar. He moved quickly to the room's door and stood outside. No one would be going into the room.

***

"Are you ready to earn your monthly stipend?" Kruger glanced over at JR and Mia as they walked to the bank of elevators.

JR remained quiet, lost in thought.

Mia looked at Kruger. "Have they found Bishop?"

Kruger shook his head. "No, not yet. We know he left the meeting room five minutes before we entered. He's not been seen since."

"He's gone, Sean." JR stared at the elevator door. His expression grim.

"I would agree, but the Director has the local police looking for him and the remaining agents with the Vegas field office are now involved. I overheard the conversation between Paul and the local Special Agent in Charge."

They entered the elevator and Kruger pressed the button for the thirty-first floor. JR watched the floor indicator. "Bet that was unpleasant for the SAC."

Kruger nodded, "His judgement about sending Dollar to head the team was discussed. Let's just say Paul didn't care for the response he was given. There may be two openings in the local office."

The rest of the ride was in silence.

When they arrived at the room, Kruger could see three agents collecting evidence. Gonzales came out of the bathroom, his gloved hands holding several evidence bags containing a hairbrush, toothbrush and a glass cup, each in its own bag. "We should be able to get DNA off these."

Kruger smiled. "Tim, get those to the forensics lab

immediately. We need proof Bishop was here."

Gonzales nodded and headed out the door.

Paul Stumpf stood by the large picture window, his back to the room. When Kruger stepped over, he stood next to the man and stared out the window as well. He waited for the director to say something.

"Well?"

"We haven't found him yet."

Nodding, Stumpf turned to look at Kruger. "I hate the bureaucracy and the politics of this job. The local SAC argued with me, claiming the personnel file he received on Dollar contained a glowing recommendation from the Director of the FBI."

"Let me guess." Kruger gave Stumpf a grim smile. "It hadn't been updated."

"No, it hadn't. When I asked him who signed the letter of recommendation for Dollar, he was silent. It was the letter from my predecessor."

"JR is here, sir. He can start looking at the computer."

Stumpf turned to the room. "Agents, thank you for your efforts. Gather what evidence you have and get it to the lab. We can finish here later. I need all of you on the street looking for this man."

The room cleared quickly. Stumpf offered his hand to JR. "I've heard a lot about you, Mr. Diminski. All of it good."

JR shook the offered hand and mumbled, "Nice to meet you."

Kruger leaned in close to JR's ear. "Relax, he's one of the good guys and he's on your side."

"Please call me, JR, sir. Mr. Diminski makes me nervous."

Stumpf chuckled. "Very well, JR." He nodded to the laptop sitting on the room's desk. "Can you tell us what's on that machine?"

JR looked at it, picked it up, and checked the model and serial number. He looked at the Director. "Give me a few minutes." Pulling his own laptop out of the shoulder bag he carried, he hooked it to Bishop's computer with a USB cable. He lifted the lid to his laptop. "I'll check to make sure he didn't set any booby traps first." With those words, JR started performing his magic.

***

Four hours later, the sun had set and the lights of Vegas sparkled through the still open curtain of room 31141. Kruger was in and out of the room several times, as was Paul Stumpf during the wait. When JR was ready to review the contents of the laptop, both were in the room listening.

"The Stephen Blair who checked into this hotel is definitely an impostor. My guess is the real Stephen is dead, along with his housekeeper. However, there's nothing on this computer to indicate he's Bishop."

"It's Bishop." Kruger showed JR a text message on his phone. "A fast DNA exam confirmed it about ten minutes ago."

JR looked at the message and nodded. "He has money stashed all over Zurich and the Cayman Islands. Most of it I can get to, some of it I can't."

Stumpf crossed his arms and raised a finger to tap on his lips. "How much does he have?"

"Almost two hundred million. About sixty percent of it is from the sale of Blair's stock in New Age Software, the other is from a lot of different sources. Apparently he's been talking to a lot of investors about his supposed venture in artificial intelligence."

"What about his emails, any mention of accomplices?" Kruger asked, looking over JR's shoulder.

Mia looked up from the laptop she was working on. "I've been going through those. He's still communicating regularly with someone in Taiwan. They never use names, and the email accounts change monthly."

JR looked up from Bishop's laptop. "Given time, we can isolate the emails."

Stumpf nodded. "Any information on his exit plans?"

Shaking his head, JR glanced back at the screen. "Not on this computer. Since there wasn't a cell phone found in this room, I would assume he has it with him."

Kruger was staring out the window at the lights of Vegas. "They found his rental car at McCarran. It's possible he had another car parked there. No records of Blair or Stewart Everett flying in or out."

JR looked up from the laptop. "I can start monitoring his cell phone. The number is on a bill he gets via the internet. But he'll know we have his computer. He's very smart, so my guess is he'll stop using it."

Stumpf frowned. "For now, freeze all the accounts you can."

JR nodded. "One other thing."

Kruger looked back at JR. "What?"

"He leased a condo in Dallas and rents a small office in a shared office complex."

"How?" Stumpf put his hands on his hips and stared at JR. "We've been monitoring any financial activity of Stephen Blair. It didn't show up."

"Shell company. It leased the condo and office space."

Stumpf shook his head, reached into his suit coat inside pocket, pulled out his cell phone, and walked out into the hall to make his call.

"Good work, JR. You've earned your pay this month."

JR smiled grimly, turned back to his laptop, and let his hands start playing the computer like a master pianist.

***

It was 10:30 p.m. Pacific Time when Stumpf made the decision to spend the night in Vegas and leave early in the morning for Dallas. Kruger was alone in one of the many bars in the resort, writing an email on his cell phone to Stephanie. Franklin Dollar sat down next to him and cleared his throat.

"Are you proud of yourself, Kruger?"

Kruger looked up and pressed an icon on his cell phone. "Excuse me?"

"Are you proud of yourself?"

"For what?"

"Getting me suspended."

Kruger chuckled. "I had nothing to do with your getting suspended, Dollar. You accomplished it all by yourself. It's the only thing I recall you doing well since you've been with the agency."

His face grew crimson, but Dollar took a breath and let it out slowly. "I'll be back in good standing as soon as the review board convenes. Then, watch out."

"Is that a threat, Dollar?"

"Consider it a warning. You've never played by the rules, Kruger. I've been following your career, and there's no way you're as good as you appear to be. No one is. I'm going to expose you for the fraud you are."

Smiling, Kruger shook his head. "When you have standards as low as yours, everyone will appear to be Superman."

Dollar snorted and stood. Giving Kruger a scowl, he walked toward the front of the bar. As Kruger watched, Dollar discreetly nodded to a woman sitting near the bar's entrance. She stood and slowly wandered over to his table. She was a tall woman in her mid-to-late twenties, with blond hair hanging down to her waist, long legs, and a form-fitting beige dress with a plunging neckline.

"Mind if I sit down?"

Kruger was staring at his cell phone. "Free country, sit where you like."

"I like it here."

When she sat down, Kruger looked up. "How much did Franklin Dollar offer you to get me in bed?"

"I beg your pardon."

"Simple question. How much is he paying you?"

"You're not being very friendly."

"I'm not in a friendly mood." He placed his cell phone on the table, the recording app still operating. "I hope you got paid up front. He's not known for keeping promises or fulfilling an agreement."

She nodded.

"I'll take the nod as a yes."

"He said you were an old friend going through a rough time and needed a companion for the night."

"He was blowing smoke up your dress. He's not an old friend, or a new friend, for that matter."

She folded her arms under her breasts, exposing more cleavage. "Doesn't mean you and I couldn't have a good time anyway. You know what they say, what plays in Vegas, stays in Vegas. No one would know."

"I'd know." He stood. "Don't follow me to my room. Oh, and when you see Franklin Dollar again, tell him I recorded his conversation and the one you and I just had." He pressed an icon on his cell phone and showed it to her. "I just sent both to the Director of the FBI."

Her eyes grew wide as he walked away.

CHAPTER 25

Flagstaff, AZ

Sleep eluded him as he lay in the creaky bed watching the lopsided ceiling fan turn. The hotel was cheap and the room cheaper, smelling of stale cigarettes and Lysol. His hasty departure from the Mandalay Bay created an issue with cash. Cash needed to fund his un-timely departure from the United States. His emergency money was still available, but he would need more once he got to his post-Stephen Blair location.

Unfortunately, he was running into an issue with his bank accounts. Each time he checked, his anger grew. "Zero Balance" or "Account Frozen" was the response from nine of the ten accounts scattered around the globe. One account in Dubai was still accessible, and he immediately transferred those funds to a brand new account in Zurich. With less than ten million dollars available, he needed to find a way to get his two hundred million dollars back. With his anger changing rapidly to fury, Bishop resorted to breathing exercises, learned in Thailand, to reign in his emotions.

Leaving the laptop behind was an unavoidable mistake. Apparently the FBI used it to find his accounts and compromise them. His exit from Mandalay Bay was chaotic.

After walking out the hotel entrance into the circle drive and having his car returned, he drove straight to the airport. It took fifteen nerve-wracking minutes as he continuously checked his rearview mirror for any sign of pursuit. After leaving the rental with Hertz, he took the shuttle to the departure terminal. Without stopping, he immediately walked to the arrival area and took the shuttle to Terminal Three long term parking. Twenty minutes later, after paying for his parking, his Jeep Grand Cherokee was exiting the airport. He found I-515 West, which led to US-93 South. At Kingman, Arizona, he took I-40 East. Four hours after leaving Vegas, he drove past a city limit sign for Flagstaff, Arizona. At the first Walmart he saw, he used cash to buy an HP laptop, a duffel bag, two changes of clothing and a few personal grooming items. After everything was packed into the duffel, he drove to a two star hotel with a sign out front claiming free Wi-Fi near the downtown area.

Paying cash, he checked into the hotel under his Everett Stewart ID and sequestered himself in the room. Without knowing if the Stewart ID was compromised, he decided he would leave early evening for the drive to Mexico. But first on his priority list was finding more information on the FBI agent who seemed always one step behind him.

He sat at the computer and Googled the name Sean Kruger. The results shocked him. He expected an FBI functionary, but found a dynamic, prolifically efficient investigator. He sat back and for the first time in several years, felt concern. A year earlier, Kruger unearthed and stopped a plot to blow up an auditorium with 15,000 souls attending a meeting. Prior to this, he spent two decades at the forefront of tracking down and bringing to justice numerous serial killers.

Bishop sat back in the desk chair and placed his right hand under his chin.

"I have to find his weaknesses."

He didn't realize he had said it out loud.

Searching Facebook, he discovered the FBI agent did

not have a presence on the site, but he found someone who claimed to be his ex-wife. The ex-wife lived in Aurora, Colorado. A twelve-hour drive from his location. The ex-wife was extremely chatty on Facebook, most of it uninteresting. Within some of her posts, there were hints about a son. Nothing concrete, but hints. When he searched for the son, he found nothing. Just like the father, the son did not seem to have a presence on social media, something he found strange assuming the boy's age.

Frustrated with the lack of finding anything further about the FBI agent, he walked to the parking lot and lifted the back gate on the Jeep. Making sure no one was watching, he lifted the floor board to reveal the spare tire, jack and tools. Once the screw holding the spare tire in place was loosened, he lifted the donut tire and removed one of three narrow brown paper bags used in liquor stores to cover wine. He then re-secured the spare tire and replaced the floor board and carpeting. Once back inside the Jeep, he opened the paper bag and pulled out one of three bundles of hundred dollar bills. In all, nine bundles of emergency money were stashed in the car. Ninety thousand dollars would have to last him until he could acquire a new set of IDs in Mexico and establish an account to transfer funds from his last remaining account in Zurich. Then, and only then, he would get his revenge on the FBI agent Sean Kruger.

He left the hotel parking lot, returning to the Walmart a mile and a half south. He walked to the back of the store to the electronics department where he bought a Virgin Mobile Galaxy 4 prepaid smartphone. He also purchased a wheeled suitcase and additional clothing. His next stop was a Target store on the way back to the hotel. There he purchased two cheap prepaid phones, these he would use only once.

Back in this hotel room, he used the Virgin Mobile phone to call Thailand. By the end of the call, he knew where to go and how much it would cost to become someone else.

***

For an American, entering the tourist area of Nogales, Mexico, was easy. For someone like Randolph Bishop, it was daunting. Unsure of his Everett Stewart Australian credentials and confident his Stephen Blair identity was blown, he sat on the American side of the border in a small café pondering how to get across the border. He watched tourists park their cars in lots around the border crossing, pay for the parking, obtain their Mexican Tourist Card and walk across the border. While he was in the café, several tourist buses from Tucson arrived and disgorged their passengers—all of which walked across the border.

He checked his watch and decided he would get his Mexican Tourist Card as Everett Stewart and cross the border when the next bus arrived. If his luck held out, when his transaction was done in southern Nogales, he would be someone else. Everett Stewart would disappear in Mexico, never to be heard from again.

His gamble paid off. The Mexican Immigration Officers barely looked at his passport and card. When asked, he told them he would be in Nogales for less than twenty four hours. The man smiled and stamped the Tourist Card.

Once past the touristy section of Nogales, he found a cab. The address he gave brought a frown to the driver's face, but he nodded and headed south. Bishop was dropped off in what seemed to be an abandoned industrial park with dilapidated buildings. Checking the GPS map on his cell phone, he located the correct building and walked through a door next to a loading dock.

Four hours later, the small man who identified himself as Juan handed Bishop a California driver's license, a United States passport and an American Express Platinum card in the name of Gary Yates of San Diego, California. They looked authentic.

Bishop nodded. "Cuanto cuesta?" How much?

"Diez mil…americano." Ten thousand, American.

Bishop shook his head. "Demasiado." Too much.

Juan reached for the items just given to Bishop. Holding them back, the new Gary Yates offered, "Nueve."

Juan stared at Bishop for a few moments, tilted his head slightly to the left. "Noventa y cinco."

Bishop smiled and handed the man a bundle of one hundred dollar bills.

Juan smiled a toothy grin. "Gracias."

As Bishop walked toward the exit door of the expansive empty warehouse, Juan said in heavily accented English, "The American Express is good for month. Owner on cruise in Mediterranean."

Bishop turned and smiled. After hesitating for a second, he walked back to Juan and handed him the remaining five one hundred dollar bills from the bundle and the Everett Stewart passport and driver's license. "Thanks for the tip, amigo."

Juan nodded and slipped the money into his jeans pocket. He opened the passport Bishop handed him and smiled.

"This made in Thailand; it is good. I do better."

Bishop stared at the diminutive Mexican for a few moments, smiled, shook his head and walked out of the warehouse.

Two hours later, Gary Yates crossed the border from Nogales, Mexico, to Nogales, Arizona, without so much as a second look from the US Border Patrol officer. He got behind the wheel of his Jeep Grand Cherokee and drove north toward Phoenix.

All of the stashed money from the spare tire area was now in the rolling suitcase purchased at the Flagstaff Walmart, as were his clothes, laptop, cell phones and personal items. Before crossing back to the US side, he picked up two additional cell phones with prepaid minutes from a Mexican cell phone company.

He parked the Jeep in a heavily used long-term parking area at the Phoenix Sky Harbor International Airport, leaving the keys in plain sight and the doors unlocked.

The shuttle took him to the departure terminal. He immediately went to the Hertz counter in the arrival terminal and thirty minutes later, using Gary Yates' American Express card, he was exiting the airport driving a Dodge Charger. He checked into the Four Seasons resort in Scottsdale using the American Express card and settled in for a few days of planning and shopping.

CHAPTER 26

Springfield, MO

"Stephen Blair's Jeep Cherokee was found stripped and abandoned in a really bad part of Phoenix last night." JR stood from his seat at the cubicle and walked to the Keurig. "Everett Stewart entered Mexico at the Nogales crossing under a forty-eight-hour Tourist Ticket and never left."

Looking up from the report he was reading in the next cubicle, Sean Kruger asked, "When did they find the Jeep?"

"About 3 this morning, their time. Police report thinks it's been there at least a day."

"How did you find that out?"

"Snooper program. Similar to a Google search engine, but without all the ads."

"I thought we were supposed to be notified when anything about Blair, Bishop, or Everett Stewart was discovered by local police departments."

"We will, but it still takes a few days. That's why I'm using the snooper program."

"Shit." Kruger was now pacing. He watched JR start to make a cup of coffee and drifted over to the machine and waited for him to finish. When JR took his cup back to the cubicle, Kruger started his own cup. "Have you ever heard of a drip coffee maker?"

"Sure, but you have to clean them. All you have to do with a Keurig is fill it with water."

Kruger frowned and stared at the finished cup of coffee. He shrugged and walked back to JR's cubicle as he sipped the hot beverage. "This is like fast food. It takes time to make a good cup of coffee." He frowned as he sipped it again. "So what where you saying?"

"I like the convenience of the Keurig…"

"Not about the coffee machine. About Nogales."

"I'm saying Bishop probably got a new set of IDs in Nogales and is back in the US with a completely unknown identity."

"Okay, how?"

JR chuckled. "How long have you been an FBI agent?"

"Is it that easy?"

"Uhhhh, yeah."

"How much?"

"It's expensive, at least five figures."

Kruger stared at his friend. "How do you know?"

Shrugging, JR took a sip of coffee. "Before you and Joseph helped with my identity crisis several years ago, I contemplated changing Mia's and my identities and moving to Australia."

Kruger was silent.

"Of course, I didn't have to. But through my connections within the hacker community, I discovered some of the best forgers are in Nogales, Mexico. Close to the border and all that. They usually charge at least ten thousand. Usually more, depending on what they are offering their clients."

"Huh."

"Which tells us Bishop has access to cash."

"Huh."

JR turned to look at Kruger, who was staring at his coffee cup. "You okay?"

"Yeah…"

Crossing his arms over his chest, JR kept his attention on Kruger.

"How did he know about a forger in Nogales?" Kruger asked. "I don't see him having that kind of information at his fingertips. Who'd he call?"

JR's eyes widened, and he turned to his computer. "Damn. Damn, I should have thought of that."

Watching JR work the computer never ceased to amaze Kruger. His fingers danced over the keys, and his head swiveled between three flat screen monitors like spectators watching a tennis match. Two minutes after he started, he sat back, lifted his coffee cup and took a sip.

"The number in Thailand we know about was called by a Virgin Mobile number three days ago, just before Everett Stewart's trip to Nogales."

Kruger took a deep breath and let it out slowly. "Bishop's bought new phones."

"I would agree. I can trace the Virgin phone, now that I know about it. But he's turned it off and hasn't used it since."

"He probably bought several throw-aways in Mexico. I would."

"So would I." JR placed his elbow on the desk and his hand under his chin as he stared at the computer monitors. "I'll place a tripwire on the Thailand phone, then I can monitor any phones that call it."

Kruger walked closer to JR's cubicle. "Where did the Virgin phone call Thailand from?"

"Flagstaff."

"The Vegas office assumed he went north."

JR was typing on the keyboard again. He paused, reading the left screen for several moments. "Everett Stewart checked into an Embassy Suites in Flagstaff. Never checked out. He paid cash for three days and was gone a day later."

"Damn. How can you follow him?"

"Until he uses the Virgin Mobile phone again, I can't."

"I was afraid you were going to say that."

JR glanced at the time on the lower right corner of his computer screen. "I'll get as much information before the conference call as I can. When Joseph arrives, we can bring him up to speed."

***

The conference call was scheduled for noon, Central Time. All the local participants were sitting around JR's conference table by 11:45. Sandy Knoll was in town, so he sat next to Joseph. Kruger and JR sat across from them. JR's version of a conference call speaker box was a modified Polycom Voice Station fed through a laptop. Not because it mattered, but because he was JR, no one on the other end of the call would be able to trace where the call originated.

Joseph clasped his hand on the surface of the conference table. "In three days, with an unknown identity, Bishop could be anywhere in the United States, or the world for that matter."

Kruger nodded. "He hasn't used the one phone we know about again. He may have already ditched it."

"I don't think he has." JR shook his head. "According to records I found in the Virgin Mobile server, he bought a Samsung smartphone with cash at a Walmart in Flagstaff. He also paid for five hundred minutes of calling time. I wouldn't think you would pay for that much time, use four minutes, and throw it away. Doesn't make sense."

"I would agree. Keep an eye on it. He'll use it again, and we'll know more about what we're up against. In the meantime, the purpose of this conference call is to bring the President up to speed on our other projects. Sean, will you be covering those?"

Kruger nodded, but was obviously concentrating on something else. Joseph stared at him. "Sean?"

Looking up, Kruger returned the stare. "Yes."

"Let's get a cup of coffee." Joseph stood and left the conference room. Kruger followed.

Kruger went to the Keurig and placed a coffee pod in the machine. Joseph crossed his arm over his chest. "Care to tell me what's keeping you so quiet?"

"Bishop."

"I gathered that. Do you want me to take the lead on the phone call?"

"Yeah, you probably should today." He raised the coffee cup to his lips, sipped the hot beverage and grimaced. "We've transferred funds and frozen most of his assets, so he's going to be pissed. He knew we were in Las Vegas to arrest him, thanks to Franklin Dollar. The question I keep asking myself is, if he feels desperate what's he going to do next?"

Joseph was pouring water into the Keurig from a gallon jug JR kept under the coffee service area. "Does he know who you are?"

Kruger nodded. "He used my name in Atlanta to gain access to Tom Zimmerman's condo."

"So, what precautions do you want to take?"

"Stephanie and I don't do Facebook or any of the other social media, and we don't talk to reporters. My name was all over the news channels last year after the Fayetteville thing, but we never identified where we lived. Plus we've moved since then. JR has helped to keep our internet presence non-existent. Brian and his fiancée don't have a social media presence either. It drives them nuts, but they understand why. These days, it's hard not to be found, but I think we've taken the right precautions. I've made a few enemies in my life Joseph, though most of them are in jail or dead. But they're out there. Bishop is different. He's the most dangerous and cunning foe I've ever faced. This is the second time he's eluded me. It's almost like he can sense I'm getting close."

Sandy Knoll stuck his head out of the conference room. "President's running late, ten more minutes."

Joseph smiled. "Thank you, Sandy, we'll be right there." He turned back to Kruger. "Only cats have nine lives, Sean. He's going to make a mistake and you'll be there when he does."

"Let's hope so. A mistake I made six years ago has cost innocent individuals their lives. There are at least three we're sure of. I assume the woman they found in the Chattahoochee River was killed by Bishop, and we can't find the body of Stephen Blair. Who knows how many he killed while overseas. I have to live with that knowledge, Joseph. I need to find him and put him away before more people pay for my mistake."

Joseph was silent as he looked at his long-time friend. He put his hand on Kruger's shoulder, smiled, and then walked back into the conference room.

Chapter 27

Aurora, CO

Bishop sat in his rented Dodge Charger on the street in front of a ranch-style home on Newark Street in Aurora, Colorado. The exterior was red brick with a large picture window between the front door and the garage. The landscaping was mature and in bad need of trimming. The owner was currently at work. She was an associate professor at the University of Denver nine miles west of the house. If she followed her normal schedule, she would be arriving within the next fifteen minutes.

His dark gray suit was from a local Men's Wearhouse store and the Aurora Police Department IDs were as fake as his Gary Yates passport and driver's license. The occupant of the home was the woman who claimed to be FBI Agent Sean Kruger's ex-wife. She had shared numerous Facebook posts about their past relationship after his successful thwarting of a terrorist plot in Fayetteville, Arkansas. Her name was Christine Daniels, the former Christine Kruger.

The black Dodge was parked so she would see the car as soon as she pulled into the driveway. Ten minutes later, she did. As soon as she drove into the now-open garage door,

Bishop exited the Dodge and walked toward the woman, who was now standing behind her car watching him approach.

"Can I help you with something?" Her tone was sharp and distrustful. She was a tall woman, slender, with short stylish blond hair and dark roots. She wore a gray pantsuit with a silk blouse. Her blue-gray eyes were narrow as she stared at the man approaching her.

Bishop smiled, held up the fake badge and ID. "Detective Barry Miller, Aurora Police Department. Ms. Daniels, may I have a word with you?"

She crossed her arms over her chest. "What's this about, Detective?"

"It's about your ex-husband. May we step inside?"

"I haven't seen or spoken to my ex-husband in over twenty years, Detective. No, we may not step inside. You can tell me what this is about out here."

Bishop frowned, turned around and quickly scanned the neighborhood. Seeing no one, he slipped his hand inside his suitcoat jacket and pulled a Sig Sauer P224 from its holster on his belt. He returned his attention to Christine Daniels. Pointing the pistol at her chest, he smiled. "Get in the house, bitch."

***

"When did you last speak to your ex-husband?"

Christine was duct-taped to a wooden chair, moved from the dining room to her bedroom. She shook her head and stared at the floor. "I've told you over and over, I haven't seen the man for twenty years. Can't you get it through your head?"

Bishop slapped her harder and bent over. Getting close to her face, he screamed, "I don't believe you."

Frustration overcame her fear, and she stared into Bishop's eyes. "Believe what you want. I don't have contact with the man."

Bishop straightened and pointed at all the pictures on the

wall of her bedroom. "Then who is that?"

Christine sobbed, "My son."

Bishop stood perfectly still. He stared at the woman, than back at the pictures on the wall. There were a few pictures of a young boy, but the rest of the pictures were of a tall slender man. The pictures appeared to be natural, without the subject posing. "He looks remarkably like his father."

She nodded and took a deep breath as she sobbed. "They look more like twin brothers than father and son."

"Where does he live?"

She shook her head.

Bishop slapped her hard. She screamed, but did not answer his question.

"You don't know, do you?"

She shook her head again. "I hated being a mother. I left when he was less than a year old. I haven't spoken to him since he graduated from high school."

"But you have feelings for him." Bishop walked closer to the wall and examined the pictures more carefully. Each was an eight-by-ten taken with a telephoto lens from a distance. Closer to the picture, he could tell the man was younger. "Obviously, you know where he is. You took these pictures, didn't you?"

She didn't answer.

He stopped at one picture in particular. It showed the man walking with a young woman on what appeared to be a college campus. The couple was holding hands. "Who's the girl?"

She remained quiet.

"You might as well answer me. I'm going to find out eventually."

Christine stared at the floor.

"Answer me."

She shook her head.

Bishop took a switch-blade from his pocket and flipped it open. He held the knife to her blouse and cut the first button off.

She took a sharp breath.

He cut off the next three buttons, exposing her bra.

"I would rather find out where your ex-husband is. You'd spare your son and his girlfriend a lot of pain. Tell me Christine."

She shook her head harder.

Bishop slipped the knife between her chest and the middle of her bra, turned it and cut the fabric holding the two cups together. With her breasts now exposed, she gasped and started to cry.

"I don't know where Sean lives. He used to live in Kansas City, but when he got married, they moved. How many times do I have to tell you I don't talk to him?" Tears ran down her cheeks as she looked at Bishop. "What do I have to say to make you believe me?"

Bishop grinned as he cut the rest of her clothes off.

***

Sitting in front of Christine Daniels' laptop, Bishop searched her Facebook account for any clue to the location of her ex-husband. He learned her son's name was Brian from several letters she kept in her nightstand. The letters were written in a child's handwriting on lined notebook paper, now yellowed with age. After an hour of searching, he found what he was looking for. It was a PDF file with an engagement announcement for Brian Kruger and Michele Brickman. The announcement was from the Columbia, Missouri, Daily Tribune. The announcement mentioned Brian was the son of Sean and Stephanie Kruger, Springfield, Missouri. No mention of the owner of the house he now occupied. She did tell him the truth. She was completely and totally out of the lives of her ex-husband and son. Sad.

Bishop stood and went back to Christine's bedroom. He stared at the body lying on the bed. "You could have saved yourself a lot of anguish by just telling me. Plus, you might have had a chance to reconcile with your son."

Christine was no longer able to respond to Bishop. Her unseeing eyes stared at the ceiling. He shook his head. "Sad. You made poor choices, Christine."

He shrugged and closed the door to the bedroom.

***

It was an hour before dawn. The neighborhood was quiet and the surrounding houses still dark when Bishop walked out to the rented Dodge Charger. He placed the GPS unit from Christine's car in the front seat and walked back into the house. He wiped down all the surfaces he remembered touching with anti-bacterial wipes he found in her kitchen. After turning the air conditioner down as low as it would go, he locked the front door and returned to his car. Once the GPS unit was attached by a suction cup to the front windshield, he requested the unit to guide him to Springfield, Missouri. After the route was calculated, he pulled away from the curb.

It was a little under eight hundred miles to Springfield. Glancing at the clock on the dashboard, it would take eleven hours to make the drive. He would be there just after dark. Plenty of time to do what he needed to do.

CHAPTER 28

Springfield, MO

Kruger's cell phone vibrated just as the conference call ended. He hesitated, pulled it out of his pocket, stared at the caller ID, and accepted the call. "I haven't spoken to you in a while, Alan, what's up?"

"It's not good, Sean."

Kruger didn't say anything. He stood and left the conference room, shutting the door behind him.

"Okay, what's happened?"

"Your ex-wife didn't show up at the university this morning. She had a full class schedule and didn't call in."

Walking toward the staircase on the far side of the room, he sat down in an empty cubicle. Taking a deep breath, he was afraid he knew where this was going.

"Christine has a history of abandoning her responsibilities, Alan. How does this concern me?"

"Her department chair was concerned; she'd never done this before. They sent a university security unit out to check on her. Temperature was in the mid-forties outside when they got there, and the house's air conditioning unit was running. They thought it strange and requested an Aurora patrol car to join them. Using that as probable cause, the police broke in."

Kruger was silent for several moments. "He found her?"

"Looks that way. Our agents were called once the police entered the house and found her. The agents on scene described it as unpleasant."

"How bad?"

"From what I was told, not as bad as Brenda Parker, but it was bad."

"When?"

"Sometime last night. Denver police have been there since mid-morning, and we have two agents still on the scene consulting. Both of them read your memo several weeks ago about Bishop, realized what was going on, and asked their SAC to call me."

"Do I need to go out there?"

"I think you should. If nothing else, see if you can determined what he learned while there."

"There are direct flights from here to Denver. I can probably be there before dark."

Alan was quiet for a few moments. "Sorry about this, Sean."

Kruger didn't answer right away. "As much as I've resented what she did to Brian, no one deserves their last hours on earth to be with Bishop."

The call ended and Kruger sat there, deep in thought. Joseph walked up to him, stood quietly for several moments and asked, "Bad news?"

Kruger nodded. "Bishop found Christine."

Joseph closed his eyes and leaned against the desk in the cubicle. "Oh, no. When?"

"Sometime yesterday. That was Alan on the phone. She didn't show up for work this morning and the University sent a couple of security people out. They didn't like what they saw, called the cops and the cops called the field office after they entered the house. I've seen Bishop's work..."

"I'm sorry, Sean."

Kruger glanced at his watch. "I need to get to Denver

today. You want to come?"

Joseph straightened up from the desk. "I have a charter service available; I'll call him. Get to the airport as soon as you can." With a grim smile, he headed toward the staircase.

Kruger walked back to the conference room and told JR and Knoll he was leaving and why.

Knoll stood. "Anything you need me to do?"

Taking a deep breath, Kruger stared at the large man for several seconds. Letting the breath out slowly, he nodded. "Yeah. Can you drive up to Columbia and keep an eye on Brian and Michelle until I get this figured out?"

Walking over to Kruger, Knoll reached into his pocket and extracted a plastic Zip-lock bag with two cylindrical objects. He handed it to him. "I originally planned to give these to you in private. As an agent with the FBI, you're not supposed to have stuff like this. But if you need them, you have them. Trust me, you might need them."

Staring at the plastic bag, he looked back up at Knoll, accepted the bag, placed it in his back jeans pocket, and smiled.

"You never know, Sandy. Thanks for keeping an eye on my son."

"No problem." Knoll nodded. "Happy to do it. I'll leave from here. My go-bag's in the car."

After Kruger left, Knoll started gathering up the files he was working on. JR turned to the large man. "When you get back from Columbia, I need you to re-qualify me on a Remington."

Chuckling, Knoll smiled. "From what Joseph has told me, you're the one who needs to teach me a few things."

JR shook his head. "I'm rusty."

The smile left Knoll's face. He stared at JR for a few moments, and then nodded.

***

"Why don't you and Kristin visit your sister for a few

days?"

Stephanie looked at her husband and blinked a couple of times. "Do you think we need to?"

"It would make me feel better. I don't know how long I'll need to stay in Denver."

"I'm sorry about Christine, Sean."

Kruger didn't say anything but turned and walked toward a bedroom window, staring out into the backyard. He remained quiet for several more moments. "Six years ago I let this monster get away."

He paused and turned back to look at Stephanie.

"I knew he was guilty of murder. I just didn't have enough proof to arrest him. So…" He took a deep breath. "I taunted him one evening, daring him to say something or take a swing at me. Anything, it didn't matter. I needed an excuse to arrest him and throw his ass in jail. At least until we could get positive proof he'd murdered those four women."

Stephanie remained quiet.

Kruger shook his head and turned back to gaze out the window. "Bishop was on the verge of taking a swing at me, I could tell. There was fury in his eyes, but just as quickly, it was gone. I watched him get into his car and drive away. He disappeared along with six million dollars he'd embezzled from his company. Now four innocent individuals are dead. Plus, I've put you, Kristin, Brian and Michelle in jeopardy. All because of that one mistake."

"Sean, it's not your fault. He's the one who killed those people."

Kruger shook his head. "But I could have prevented their deaths." He turned to his wife. "If I had left the guy alone, he would have showed up for work the next morning. We received the results from a DNA test early the next day. A match from one of his victims." He closed his fist and held it up for emphasis. "We had him. We could have put him away for life. Except I warned him."

"You didn't know he would vanish."

"No, I didn't know. But I let my ego get in the way and

I…" He didn't finish. He put his arms around Stephanie and hugged her. "I need to correct my mistake."

***

Kruger scrolled through crime scene photos on a Samsung tablet. FBI Special Agent Marcie Kincaid stood next to him while he looked at a photo, then the room. He repeated the process with the next photo. Stocky and several inches shorter than Kruger, with medium-length brown hair tied back in a ponytail, Kincaid was a ten-year veteran of the Bureau. She stood silently with her hands behind her back as she waited for Kruger to finish.

"Thanks for having the body removed before I got here, Marcie."

She nodded her head. "We were informed about your relationship to the victim."

"Her name was Christine, and the relationship ended twenty years ago. Still, I appreciate your concern."

Marcie nodded again, her demeanor not changing.

Charlie Craft walked back into the bedroom. "We've found a lot of DNA and a few fingerprints. Looks like he tried to wipe most of the prints, but missed some."

Kruger looked at Charlie. "Can you confirm it was Bishop?"

"Officially, not yet. But, yeah, it was Bishop."

Kruger nodded. "Can I look at the laptop in her office?"

"Sure. We checked it first. We didn't find Christine's or any fingerprints on it, lots of cleaning residue from being wiped within the last twenty-four hours."

Sitting down at the laptop, Kruger turned it on. As he waited for it to boot up, he stared around the office. Pictures of Brian were everywhere. On the wall, on her desk and when the computer opened, her desktop background picture was a long distance shot of him on stage accepting his bachelor's degree diploma. Kruger was at the ceremony, but did not remember seeing his ex-wife. He shook his head. The sadness of her decision not to be involved in her son's life now even more apparent.

The computer was not password protected, so it indicated Bishop would have been able to access any of the files on the computer. He called Charlie into the room. "If I wanted to look at the most recent files accessed, what would I do?"

Charlie explained how to do it and stood with his arms folded across his chest as he watched his old mentor work the keyboard.

"Oh, shit." Kruger stared at an open PDF file displayed on the computer screen.

"What?"

Kruger pointed at the screen showing the last file Bishop looked at before closing the computer. It was a scanned copy of Brian and Michelle's engagement announcement from the Columbia newspaper.

"He knows Brian lives in Columbia, and I live in Springfield."

***

On the drive back to the airport, Joseph drove while Kruger spoke to JR on his cell phone. "Sandy Knoll is in Columbia with Brian and Michelle. They're safe. How easy will it be for Bishop to find my house?"

"He won't be able to find yours, Joseph's or my address online in any search engine. I made sure of that when you moved here." He was silent for a moment. "Uh, oh. I forgot about something. Let me check." Kruger heard the clicking of JR's keyboard and then silence. "I was afraid of this. All he would need to do is access the county assessor's webpage and search local property records. They're public records so there isn't much I can do about it."

"Can he do it online?"

"Yeah, I just did. Type in your name, and it gives the address of real property in the county."

"Do you think he would know to look at the website?"

"I wouldn't bet against him. Bishop has proven to be adaptive and elusive in the past."

"Yes, he has."

"Sean."

"Yeah."

"Assume the worst."

CHAPTER 29

Springfield, MO

As Joseph and Kruger walked through the parking lot at the Springfield-Branson National Airport's General Aviation Terminal after returning from Denver, Kruger's phone vibrated. He glanced at the caller ID and saw a 928 area code. Thinking it might be one of the agents from Las Vegas, he accepted the call.

"Kruger."

"Agent Sean Kruger?"

"Yes." He paused briefly, not recognizing the voice. "Who is this?"

"I'm surprised you don't remember me."

Kruger's heart froze. He stopped walking and stared at Joseph. "Sorry, I'm getting old, my memory isn't what it used to be. Please, tell me who you are." He snapped his fingers, pointed to the phone and mouthed, "It is Bishop. Call JR."

Without hesitating Joseph turned his back to Kruger, took out his cell phone, and punched in one of JR's numbers only he knew. It was answered immediately. Joseph's voice was low. "JR, Bishop is calling Sean. Trace the number."

"Got it. You wanna stay on the line?"

"Yeah." He turned, looked at Kruger and nodded.

Kruger stared at Joseph, waiting, the caller silent. "Are you still there?"

"Yes, trying to decide what to tell you. I think you know who this is, so I won't say it out loud."

"I could be wrong."

"You have a nice house, Agent Sean Kruger."

Kruger closed his eyes, took a breath and let it out slowly, thankful Stephanie and Kristin were in Kansas City.

"What do you want, Bishop?"

"Good, you do know who it is. Let me explain something to you, Agent Sean Kruger. I will always be one step ahead of you. Try to understand that…"

"I'm not going to play your game, Bishop. Why are you calling?"

The phone was silent again. Kruger frowned, glanced at the phone's screen to see if the call was over. It wasn't. Finally he heard, "It's really a curtesy call, more than anything. Maybe a warning. Yeah, I'm calling you with a warning. Return the money. If you don't, you won't like the consequences." The call ended abruptly before Kruger could respond.

He took the phone away from his ear and stared at the screen. Joseph walked closer. "JR says the call was made by the phone purchased in Flagstaff. He couldn't pinpoint the location, but he said it was local."

"I know. He told me I have a nice house."

Joseph stared at Kruger. "I'll call the police, they can meet us. Maybe he's still there."

Kruger turned and started walking toward his car. "No, he's long gone. I wonder if he found what he was looking for."

Three patrol cars and a detective's car—their light bars rotating—were parked outside Kruger's house when they arrived. Yellow tape was being strung around Kruger's yard. Joseph knew the detective who was sitting in his car talking on a cell phone. The car's door was open, and both of his feet were on the ground. When he saw Joseph approaching, he stood and extended his hand, but did not stop his phone conversation.

Joseph shook the man's hand and waited for him to end the call. "Yeah, I need someone from the crime lab here immediately." He paused as he listened. "The owner just showed up." Another pause. "Okay, I'll call you back after I talk to him."

The detective ended the call and smiled. "Good to see you, Joseph. Wish it was under better circumstances."

Joseph nodded. "Bob, this is Sean Kruger. Sean, this is Detective Robert Morris."

Kruger shook the man's hand. "What's going on inside, Detective?"

Morris looked at Kruger. "You used to be with the FBI, right?"

Kruger nodded. He didn't feel like getting into details concerning his status.

"You think someone from your past was here?"

Again, Kruger nodded.

"There doesn't appear to be anything missing. All the electronics and stuff burglar's normally take are still there. But someone tore the place apart looking for something."

Kruger looked at his house, took a deep breath. "May I go in? I might see something you don't."

Morris nodded, "Your house."

Walking through the rooms of their home, Kruger noted the systematic method Bishop used to search for whatever he was looking for. He kept his breathing steady, controlling the rhythm, fighting the inner turmoil. Files were scattered in his home office, so determining if anything was missing would be difficult. Storage boxes in one of the spare bedrooms were dumped on the floor, the contents strewn about. Kristin's room was ransacked, for no apparent reason other than he was there and could do it. Finally he walked into Stephanie's and his bedroom where the chaos intensified. Pillows were cut and ripped apart, and the bedding wadded up and thrown into a corner. Lamps were thrown against the walls and shattered. As he surveyed the room, he noticed several objects missing.

Turning to Morris, his voice in a barely controlled whisper, "Stephanie's tablet is missing, as is a picture of her and Kristin I keep on my nightstand."

He returned his attention to the nightstand and walked closer. On the floor, under a ripped pillow case, he saw broken glass and the twisted remains of the frame he kept the picture in. Kruger pointed to it. "He took the picture, left the frame."

Morris bent over and using the tip of a pen lifted the pillow case. "I'll have them dust it for prints. I'll need yours for elimination purposes."

Kruger nodded. "There is a bottle of facial cream on her side of the vanity. It doesn't look disturbed. You can get her prints off it."

Morris smiled slightly. "Good, thanks. Sorry you had to see this, Sean, but we appreciate your help."

Remaining quiet, Kruger turned, walked out of the bedroom, and returned to his car outside on the street. He leaned against the hood, closed his eyes, bowed his head, and crossed his arms tight against his chest. He took a deep breath and let it out slowly.

Joseph walked up and leaned against the hood next to Kruger. "How bad?"

"Not as bad as Brenda Parker's house, but bad enough."

Joseph nodded. "I called Sandy. He'll be calling in four more members of his team. They'll fly into Columbia and take over protecting Brian and Michelle. More boots on the ground, so to speak. Sandy will be back early tomorrow morning. He'll be at your disposal."

"Thank you, Joseph." Kruger looked up. Dusk was turning to night and the street lights of the neighborhood were starting to glow. "I need to go back in there and get something. Then I'll stop at JR's before I drive to Kansas City. I'll feel better when Stephanie and Kristin are with me."

"Good idea."

CHAPTER 30

Kansas City, KS

The house was dark. No external lights were visible from the driveway, and all the windows in the front of the house were unlit. Kruger parked the Mustang behind Stephanie's Jeep Cherokee on the right side of the driveway. He glanced at the clock on the Mustang's dash. It was 11:03 p.m.

Before leaving Springfield for the drive, he called. She told him her sister and husband would be out attending a company function. She would leave the front porch light on for him and wait up. Placing the Mustang in park, he stared at the dark house, his stomach clinching. He stepped out of the car and walked toward the Cherokee, touching the hood as he passed. It was cold to the touch.

The house was on an oversized lot in an upper-income neighborhood of Overland Park, Kansas. The lot contained numerous mature oaks and maples, allowing only the partial glow of a distant street light to penetrate the gloom. The garage was on the right side and opened to the side, allowing a wider than normal driveway. Two large picture windows featured prominently on the left side of the home, while a covered porch dominated the center of the structure. As

Kruger approached the front door, broken glass reflected light from the street lamp. He glanced up. The front porch light was shattered.

The tightness in his stomach increased as he reached for the Glock 19 in his belt holster. Curtains adorning the two large picture windows were open, something he knew his sister-in-law did not allow at night. As he approached the front entrance, he could see the jam was shattered and the door slightly ajar. A cold shiver coursed through him as unthinkable possibilities reached his consciousness.

Holding his Glock with both hands pointed down, he leaned his shoulder against the door and increased the opening.

"Steph… it's Sean, are you here?"

His answer was silence from the pitch black interior. As he peered into the darkness, his cell phone vibrated. He looked at the caller ID. Unknown.

"Yes."

"They not there, Agent Kruger."

"Who is this?"

"Not important…"

"Where are my wife and daughter?"

"Safe… for now. Maybe you cooperate. Maybe you see them again." The voice, deep and gruff, spoke English with a heavy accent Kruger could not immediately recognize.

Remaining silent, Kruger fought to tame his growing panic. The only way to save Stephanie and Kristin was to think logically. "What do you want?"

"My employer very upset with you."

"Yeah… So?"

"He want you to return his money and stop trying to find him. Back off. Very simple."

"I want proof of life first."

"They are fine. I will call back in one hour. You talk to wife then."

The call ended, Kruger stared at the screen, trying to think. Pushing down the panic, he took a deep breath and sent a text message to a number he knew from memory.

His phone rang fifteen seconds later. "Did you get the call?"

"Yeah, good decision having your phone cloned before you left." JR's voice was tense.

"Can you start tracking his location when he calls back?"

"Already on it."

Kruger opened his recent call screen and returned the phone to his ear. "He was on the call less than two minutes."

"Smart. It might take several calls. But I'll be able to get a general location on the next one. Why did he say an hour?"

"I think he was watching; he knew when I got here. He's probably moving toward a safe house, so it won't be too far from Kansas City."

"I would agree. While we've been talking, I hacked into Verizon's system and found his number. It's a burner, sold at a Qwik-Trip. Could be a problem."

"Yeah, well, you've done it before."

"Tricky, but doable. Let me see what I can find. I'll call you back."

The call ended, and Kruger took a deep breath. His earlier panic remained, but having JR's assistance eased the sharp edges.

While the minutes crept by, he went to the trunk of his car and grabbed the old duffel bag he kept packed. A habit from his Bureau days. It was the object he retrieved from their ransacked house and placed in the Mustang's trunk before leaving.

Returning to the interior of the darkened home, he stood in front of one of the picture windows and watched the street. As he waited, he started changing clothes. He wanted to be ready to leave the house as quickly as possible, anticipating JR would be able to steer him toward Stephanie. He put on a black pair of jeans, a long-sleeved black t-shirt, black socks and black Nike running shoes. He found his black watch cap tucked away in a side pocket of the duffel bag.

Using a flashlight from the duffel, he walked to the laundry room of the darkened house. After rummaging around, he found a can of black shoe polish in the cabinet above the washing machine. Not what he preferred, but it would do. Returning to the front window, he withdrew several items from the duffel bag. One was his ankle holster, which he strapped to his right leg just above his shoe. He opened a small plastic gun case containing his Glock 26 and secured it in the ankle holster. Next he strapped a Gerber 06 Fast knife to his left calf with two strips of Velcro. He pulled his jeans down over it. Kneeling next to the duffel, he loaded four magazines for his Glock 19 and one for his 26 with 9mm hollow points. When he completed this task, he found the Zip-lock bag Knoll gave him. Opening the bag, he removed the two cylindrical objects. The first was a threaded barrel for his Glock 19, and the second object, a Gem-Tech GM 9 suppressor. He field stripped the Glock 19, replaced its original barrel with the threaded one, and reassembled the gun. He screwed the suppressor on and checked the feel of the pistol. Longer, but not unmanageable. Removing the suppressor, he slipped it into his left sock.

Exactly fifty nine minutes after the first call, his cell phone vibrated. The caller ID was the same as the previous call.

"Yes."

He heard Stephanie's voice. "Sean, we're both okay. I'm sorry, I didn't take the precautions you taught me." She sounded strained, but steady.

"I'll find you. Try to stay calm and do what he tells you, okay?"

"Okay, I'll…"

The phone was taken away from her, and he heard, "There is proof of life. Now, I will call you back in fifteen minutes with more details."

The call ended. Ten seconds later it vibrated again.

"Where is he?" Kruger knew it was JR on the other end.

"He's in north Kansas City, somewhere between 435 and

169, north of 152. If you can keep him on the phone longer than thirty seconds next time, I can narrow it down even further. Possibly to a street and house."

"Got it, I'm heading that way."

The call ended, and Kruger took a deep breath. He remembered one more item he might need. Returning to the old duffel bag, he found a pair of thin black cotton gloves and put them in the back pocket of his jeans. He dropped the shoe polish in the duffel bag and retrieved a double magazine pouch. Two of the newly loaded extra clips were secured in their slot. He attached the unit on his belt above his left hip. He extracted the magazine from the Glock in his holster, checked it again for the fourth time and slapped it back into the butt of his gun. He then charged the weapon and returned it to his holster.

He took a deep breath, placed his ID and badge wallet in one of the side pockets of the duffel bag, and exhaled slowly. Tonight he was not an FBI agent. He was a husband and father going after the person responsible for kidnapping his family.

When the next call came, he was on State Line Road getting ready to merge onto East 435. He answered with, "Yeah."

"Here is what you will do, Kruger. You will dismantle the search for Bishop. You will then return all of his money."

"Just how in the hell am I supposed to do that? Bishop's on the most wanted list. Nobody is going to call off the search until he's in custody."

"Not my problem. You have the problem. The consequences of not ending search and returning money are not good for family. Once money returned, your family will be returned."

"Yeah, you've mentioned that."

"Are we clear about what you must do?"

"Very. How do I know you'll keep your end of the deal?"

"You do not. This is beauty of arrangement. I control

it."

The call ended before Kruger could respond. As he followed the highway, 435 turned north and his cell phone vibrated again.

"Talk to me."

"He's within a few hundred feet of North Oak Trafficway and North East 114th Street."

"Can you narrow it down any further?"

"Maybe, if he makes another call, but not until."

"I don't think he will. I can work with what you've found."

"Hold on, he's making another call. Don't hang up. He's calling Bishop's Virgin phone."

The phone was silent for three minutes as Kruger waited and drove north. Finally JR came back on. "The house is about two hundred feet east of North Oak Trafficway on 114th. That's as close as I'm going to get you."

"That's good enough. I can take it from here. Keep monitoring his calls."

"You got it. Good luck, Sean."

"Thanks."

The area in north Kansas City was unfamiliar to him. Using a map app on his cell phone, he located a Casey's General Store about a mile from the location of the houses. He parked the Mustang in the lot and used the cell phone's Google Earth feature to look at the area. It was an older neighborhood with mature trees and small older homes.

The street level portion of the app allowed him to view the neighborhood in detail. As he studied the area, an idea of how to proceed became clearer. It was approaching 1 a.m., and the area was quiet. He drove his car behind the store, put the watch cap on and smeared black shoe polish on his face using the rearview mirror to make sure he was properly covered. He removed the suppressor from his sock and screwed onto his weapon. Satisfied with the results, he took a deep breath and put the car in gear. He carefully drove south and then east to find North Oak Trafficway.

Ten minutes later, his car was parked behind several other cars in the yard of a house on an adjacent street. He flipped the switch on the dome light to off and slipped the black cotton gloves on. He exited the Mustang and stood up. Looking around he walked toward the area found on the Google Map search, avoiding street lights and houses with porch lights on.

JR's instructions mentioned the house was two hundred feet east of Oak Trafficway. He saw two homes within this distance. Both were on the south side of 114th, while the north side was vacant. The mature trees and landscape of the neighborhood provided cover while he surveyed the two structures. Six cars were parked in the driveway and yard of one house, while the other house's driveway was empty. His best guess was the one without cars.

Carefully and slowly he circled the building. Disturbing a dog was a concern, but so far none were barking from the surrounding homes. The structure without cars was a plain dirty beige craftsman in serious need of a paint job. Untrimmed bushes dominated the front and the sides of the building. No lights were visible in the front. As he circled around to the back, he noticed lights shining through a basement window. The yard to his right was heavily landscaped with a chain link fence separating the lot of his target house from its neighbor. The bushes and trees provided cover preventing anyone next door from seeing his approach. Even though he was dressed totally in black, he was glad for the cover.

Peering through the basement window, he saw an unfinished room with an old washer and dryer against one wall left of a staircase. On the other side of the stairs was a wood paneled wall with a closed door three feet from the bottom stair. Moving toward the back of the house, he could see a blue flickering light in a back window. As he got closer, the muffled sound of a television was discernable through the walls of the house. Carefully, he backed up to a point where he was out of the glow from the window, but could see in. A man in his mid-thirties sat in front of the TV drinking a beer. He was slender, dark skinned, with black, stringy hair. Kruger guessed his nationality as either from Southeast Asia or the Pacific basin. On the side table next to him was a cell phone and an automatic pistol.

A rustling sound could be heard in the yard to his left. As the sound grew louder, a large mixed breed dog poked its large head through the bushes next to the chain link fence. Kruger stood still and watched the dog as it backed away from the fence and moved further down to another opening in the hedge. The dog continued to move further away, so Kruger went back to watching the man in the window.

When the dog started barking furiously, Kruger retreated further into the shadows of the backyard. The man in the chair, got up, grabbed the pistol and came to the back door. He opened it, stepped out to the wooden back porch, and stood listening. Shaking his head, he yelled, "Shut up, stupid dog."

Kruger smiled. It was the voice from the cell phone calls. He stood in the darkness as the man yelled several more times for the dog to stay quiet. The man remained on the porch until the dog grew silent, then stepped inside the house, and closed the door.

Waiting until the man settled back into the chair before moving, Kruger silently crept through the shadows until he was beside the wooden porch. Carefully, he put his foot onto the bottom step. As he added weight, the board did not squeak. Satisfied, he climbed the remaining two steps. With his Glock 19 in his right hand, he grasped the door knob with his left hand and slowly turned it. It was unlocked. Looking through the door's glass pane, he could see it opened into a small mud room with a door slightly ajar leading to a kitchen. Kruger opened the door to the mud room, being careful not to let the hinges squeak. Once inside, he glanced into the kitchen area through the open door. Far to the left of the kitchen, he could see the flickering light of the television and the back part of the chair where the man sat. He opened the door wider and prepared for his next move.

He rushed through the kitchen, keeping his eye on the man sitting in the chair. As he emerged, the man's eyes grew wide and stared at him. Kruger trained his Glock on the man. "Keep your hands where I can see them." The man sat still with his hands resting on his legs. "Where are they?"

A perplexed look turned to anger. "How did… How did you find me?"

Kruger moved closer to the man. "Where the hell are they? You've got five seconds."

The man continued to study Kruger. The dog next door started barking louder than before. The staring contest continued until a crazed smile came to the kidnapper's face and his eyes narrowed. He made a fast grab for his gun just before Kruger shot him above his left eye. The man's head snapped back as blood and gray matter spread over the cloth of the cheap easy chair. Shaking his head, he grabbed the man's gun, secured it in his belt next to his back and placed the phone in his back pocket. Quickly locating the stairs to the basement, he ran down two at a time to the closed door. It was locked. He stood back and kicked it with his right foot. The jamb shattered and the door flew back and banged into a wall. Inside the room Kruger saw Stephanie huddled on the floor holding Kristin. Stephanie looked defiantly at him as Kristin whimpered, snuggled in her arms.

At first, Stephanie didn't recognize Kruger with the blackened face and watch cap. Shock and anger changed to relief as she realized who it was. She stood and rushed into his arms. "I knew you would find us."

Kruger took Kristin in his left arm and held Stephanie in his right arm. "We've got to get out of here."

He quickly led them up the stairs and back to the kitchen. Kristin's head was buried against her father's shoulder and Kruger held her so she would not see the carnage sitting in the chair. Stephanie looked at the man with the bullet hole above his left eye. She kicked his leg violently and screamed, "I hope you burn in hell, motherfucker."

Kruger frowned. While justified, it was the first time to hear his wife say anything remotely similar. He decided it would be a topic for a later conversation.

Kruger stopped just before they entered the kitchen, glanced around, saw what he was looking for and pointed at it.

"Steph, grab that."

She bent over to pick up his spent bullet casing and handed it to him. He stuck it in his right jeans pocket and hesitated. He turned back to the chair and used his cell phone to take a picture of the man in the chair. With this accomplished they hurried through the kitchen.

As they approached the back door, Kruger glanced out. Not seeing anyone being curious about the noise, he took a breath. "I think the dog barking might have masked the sound of the gun shot. Let's hope so."

Exiting the house through the back door, he hurried them around to the front and down the street to his Mustang. Even though numerous dogs were barking furiously throughout the neighborhood, no one yelled at him or turned a porch light on to check the commotion.

Fifteen minutes later they were on 435 heading south. During this time Stephanie held Kristin and remained silent, staring out the front windshield of the Mustang. Finally she turned to look at him. "How'd you find us so fast?"

"JR."

She nodded. "Remind me to give him a hug."

"We're going to his place, not home. I've got to get you and Kristin to a safe location."

Kristin was asleep in her mother's arms, seat belts and child seats forgotten. Stephanie faced the front window almost in a hypnotic stare and silence dominated the interior of their car again. Finally Kruger took a quick glance at her. "I'm going to find him, Steph."

She looked at him. "What do you mean? You shot the man."

"No. Bishop's involved. The man who kidnapped you

was hired by Bishop. My failure to arrest him six years ago was the biggest mistake of my life. I have to find him and take him down. It's the only way our family will ever be safe."

She looked at her husband, started to say something, but remained quiet. She returned her attention to the front windshield. Finally after several moments, she nodded.

CHAPTER 31

Springfield, MO

It was just after four in the morning when Kruger parked the Mustang next to the main entrance of JR's building. JR, Mia, and Joseph were waiting for them. Mia helped Stephanie with Kristin and escorted them into the building.

Joseph examined Kruger's face, still black with the shoe polish. "Shoe polish… Really?"

"Necessity demanded improvisation."

"I'm going to enjoy watching you get it off." Joseph grinned.

His mood grim, Kruger stared at his old friend. "It worked and that's all that matters."

Nodding, Joseph started walking to the door of building. "JR's made progress while you were driving, and I've got several friends watching this place. You'll be safe until we get you three moved."

"Thanks, Joseph." Kruger took a deep breath. "I'm not taking Steph and Kristin back to the house until its back to normal. I don't want her to see what Bishop did."

It took several minutes to get Kristin settled in a spare bedroom on the third floor of JR's building. Mia closed the door and went to the kitchen to make coffee. Stephanie followed, allowing the three men some time alone.

"I've been able to isolate Bishop's Virgin Mobile number," JR was standing at the top of the staircase. "He's west of St. Louis at the moment."

No one spoke for several minutes. Kruger stood, went to his duffel bag and retrieved the cell phone taken from the house. He handed it to JR. "The kidnapper had this on him."

JR popped the back cover off, stared at it for several seconds, and pried the battery out with his fingernail. Smiling, he eased the SIM card out and held it up like a trophy. "This is good. I can get phone numbers off this, check on who the guy was calling and who called him."

Kruger sighed, "I'd better call the Kansas City police department and leave a tip about the house."

Joseph shook his head. "Not necessary."

"Why?"

"It's taken care of."

Kruger looked at Joseph and blinked several times. After a few moments the meaning of what he heard registered. He nodded. "Did you find out anything about him?"

"Not much. We know his name, Mufliha ben Amal, went by the name, Ben."

Kruger stood and started pacing. "Muslim?"

Joseph nodded slightly. "Malaysian Muslim to be exact. He's known to the Kansas City police as a part-time pimp and drug dealer. Your bureau thinks he's a member of Jemaah Islamiyah."

Kruger stopped pacing and turned to his old friend. "They think?"

Joseph nodded.

"The person Bishop called in Taiwan, is he aligned with this Jemaah Islamiyah?"

Joseph shrugged. "We don't know who he is calling. But, the group Amal claims allegiance to is aligned with ISIS."

Turning to JR, Kruger asked, "Can you dig into this a little further?"

JR nodded.

"I'm not up to speed on Jemaah Islamiyah." Kruger stared pacing again. "The Bureau's current thinking is Bishop spent most of his time overseas in Thailand, Malaysia and Indonesia. What if this whole takeover of Stephen Bishop and artificial intelligence scam was to provide funding?"

Joseph shook his head. "Don't know, maybe."

"After the sale of Blair's company and the ninety million he has pledged in the scam, we're talking real money, Joseph. Way over a two hundred million."

"Still…" He paused, checked his watch and continued. "Let's find out more about this Mufliha character before we start jumping to conclusions. JR, do you have anything else on him?"

Nodding, JR motioned for them to follow as he walked back down the stairs.

Once he was sitting in his cubicle, he started reading from his computer screen. "He's been arrested several times for petty thief, possession with intent to distribute, and running a few girls on Troost Avenue. The KCPD didn't considered him a big time pimp, just a nuisance. I doubt there will be too many tears shed. The house is owned by a large investment group and rented out by a property management company." JR switched his attention to the adjacent screen. "I found employment documents for him in the management company's computer. He's listed as a part-time maintenance man, he mows lawns. I'm guessing he probably knew the house was vacant."

Kruger's eyebrows rose. "What about the house? There could be evidence left behind from Stephanie and Kristin's presence?"

Joseph shook his head and gave Kruger a grim smile. "No, not really." Joseph looked at his friend. "They weren't there long enough, and the KCPD will have no reason to check the house because Amal can't be linked to it."

Kruger studied his old friend. "Why?"

"Because he and the chair are no longer at the house."

"Should I ask how you accomplished that?"

"You can ask…"

Nodding, Kruger understood. "But, you won't tell me."

Joseph gave him a blank stare.

"Then it never happened."

With a slight nod, Joseph smiled. "Not unless you tell the Bureau."

Stephanie came into the living room, said nothing, and sat on the sofa next to Kruger. She yawned and put her head on his shoulder as he wrapped his right arm around her. He yawned immediately. "Adrenaline's wearing off."

***

Stephanie was still snoring softly when Kruger woke at eleven. Disorientated at first, the presence of Kristin between them brought him back to reality. JR's guest bedroom. Kristin was curled up next to her mother. He rose, put on his jeans and the black t-shirt, and went into the bathroom to brush his teeth. As he brushed, he stared at his face in the mirror. Blood shot eyes with dark circles underneath stared back at him. The gray in his hair was more pronounced, and his skin retained an ashen tint from the shoe polish.

In the mirror, he saw Stephanie stagger into the bathroom, her eyes barely open. She wrapped her arms around his waist and placed her head against his back. "Sorry about last night. I never thought it would happen. All those years of you pounding into my head on how to protect myself, and I forgot everything."

He twisted around in her embrace and put his arms around her. "Don't blame yourself. I should've been there for you."

"I've been a bitch the last couple of weeks, I'm sorry."

"No, you haven't. I've been gone too much."

He could feel her head shaking. "No… it's something else."

Frowning, he pushed her away from his chest and

looked into her eyes. "What?"

"I'm pregnant."

"How… I thought you couldn't… Are you sure?" He pulled her to his chest and hugged her tightly.

"My doctor confirmed it Monday. I was going to tell you, but with all the commotion with this Bishop thing, I never found the right time. I'm scared, Sean. I want the baby to be healthy." A tear slid down her cheek. "What if I'm too old?"

"Nonsense, you're healthy and take good care of yourself. You'll do fine."

"That's what my doctor said, but she didn't say it with…" She didn't finish her sentence.

He took a deep breath and looked down at her. She stared up at him, tears in the corners of her eyes growing heavy. They stood in the embrace for several minutes. "I probably need to reevaluate my arrangement with the Bureau."

Surprisingly, she nodded.

***

While she took a shower, he lay next to the still sleeping Kristin. He placed his hands behind his head as he lay on the pillow staring at the ceiling. Too many thoughts swirled in his mind as he tried to prioritize his next steps. He couldn't leave Stephanie and Kristin alone again. She needed calm for the next eight months. But Bishop had to be stopped. .

Kruger heard the shower stop and watched as Kristin opened her eyes, saw him, giggled, smiled, and stretched. Her blues eyes sparkled and her long blond hair was disheveled from a restless night. He hugged her. "Good morning, sleepyhead." She giggled again and sat up. When she saw Stephanie step out of the bathroom, she squealed with delight. Stephanie was dressed only in a bra and panties with her hair wrapped in a towel. The little girl reached up and laughed as Stephanie scooped her up and held her, their hug lasting longer than usual.

Kruger watched as mother and daughter embraced each other. Guilt and envy swept over him as he realized his numerous absences of late were preventing the bonding between him and his daughter. He smiled, but there was very little joy in the smile. Stephanie said to Kristin, "I bet you're hungry, let's go see if we can find some breakfast for you."

It was close to noon when they emerged from the bedroom. Stephanie still wore the robe she borrowed from Mia, and Kruger remained barefoot. As they entered the living room, Kruger saw a large man sitting on a sofa reading a newspaper. When the man heard them enter the room, he stood and smiled.

"Good morning, sir."

Kruger smiled. "When did you get back, Sandy?"

"Early this morning. I enjoyed meeting Brian and Michelle. Thank you for the opportunity."

Kruger shook the man's hand. "Thanks for going up there on such short notice."

Sandy Knoll nodded toward several suitcases and a duffel bag on the floor next to a love seat across from where he stood.

"We went by your house this morning, secured it, and brought a few things for you and your family." He reached down to the sofa, picked up an object, and handed it to Kruger. "I found this in your duffel. Thought you might need it."

Kruger stared at his FBI ID billfold, the one he placed in his duffel bag the night before. Silently, Kruger nodded and took the folded wallet. He cleared his throat and turned to Stephanie. "Excuse my manners. Stephanie, this is Major Sandy Knoll, he's a good friend of Joseph's."

Stephanie was holding a shy Kristin, whose face was buried in her mother's neck and hair. "Nice to meet you, Sandy. Excuse me, this little girl is hungry."

She retreated toward the kitchen, and the two men watched her go. When she was out of the room, Sandy turned back to Kruger. "I have a man on your house, plus several securing this building."

Kruger smiled grimly, "Thanks."

Sandy nodded and remained quiet.

JR appeared at the top of the steps leading to the second floor, he saw Kruger and Knoll. "You both better come downstairs I've found something."

CHAPTER 32

Columbia, MO

Randolph Bishop cursed under his breath as he bit into an apple and stared at the ancient tube-style TV. It was going on twenty-four hours since Amal last answered his phone. Numerous calls to the man's cell phone went straight to an automated announcement telling him the phone's voice-mail was not set up. With no way to leave Amal a message, Bishop's frustration level increased by the minute. Now the idiot had missed three scheduled check-in times. The only reason Bishop could surmise for Amal's silence was he'd been caught, or he was dead.

So far there was nothing mentioned in the media about the abduction of the FBI agent's wife and child, or the capture of the kidnapper. Even in the online version of the Kansas City Star, there was no mention.

His drive from Springfield to Columbia took most of the night, as he traveled back roads and little used highways. When he did a cursory survey of Brian Kruger's apartment, he spotted several security types guarding the building. After watching the apartment for several minutes, he drove to the local regional airport and turned the rental car into the Hertz counter.

A taxi took him to an American's Best Value Inn on the north side of Columbia. The clientele consisted of cost-conscious travelers looking for a cheap hotel with even cheaper furnishings. The hotel and rooms were decorated with colors designed to hide dirt. The smell of Pine-Sol, stale cigarettes, and a faint background of cheap beer assaulted his nose as he opened the door. Signing in as Gary Yates, he paid cash for one night and became just another anonymous guest. The main reason he chose this hotel was the car lot next to it.

As he watched CNN, his cell phone vibrated. Only one person, besides Amal, knew the number. The caller ID showed an international number. He accepted the call.

"My man in Kansas City may have been compromised."

"He hasn't called me, if that's what you're referring to. Where is he?"

Bishop prepared himself for the rant he knew was coming. He was not disappointed.

The man from Bangkok sighed. "My friend, how can I continue to trust your judgment in these matters? You owe our organization millions of your American dollars, yet you have delivered nothing. What am I to do?"

"What you were supposed to do was refer me to someone competent."

There was silence on the other end of the call. "Your problem, not mine. We have spent a lot of time and money to get you back to the United States. Yet, you continue to push back about paying your debt."

"I will provide the funds we discussed. You are the one who recommended Amal. How do I know he hasn't used the woman for his own pleasure and killed her?"

"He is a loyal member of our society. He is disciplined. And if he has, Allah have mercy."

"Yeah, well, how come your loyal member hasn't checked in for twenty-four hours?"

"As I mentioned earlier, he may have been compromised."

"I need this meddlesome FBI agent out of the way. The woman and child were to be used as bait. With them, he would have walked into my trap. Now I'm left with one conclusion. The person you recommended screwed up."

"Pay your debt, Mr. Bishop. If you don't…" There was a long pause. "Our reach is long and you will have nowhere to hide."

"Yeah, yeah, so you've told me…" The call had ended without the man hearing Bishop's response.

Bishop felt rage rolling up from his lower body, his stomach clinching, his lungs constricting, and his throat tightening. He stood and rapidly paced the room, taking short breaths and closing his eyes. He stopped pacing, took a deep breath and stood still. Finally, control of his breathing returned, and he stood in the middle of the depressing room with his eyes closed. After ten minutes, he opened them and sat down on the bed next to the nightstand. Reaching for the cell phone used to talk the man in Taiwan, he removed the battery and SIM card, which he dropped to the floor. Using his heel, he crushed it into small pieces. After gathering the pieces, he flushed them down the toilet.

Afterward, he sat down at his laptop and starting searching the internet. An hour later, he found a reference to the person he was looking for. His Facebook page indicated he worked as a bartender at a high-end restaurant near the Sprint Center in downtown Kansas City. Using the second burner phones he bought in Mexico, he called the restaurant and asked for the man. The person answering the phone acted like Congress would need to pass a law for him to grant Bishop's request. But, he took the phone to the man anyway.

"Yeah, this is Reggie."

"How you doing, Reggie. It's Bishop."

"Damn, son, it's been awhile. Ten years?"

"Probably."

"From what I hear, you're a hot commodity. Not sure I should be associating with you." There was a note of humor in the man's voice.

"How would you like to make an easy five grand?"

"Love to. Is it legal?"

"Just a field trip. Information gathering."

"Sure. What do you need?"

"Call this number when you get off. I'm not in KC." He told Reggie the number.

"Cool. Talk to you later."

***

The call came at 2 a.m.

"So, Bishop, why do you want to pay me five big ones?"

"I need you to check on someone."

"Who?"

"A former employee of mine."

"Former?" Reggie chuckled. "What did he do?"

"He was supposed to call me twenty-eight hours ago and hasn't."

"What was he doing for you?"

"Babysitting."

When Reggie stopped laughing, Bishop heard, "He sounds dead, or he skipped. What do you think?"

"Dead. But I need to be sure. I need you to go to the morgue and see if he's there."

"Disgusting. But I'll do it for five." He pause for a second. "Up front."

"Give me an account number. The money will be there in the morning."

"Cool. Give me the details and a phone number to reach you."

Bishop gave him a quick summary and a number. "Keep it low-key."

"Always."

The call ended, and Bishop put the phone in his pocket. He stared again at the television set.

***

The next morning, around ten, he wandered next door to the car lot. A tall, skinny, acne-scared, twenty-something greeted him. "Good morning. Looking for an SUV?"

Bishop shook his head. "Looking for a something I can depend on with less than a hundred thousand miles on it."

The salesman struck out his hand. "I'm George."

Bishop shook the man's hand. "I'm Gary. Tell me about this one." He pointed toward a white 2012 Chevy Equinox.

George smiled, "You won't regret buying that one."

The salesman droned on about the quality of the car, its low miles, maintenance records, and being named most reliable SUV. Finally, without letting the man take a breath, Bishop interrupted, "Ninety-five hundred, cash, and new tires."

The young salesman stammered, "Ah, well, I, uhhh… I can't say yes or no. We'd have to talk to my sales manager."

"Well…" Bishop pointed toward the building. "Go talk to him."

An hour and a half later, Gary Yates owned a Chevy Equinox, which Bishop drove off the lot. He'd paid ninety-nine hundred dollars cash for the SUV with brand new Firestone tires and an oil change. No one, even if they checked, would be able to associate the SUV with Randolph Bishop.

***

Bishop paid for another day at the motel as he waited to hear from Reggie. It was close to 9 in the evening when his cell phone vibrated. Glancing at the caller ID, he accepted the call. "What'd you find?"

"I found him. In the morgue."

Bishop was silent for a moment. "Go on."

"The body was found Tuesday morning, no ID, and a bullet hole just above his right eyebrow. They have him listed as John Doe."

"Did you identify him?"

"Hell no! You think I'm stupid? I gave the morgue attendant two hundred bucks, told him I was looking for my missing brother. By the way, you owe me fifty two hundred."

"Fine. Where did they find him?"

"You're going to love this." The voice on the other end of the call laughed. "The body was sitting in a bus stop across the street from City Hall and the police department in downtown Kansas City."

Bishop did not find any humor in this fact. "Was he killed there?"

"No, police report says he was killed elsewhere and moved to the bench. No one saw anything. Time of death was somewhere around midnight the previous night. Lots of security cameras around. Police are scratching their heads; all the cameras have a ten-minute gap around 3 a.m."

"What about the FBI agent?"

"No idea. He wasn't mentioned."

"Damn. How did they find Amal so fast?"

"Was that his name?"

"Don't worry about it. I need you to find someone else."

"Sure, for another five thousand."

Bishop was silent for a long while. "Fine."

"Who am I looking for?"

"An FBI agent named Sean Kruger."

"How do you spell it?"

Bishop spelled the name. "Try to find out where he is and get back to me."

"It may take a few days."

"Yes, yes, yes. Just find him."

After the call ended, Bishop let out a long breath. He doubted Kruger would take his family back to their house. He would find someplace safe and out of the way. If anyone could find the place, Reggie would.

In the meantime, he needed a place to stay for a while. The perfect solution presented itself that evening as he ate dinner in a restaurant next to the hotel

***

Rosie Singleton lived in a small cookie-cutter ranch-style home in Hallsville, MO, twenty-two miles north of Columbia. Life had slapped her in the face more times than it had patted her on the back. Now in her mid-forties, twice divorced from abusive husbands, childless, and working at a dead-end job with the city of Columbia, she still shared a smile with everyone. Another attribute passed on to her from her mother was a natural high metabolism, which kept her relatively slim. Her hair was prematurely gray, but still dark brown, thanks to a box of Miss Clairol purchased each month at a Columbia Walmart.

She kept her hair shoulder length and straight, sometimes pulled it back in a ponytail, sometimes not. Her face was oblong, with a small nose supporting black-rimmed glasses in front of hazel eyes. Her father was half Cherokee, which gave her an exotic skin tone. Combined with her five-foot-eight-inch height, getting attention from men was not a problem. Having to deal with the attention was.

One of her favorite activities was meeting several girl friends on Tuesday and Thursdays for dinner at a local Country Kitchen close to her office. It was Thursday, so the four friends sat in a booth laughing and sharing the latest gossip.

Randolph Bishop was eating at a table next to them.

"I've been saving for this vacation for five years," Rosie announced as the laugher subsided from one of Betty's jokes. Betty was several years older than Rosie and her best friend.

"You've been talking about it for at least ten, girlfriend," Betty sat next to Rosie and put a hand on her arm. "Aren't you scared to take a cruise by yourself?"

Shaking her head, Rosie straightened in her chair. "Nah. It's a Christian-based cruise for singles only. I'm hoping the men aren't too religious, if you know what I mean."

All the girls laughed again.

Rosie continued, "Besides, once the cruise is over, I'll

never have to see them again."

More laughter.

"When do you leave?" another friend asked.

"I have to drive to St. Louis in the morning to catch a Southwest flight to Houston. I'll be gone for two whole weeks." Rosie smiled. "I've never taken two weeks at a time before. I figure one week of cruising, then another week to recuperate."

They all laughed again.

Randolph Bishop heard every word the booth full of middle-aged women said. He lingered at his table staring at his cell phone until they were done. When they started splitting up their bill, he stood and walked to the cashier to pay his check. He waited in his new SUV and watched until Rosie Singleton walked to her car. After she waved to her friends, she opened the door of her Honda Civic, sat down, and drove out of the restaurant parking lot. Fifteen seconds later a white Chevy Equinox followed.

CHAPTER 33

Springfield, MO

Kruger and Knoll followed JR down the stairs to the second floor and to a cubicle where Joseph stood. He smiled. "Good to see you this morning, Sean."

"Thanks for everyone's help last night."

"Our pleasure."

JR positioned himself in front of a dual set of computer screens, using a mouse to click on an icon on the screen. "Listen to this."

"My man in Kansas City may have been compromised."

"He hasn't called me, if that's what you're referring to. Where is he?"

"My friend, how can I continue to trust your judgment in these matters? You owe our organization millions of your American dollars, yet you have delivered nothing. What am I to do?"

"What you were supposed to do was refer me to someone competent."

There was a lengthy moment of silence, Kruger started to say something, but JR raised his index finger and said, "Wait."

"Your problem, not mine. We have spent a lot of time and money

to get you back to the United States. Yet you continue to push back about paying your debt."

"I will provide the funds we discussed. You are the one who recommended Amal. How do I know he hasn't used the woman for his own pleasure and killed her?"

"He is a loyal member of our society. He is disciplined. And if he has, Allah have mercy."

"Yeah, well, how come your loyal member hasn't checked in for over twenty-four hours?"

"As I mentioned earlier, he may have been compromised."

"I need this meddlesome FBI agent out of the way. The woman and child were to be used as bait. With them, he would have walked into my trap. Now I'm left with one conclusion. The person you recommended screwed up."

"Pay your debt, Mr. Bishop. If you don't... Our reach is long, and you will have nowhere to hide."

"Yeah, yeah, so you've told me..."

The conversation stopped.

Joseph crossed his arms over his chest. "NSA?"

JR nodded. "I found the number on the SIM card from the kidnapper's phone. Both numbers for Bishop and the man in Thailand were previously unknown to me. They're using different burner phones on almost every call."

"How are they communicating the numbers to call?" Kruger asked.

"Don't know, haven't figured that out yet."

Kruger started pacing. "At least we have the answers to a lot of questions about Bishop."

Joseph nodded. "He was sent here to raise money to pay a debt of some kind."

Shaking his head, Kruger stopped and looked at Joseph. "No, I think he's running a scam on them. He needed help getting back into the states. His ego is such, he figured once he was here, he could outsmart them. He'd buy another identity, one they don't know about, and disappear again."

"Do you have a recording of the call to Amal from Thailand?"

JR smiled. "It's in Thai, but I've run it through a translation program, so it's going to sound mechanical. I'll play the pertinent parts." His hand moved the mouse until it was hovering over another icon on the computer screen and he clicked it.

"Do you still work for the property management company?"

"Yes."

"Good. There is a man, his name is Bishop, he has job for you."

"What is job?"

"He needs you to take a woman and a child from an address in Overland Park and keep them at one of those rental houses you work on."

"How long do I keep them?"

"A few days."

"Then what?"

"Use your imagination."

"Ahhh... How much do I get paid?"

"You will need to negotiate with Bishop. I am a mere functionary getting you and him together. He will have all the details."

Kruger sat down. "He had no intention of letting them go."

Joseph looked at his old friend. "You didn't think he would, did you?"

"No. I knew he wouldn't." Kruger frowned. "JR, did you find any of the calls between Bishop and Amal?"

"Nope, the only recordings I have access within the NSA system are foreign to domestic and domestic to foreign. They say they don't record domestic calls." A smirk appeared. "Right..."

Sandy Knoll crossed his arms over his wide chest. "We're wasting time. Where's Bishop?"

Kruger hid his smile with a hand while Joseph's eyes showed agreement.

Oblivious to Knoll's frustration, JR replied, "Glad you asked. Bishop's phone is still in the Columbia area. At least it was until a while ago. The phone he used to talk to Thailand is dark, which means he's destroyed it, or taken the battery out."

Kruger's eyes widened, and he stood up. "He's still in Columbia?"

Knoll placed his hand on Kruger's shoulder. "My men are still there. Brian and Michelle are under their protection and safe."

JR was typing on his keyboard, his head staring at only one screen. "All the phones I know about are dark. I'm having them pinged every five minutes. But none are showing active. He could be anywhere."

Taking a deep breath, Kruger pulled his cell phone out of his pocket and walked away from the cubicle. Joseph followed.

With the cell phone against his ear, he was silent waiting for his call to be completed.

"Alan, it's Sean."

"Any word on Bishop?"

"No, nothing concrete. We think he's in the Columbia, Missouri area. Can you ask the KC office to have them notify the Columbia PD to be on the lookout for stolen cars and missing women?"

"I'll have them send a couple of agents over for a few days."

"It could be nothing, Alan. He may be long gone."

"Do you want to take that chance?"

"No."

"I'll call you when they have someone there."

Kruger ended the call and looked at Joseph. "I feel like I'm spinning my wheels. Bishop's out there somewhere just beyond our reach. I'm worried some poor soul is going to pay for our incompetence with their life."

"Maybe not."

Kruger gave Joseph a scornful look. "You and I both know he's going to hold up somewhere. For how long, who knows? If we don't have some kind of contact with him in the next few days, someone will be dead, and it will be my fault."

***

Rosie Singleton didn't drive to St. Louis on Friday morning. She couldn't. She was tied up. Each of her arms and legs were tied to one of the four cherry wood posts on the bedframe she inherited from her grandmother. Her left eye was swollen, turning black and blue from the first blow Randolph Bishop landed as she opened the door the previous evening. Subsequent strikes with a belt on her body had left welts and a few cuts. She was naked, except for her panties and a strip of duct tape across her mouth.

Bishop stood at the bottom on the bed looking at the partially conscious woman. The smile on his face grew as he used a pair of scissors to cut away Rosie's underpants. Once they were off, he unzipped his pants and climbed onto the bed. Rosie suddenly realized what was going to happen, stared at him, and tried to scream.

***

JR stared at the computer screens without blinking for fifteen minutes. Mia stood behind him rubbing his shoulders. "You're awful tense, JR."

He nodded.

"How long are you going to stare at it?"

"All night, if I have to."

"Again, what are you looking for?"

"Bishop's left a trail somewhere. There has to be some trace of him. It's not possible in this day and age to do anything and not leave an electronic crumb."

Mia continued to rub his shoulders. "How's he getting around?"

"Rental."

"If he's in Columbia, could you check to see if someone has turned in a rental in the past couple of days from, let's say, out in the west?"

JR whipped around and stared at Mia. "Most rentals are local, returned to the location it was rented from." He returned to the computer keyboard and started typing furiously, the shoulder rub forgotten.

***

An hour later, Kruger, Joseph, and Sandy Knoll stood behind JR as he explained the files on the computer screen. "After searching one-way rentals made over the past six days, I came across this one in Columbia." He pointed to the left screen. "A Gary Yates returned, without prior approval from the rental company, a Dodge Charger rented in Phoenix, Arizona, to the Hertz counter in Columbia. The Charger was rented two days before Bishop's Jeep was found stripped and abandoned. There is a note by the rental agent. The renter did not complain about the stiff fine he paid and then walked to the taxi queue and left via a cab."

Kruger murmured, "Huh."

Knoll leaned over to look at the file closer. "What are the odds?"

JR tapped a few more keys and pointed to another file. "This is the paperwork sent to the Jefferson City office of the Missouri Department of Revenue by Joe Maxim's Ford in Columbia. Gary Yates paid ninety-nine hundred dollars, cash, for a white 2012 Chevrolet Equinox the next day."

"It's him, JR."

"I would agree."

"But where is he now?" asked Sandy.

JR held up a finger and smiled. "There is a hotel next to the car lot. I hacked into their registration system and guess what?"

"Gary Yates was registered," Kruger folded his arms across his chest.

JR nodded. "Checked out this morning."

Kruger turned away from the group and stared out one of the windows close to the cubicle. After several minutes, he turned back and put his hands on his hips.

Joseph spoke first. "I've seen that look before. What are you thinking, Sean."

All three of the other men in the room looked at Kruger.

"In the late nineties, Chevrolet started putting On-Star service on their vehicles. Now the units are standard equipment. On-Star has many functions, but one of the main functions is to provide hands-free GPS directions to drivers. To do that, the On-Star system has to…"

"…Know where the vehicle is at all the times," JR finished, his eyes widening.

Kruger nodded.

Without another word, JR turned back to his computer and started doing what he did best—hacking into a corporate server.

***

An hour later, the four men sat in JR's conference room. JR turned his laptop so the rest of the group could see a map on the screen. He pointed to a dot north of Columbia, in a small town labeled Hallsville.

"That is the current location of the Equinox purchased by Gary Yates. According to the Boone County Assessor's office, the house at that location is owned by a woman named Rosie Singleton. Rosie works for the City of Columbia as an admin for the City Attorney. Mia called the office and asked for her. She was told Rosie was on vacation for the next two weeks." JR looked at each of the men seated at the conference table. "I would say she's in trouble."

Knoll stood up and left the conference room.

Kruger stood as well. "I've got my go-bag in the car, Steph and Kristin are safe here. I'm going to Columbia, and hopefully, I can stop this psychopath from killing again."

JR looked up at him. "I'm going, too."

Kruger stared at his friend. "We need you here for the information."

JR pointed at the laptops. "They're portable, Sean."

Kruger looked at Joseph, who nodded. "I'll stay here. Besides, I'm getting too old for this stuff."

Knoll stuck his head back into the room. "I've pulled three of the six guys I have in Columbia heading toward the house. They'll put it under surveillance until I get there."

"JR and I are going. You can follow me with your Denali; we'll need your equipment. I'll call a buddy of mine with the Highway Patrol and clear the way. He might even provide an escort."

Knoll smiled, nodded, and headed toward the stairs.

Kruger turned to JR. "Go pack something fast."

JR nodded toward a backpack in the corner of the conference room. "Already did."

***

"We think we've found Bishop."

Stephanie stood staring at her husband, her arms crossed over her chest, frowning. She started to say something, but hesitated.

"Did you hear me?"

She nodded, but dipped her eyes and studied the carpet. "I heard you." She paused for a few moments. "But… I don't want you going."

Kruger took a breath and tilted his head slightly to the left. "Really. Why?"

She shook her head, "Not sure. I want Bishop out of our lives. But…"

The silence made Kruger shiver. "What are you concerned about, Steph?"

"You."

"Me?"

"Yes, you."

"Why?"

She exhaled loudly. "I don't want you taking vengeance out on this man, Sean. If you do, it will steal your soul."

Kruger stared at her for several moments. "I'm just trying to make sure he doesn't hurt anyone else."

"No, that's not it, Sean." She stepped closer to him and put her arms around his waist. Looking up into his eyes, her voice was slightly shaky. "I love you, and I've grown to know you better than you know yourself."

He did not respond.

"If you go to Columbia and find Bishop, you'll execute him without hesitation. You'll become judge, jury, and executioner within the time it take to blink an eye.

Kruger was silent, his arms around her waist. Finally after looking into her eyes for a minute, he shook his head. "No, I won't."

"Yes, you will." She laid her head on his chest. "You're still scared Kristin and I will be abducted again. The only way you can prevent another episode is to execute him."

The truth hurts sometimes. It was a first time for Kruger, his voice caught as he spoke. "I'd never…"

"Never what, Sean?"

He turned his head and stared at nothing. "When I received the call about you and Kristin being abducted, I faced a real possibility I'd never see either of you again." He returned his gaze to her face. "I went into automatic mode, relying on my training and years of experience on how to be prepared for all contingencies. I knew what needed to be done, so I called JR. Without him, I wouldn't have found you. It was when I realized you and Kristin might be gone forever, that I understood no one has ever been as important to me as you. No one. Trust me when I say, I will not do anything to prevent our growing old together. That includes executing Bishop."

She smiled and placed her forehead on his chest. He felt her nod.

CHAPTER 34

Columbia, MO

"Allen, I need a couple of favors."

Major Allen Boone with the Missouri State Highway Patrol chuckled. Kruger was talking to Boone through the Mustang's hands-free SYNC cell phone system. He and JR were cruising northeast on I-44 toward Lebanon, Missouri, at ninety-five miles an hour, the Mustang's custom installed police emergency lights flashing. Sandy Knoll was several car lengths behind.

"Name it, Sean."

"Remember Randolph Bishop?"

"Hard to forget. Why?"

"We think we've located him north of Columbia. I'm heading there now. The first favor I need is for you to alert your patrol units I'm running with lights only in a two-vehicle caravan. I'd like an escort once I'm heading north on 5 out of Lebanon."

"When do you think you'll be there?"

Kruger glanced at the dash clock. "Twenty-five minutes."

"Done. What's the second favor?"

"We've got three men on scene watching his suspected location. We know his vehicle. I would like some help isolating the area."

"Where is it?"

"Hallsville."

Boone was silent for a few moments. "I'll have a Rapid Response Team join your caravan as you pass through Jeff City. Plus, I'll dispatch several patrol cars toward Hallsville now."

"Thanks, Allen. One more thing." He took a breath. "I don't want to step on any toes with this operation. We have three men on scene with our task force, ex-Special Forces. Their team leader, retired Major Benedict Knoll, will be directing the scene once we arrive."

Boone was silent again. "Under what jurisdiction are you operating? We can't be a part of an illegal military operation inside the United States, Sean. You know that."

"It's not military. We're part of an FBI task force. If you need confirmation, call Deputy Director Alan Seltzer. He'll take your call and confirm it."

"Good, I'll make the call to cover both our asses."

"Thanks, Allen."

***

Rosie Singleton's house was as anonymous as the rest of the homes in her quiet neighborhood of Hallsville. Built in the late sixties, a faux brick facade and new vinyl siding gave it a pleasant appearance on the outside. Its mature landscaping included two massive oak trees, numerous smaller decorative trees, and an abundance of bushes and flowers.

Missouri Highway Patrol cars cruised the entrances to the subdivision, maintaining as low a profile as possible. Parked on the street in front of the house was a white Chevrolet Equinox, stationary since Sandy Knoll's team of three ex-special forces operatives set up surveillance five hours earlier. Rosie's house appeared empty.

With the help of the Missouri Highway Patrol Rapid Response Team asking permission from current owners, the team set up two observation posts in the house across the street and the house directly behind Rosie's home. Two members of the RRT and one of Sandy's team occupied both locations. Sandy was in the house behind Rosie's home using a state-of-the-art thermal imaging camera. Kruger and JR were with him.

"I've got one heat source in the house, besides the furnace. Lights show up as heat sources and I'm not seeing any." Sandy returned his attention to the east side of the house. "It's horizontal, about three feet off the floor."

"JR found the architect for the subdivision. It's a back bedroom. Can you tell the size of the image?"

"It's too small for a male. It's either a large dog, or…" He removed his eyes from the camera and turned to look at Kruger. "A female. She's still alive, Sean."

"No other heat signatures?"

Knoll shook his head. "She's alone in the house."

"She could be asleep." JR looked up from his laptop.

Kruger shook his head. "We're going in. I don't care if it's a mistake and she's taking a nap. I'll apologize later. If she's alive, let's keep her that way."

Sandy nodded and handed the camera to his teammate. "Keep an eye on the heat signature. If you notice anything at all change, call me."

The man nodded.

***

Sandy Knoll, Jimmy Gibbs and Kruger comprised the main entry team, while RRT members stood as back-up. Black jeans, black Kevlar vests over black long sleeve t-shirts, black watch caps and black steel-toed combat boots were the wardrobe. It was approaching 10 p.m. and the neighborhood was quiet. Knoll slipped night vision googles over his eyes and nodded at Gibbs. "I'm first in, you and Kruger breach the door. From what we can see on the thermal, it will be dark inside."

Kruger and Gibbs slipped their night vision googles down and stood ready.

Knoll held up three fingers. "On three, one, two, three…"

A loud crack was heard as the two-man breaching tool slammed into the back door jamb. Splintered wood flew as the door crashed against a wall. Knoll was in the room before the door hit the wall, moving fast through the laundry room into the kitchen. Gibbs and Kruger were close behind sweeping with their outstretched Glocks, making sure rooms were empty. Each man said, "Clear," as they moved through the house, not seeing any obstructions or opponents.

Knoll was first into the bedroom and rushed to the bed. "Female, shallow breathing, heart rate erratic." He turned toward Gibbs. "Call 911 and get your kit."

Kruger found the light switch and called, "Lights." All three men stripped off their night googles. Gibbs was on his cell phone directing an ambulance as Kruger moved back to the woman.

She was naked, curled into a fetal position, with one leg handcuffed to a bed post. He found a blanket at the foot of the bed and quickly covered her. Once she was secured, he walked out of the room to check the other bedrooms they cleared before entering the back room.

He turned a light switch on and stared at the contents. Knoll walked up behind him. "Looks like he's planning to return."

Kruger nodded, but said nothing. He moved to the center of the room, and using his Glock, moved one of the flaps of a duffel bag.

"I've got cash here. Lots of cash. He definitely was planning on returning. I'll tell Boone he's still in the area."

***

Flashing emergency light bars of four Highway Patrol and two county sheriff's cars reflected off the front bedroom walls. The sound of a medivac helicopter, with Rosie Singleton inside, could be heard receding into the night. Allen Boone stood in the doorway and leaned against the door frame.

"How'd you know?" He stared at Kruger, who at the moment, was searching files in a cardboard box from the closet.

Where Kruger was tall, slender and athletic, Boone showed the signs of a decade behind a desk. A year younger than his friend, Boone's hair was mostly gray and thinning, the last remaining strands of black surrendering to the onslaught of middle age. He was dressed in jeans and a Highway Patrol windbreaker. His slightly round face tilted to the side.

"Didn't. But I couldn't take the chance." Kruger looked up. "Too many people have fallen prey to Bishop. It stops here."

"The EMT told me she was suffering from dehydration, hypothermia and trauma. She was just hours from death, Sean. "

"Will she be okay?" Kruger's voice was steady, despite his building anger.

Boone nodded, "They started fluids before taking off. The EMT I spoke to was optimistic, she seemed to think Rosie would recover physically. She was concerned about her emotional state. There was evidence of a beating and violent, repeated rape."

Kruger looked up, his eyes staring at nothing. "I was afraid of that."

He hesitated for a moment before returning his attention to the file box. "Garage is empty." He held up several sheets of paper. "Insurance papers indicate she owns a 2011 Honda Civic. My bet is Bishop is using it to watch my son's apartment."

Boone stood up from leaning on the frame, his eyes

wide.

Kruger smiled grimly. "There are three, very competent gentlemen, watching over Brian and Michelle. I'm not worried. Yet."

"I'll dispatch some of these officers to start looking for the Honda?"

Kruger nodded and handed Boone a sheet of paper. "Here's her Department Of Revenue car registration." He pointed to a spot on the paper. "There's her license plate number."

Boone took the paper and left the room.

Knoll walked in. "I'm sending my guys back to Brian's house. I can go or stay, your decision."

"Go, Boone's men have this covered. JR and I will join you after we secure the house."

After Knoll left the room, Kruger stopped searching the file box and turned to JR. The computer genius was typing on the keyboard of a desktop computer. The old style bulky tube monitor sat on a small desk in the corner of the spare bedroom. Cables draping over the edge were attached to the computer box sitting on the floor. Kruger could tell he was focused and asked, "Find anything?"

Having known JR for several years, the lack of an immediate response was not unusual. Kruger waited. After several minutes, JR looked at him. "Maybe."

Kruger remained quiet.

"I believe I found the crossing."

"What do you mean?"

"I've been curious about how Bishop crossed paths with someone like Rosie Singleton. She lives alone in an isolated community and was planning on being gone for several weeks. No one would miss her at work because she would be on a cruise. Her tickets and packed bag are still in the living room. A plane ticket showed she was to fly out of St. Louis yesterday. How did Bishop know?"

"I've wondered the same thing."

"I found a debit in her bank account to a restaurant

Thursday night."

Kruger looked at JR and waited. This was a typical dramatic pause from his friend when explaining a finding. "Go on."

"The restaurant was next to the hotel Bishop was staying in."

Kruger stood. "Damn, he overheard her talking."

"That would be my assumption as well."

Frowning, Kruger paced in the confided space of the bedroom. "Any way to find the Civic like you did the Equinox?"

JR shook his head. "Bluetooth and Navigation were options on Hondas that year, but her car didn't have it."

"Unfortunate."

"So, how are you going to find him?"

"Well, looks like we're going to have to do it the old fashioned way." Kruger stopped pacing. "Put a BOLO out on the Civic."

CHAPTER 35

Columbia, MO

The shift change at Brian Kruger's apartment failed to occur at the normal time. Holding binoculars against his eyes, Randolph Bishop watched the two men as they maintained their vigilance outside of Brain's residence. The pattern had been two outside, one inside, rotating positions every thirty minutes. There were two teams of three, each spent twelve hours on, twelve hours off. Tonight, something was wrong. Since the missed shift change three hours ago, the two men outside were on their cell phones constantly.

Bishop watched from a wooded area east of the apartment. Surrounded by bushes and trees, he stood just behind a large scrub oak. Where he stood was dark, the lights of the apartment complex failing to illuminate him due to the thick foliage. Rosie Singleton's Honda sat in a Walmart parking lot several blocks to the south.

How to get to Brian Kruger continued to elude him. He had been watching off and on for several days. Now, after three hours of watching this disruption in the security routine, he felt any chance of getting to the son was gone. Even as he watched, four police vehicles, their sirens screaming and lights flashing, could be seen heading toward the apartment complex on Providence Road. Bishop lowered his binoculars and observed the cars turning onto Green Meadows Road as they proceeded east, skidding to a noisy stop in the parking lot of Brian's building. He raised the binoculars again and watched as Highway Patrol officers stepped out of the cars, their emergency lights still rotating, and conferred with the two men guarding the building.

Bishop's breathing rate increased, and he felt a chill crawl up his spine. He moved further back into the bushes. After several minutes of indecision, he started making his way back to the Honda. As he got within sight of the car, he noticed a Boone County Sheriff car parked behind the Civic. A sheriff's deputy stood next to the open driver's door speaking into a microphone from the car's radio and staring at the back of the car.

"Dammit." The word slipped from his mouth without thinking. He stood still as he watched the deputy return the microphone to the car's interior and place his right hand on his weapon. After several seconds, he withdrew it from his holster and stepped carefully around the hood of the patrol car. Gripping the gun in both hands, he approached the Honda's driver's side door. Once he confirmed the car was unoccupied, he returned the weapon to its holster and pulled a flashlight out of his belt.

Bishop retreated from the Walmart parking lot into the darkness of the night. He rushed across Green Meadow Road into a Kohl's department store parking lot. Checking his cell phone, he noted the time was approaching 11 p.m. The store closed at 9, but a few cars were still scattered haphazardly around the area. He checked several and found a twenty-year-old Mustang with the driver door unlocked. He climbed into the back seat and waited.

Fifteen minutes later, he heard voices, both female. He lowered himself into the back floor of the car and held his CZ P-07 9mm pistol in his right hand. One of the voices said, "G'night, Sally, I'm off tomorrow. What about you?"

"Have to be here at 4 in the afternoon," Sally answered. "Gotta close tomorrow night and do the folding thing like we did tonight. Got any plans for your day off?"

"Sleeping late. Have to be here early the next day."

Bishop felt the driver door open and the car dip as the owner sat behind the steering wheel. He waited as she started the car and drove out of the parking lot. The ride lasted fifteen minutes, with Bishop having no idea where they were. As the car stopped and she placed the automatic transmission in park, Bishop rose, reached around the driver seat and placed his hand over the woman's mouth as he simultaneously placed the pistol against her right temple and growled, "Don't make a sound and I won't kill you."

There was a gasp from the woman, but she nodded. He couldn't make out too much detail about her appearance, but he felt sweat form on her upper lip. In the rearview mirror, he only saw a round face, his hand over her mouth. The eyes were wide and her hair dark. He asked, "Do you live alone?"

She shook her head.

Without hesitation, he removed his hand from her mouth and pulled the trigger.

Bishop climbed out of the passenger door, looked around, saw no one, and started running.

***

His arms crossed, Kruger stood behind Rosie Singleton's Honda Civic as the Highway Patrol Rapid Response Team processed it for fingerprints and DNA. Sandy Knoll walked up beside him. "We're transferring Brian and Michelle to a safe house Joseph owns in Christian County. They left ten minutes ago."

Nodding, Kruger looked at the taller man. "Thanks, Sandy." He turned his attention west of the Walmart parking lot. "Allen's spoken to the Governor. The Highway Patrol is issuing a statewide BOLO for Bishop. If he follows past behavior, he'll find someplace to hold up for a while and let everything calm down."

As he finished the sentence, a Highway Patrol car skidded to a halt just behind where the two men stood. A man with sergeant's stripes on his sleeve was behind the wheel. "You Kruger and Knoll?"

Both men turned and nodded. With a neutral expression, the patrolman spoke, "A woman who works at the Kohl's next door was shot inside her car. Her roommate heard a loud pop, looked out the window, and saw someone running from her roommate's car. She called 911. First responders tell me it's bad."

Kruger shut his eyes and brought his hand up to cover them. "Ah, geez." He shook his head and then turned his attention to Knoll. "I'll head over there, you get with Boone and shut this town down."

Knoll nodded.

***

Kruger parked across the street from the duplex, left the emergency lights on his car flashing, and stepped out into the chaotic scene. Columbia police, Highway Patrol, Boone County Sheriff's cars, and a Boone County Hospital ambulance were parked in and around the older model Mustang sitting in a driveway, their emergency lights reflecting off the houses in the neighborhood. He saw a female officer talking to a young woman on the porch of the house. The woman was crying. Clipping his badge on his belt, Kruger walked toward a Highway Patrol officer who was standing next to the older Mustang.

The officer noticed Kruger and started walking toward him. The two shook hands and Kruger introduced himself. The Highway Patrol nodded. "Corporal Matt Hughes. Major Boone speaks highly of you." Hughes was taller than Kruger by several inches and broad in the shoulders. His size made him slightly intimidating, but Kruger was used to large law enforcement officers.

"Boone's a good man; I've worked with him several times. What've you got here, Corporal?"

"Contact gunshot to the right side of the head. She never knew what happened. We're guessing, but it looks like someone was hiding in the back of her car when she left work. The back seat and floor board are cluttered, but you can see where the clutter has been pushed aside. Roommate heard a loud noise, looked out the window, and saw a man emerge from the passenger side of the car and run north." Hughes pointed in the direction of more duplexes down the street. "Lots of students live around here."

Kruger nodded and took a deep breath. "If it's the man I suspect, you need to tell your fellow officers to shoot first and ask questions later. He's desperate and will not hesitate to kill a police officer."

Hughes sighed. "Major Boone already issued a shoot-on-sight order."

Nodding again, Kruger looked in the direction Hughes pointed. "What exactly is in that direction?"

"Lots of older homes, apartments, and wooded areas."

Kruger frowned as he understood the implications of Hughes' statement.

***

Bishop breathed hard as he slowed from his dash down the street. Having never been in Columbia, he had no idea where he was. He could tell it was an older part of the city. Mature trees, older two- and three-story homes, a few nice ones, but most were rundown. New and old cars lined the street with many parked in yards. The area appeared to be close to the campus of the large university and he assumed the majority were student housing.

Off in the distance he heard multiple sirens and felt a moment of disappointment. He did not expected the girl to be found so quickly. Not wanting to be seen, he left the street and made his way behind one of the larger two-story homes.

A quick glance at the only remaining cell phone he possessed showed the time was half past 1 in the morning. He turned the phone off and disappeared into the darkness of the back yards.

Keeping to the shadows behind the houses, he moved slowly into the wooded area behind them. Standing still he observed several of the older homes, keeping an eye on the ones with lights on. Ten minutes later, his vigilance was rewarded with the sight of a young woman in the second-floor window of a three-story house. Her hair was tied back in a tight ponytail, and she wore a man's shirt with the sleeves rolled up. Her back was to the window, and she appeared to be sitting on the ledge of the window. Her left hand was pressed to her head, and her right hand was animated. She was talking to someone on a cell phone.

Bishop moved through the darkness until he was directly behind the house and watched. Several minutes later, the woman stood and turned toward the window. Her shirt was open, and she wore nothing underneath. The sight of her bare breasts and slender body caused Bishop to take a sudden deep breath. His lips grew dry, his heart rate quickened, and he felt a tightness in his groin. His attention turned to the building. It was an older home, at one time a grand structure, but now subdivided into multiple apartments. Bishop noted an outside fire escape attached to the outside leading to the second and third floors of the house.

Retreating further back into the wooded area behind the home, he continued to watch her as she talked on the phone. After several moments, he approached the house, avoiding the light cast by the window. Making his way to the fire escape, he started to climb.

Once in the hallway of the building, Bishop stood quietly outside the woman's apartment, his ear to the door listening to the one-sided conversation.

"I can't believe he just left without waking me. I'm so embarrassed, Sara."

There was silence as the woman listened to her friend.

"I know, but he was so nice and we've had several dates. Uhh… I can't believe it. I feel so used."

More silence.

"No, he's not coming back. I'm done with him."

An idea came to Bishop, he gently tapped on the door.

"Hold on, Sara, I just heard something at the door. I'll call you back, maybe it's him."

He tapped the door again.

From inside he heard in a soft voice. "Is that you, Tommy?"

"Yeah, sorry I left." Bishop heard a deadbolt retracted and a chain being slid out of its receptacle. When the door started to open, Bishop slammed his shoulder into it and heard it make contact with the person behind. He heard a gasp of surprise as he rushed into the room, shutting the door immediately behind him.

The woman was now sprawled on the floor, the shirt open, exposing her nudity. Bishop knelt, clamped his hand over her mouth and growled, "Don't."

Withdrawing the CZ secured by his belt with his other hand, Bishop pointed it at the woman. When she saw the gun her eyes grew wide and he felt her body start to tremble.

CHAPTER 36

Columbia, MO

The early glimpses of dawn were evident as Kruger and Knoll returned to Rosie Singleton's house. JR had remained behind to learn what he could from Bishop's possessions.

Kruger and Knoll listened as JR summarized his findings.

"First, there's over fifty thousand dollars in the duffel bag. Two cell phones and no computer. Did you find one in the woman's car?"

Shaking his head, Kruger spoke first. "No. The witness who saw the fleeing man thought she saw a backpack on the guy."

JR frowned. "Without his computer, it will be difficult to determine how much money he has left."

Knoll stood next to Kruger, his arms folded across his massive chest. "It's been five hours since the last sighting. He could be gone by now."

"I agree." Kruger walked toward the window and watched the sky grow lighter. "I hope we don't have another casualty, but I expect we will."

"How fast did the checkpoints out of town go up?" JR

asked, returning his attention to his laptop.

"Right after Rosie's car was found."

JR nodded. "Now what?"

"I don't know." Kruger concentrated on the sunrise. "He's been unpredictable from the start. If he's found somewhere to hide, it might be several days before he feels comfortable enough to move again."

"I think he'll try to find a way out," Knoll leaned against the door jam. "We've been right behind him since he got to Columbia."

Kruger turned to look at the big man. "You may be right." He resumed studying the brightening sky. After several minutes of silence, he walked to the bedroom door, and looked at JR. "Pack your computer, we're getting out of here."

***

Sara Ferguson gently tapped on the door of her best friend's apartment.

"Mandy, are you okay?"

Silence. She tapped again.

"You didn't call back, I got worried."

Still no response. She tried the door and found it unlocked. Taking a deep breath, she gently opened the door and peeked in. The front room was dark and she didn't hear anything out of the ordinary. "Mandy, are you here?" She stepped further into the quiet room.

A strong hand grabbed her right arm and yanked her into the room. The door shut behind her. Before she could make a sound, a hand clamped over her mouth, her right arm was wrenched behind her back, and she felt the presence of a larger body that smelled of sweat.

"Mandy can't come to the door right now. Don't make a sound, and I won't hurt you. Do you understand?"

Sara nodded slightly.

"I'm going to take my hand away from your mouth. If

you make a sound, I'll break your arm. Do you understand?"

Sara nodded again.

Bishop removed his hand from her mouth and at the same time put more pressure on Sara's right arm.

"Where's Mandy? Is she okay?"

"Don't worry about Mandy. You need to worry about yourself at the moment. Do you have a car?"

"Yes."

"Where is it?"

"On the street. Why?"

"You're going to take me for a ride, Sara."

"Who are you? How do you know my name?"

"Who I am and how I know your name is not important. Now, let's go to your car."

***

JR was on the verge of shutting his laptop down, when he received a message from one of his servers in Springfield. "Hang on, Sean. A phone just called the number in Thailand."

Kruger stopped and walked back to JR, but remained quiet.

Typing rapidly on the keyboard, he stopped, read something on the screen, and started typing again. He repeated this process several times before looking up from the screen. "The phone number calling the contact in Thailand is owned by Mandy Bryant, who lives a half mile from the woman shot in the Mustang."

"Shit." Kruger was out the door and heading toward his car followed closely by JR, who was stuffing his laptop in a backpack. Sandy Knoll ran to his GMC Denali and prepared to follow. As Kruger accelerated toward the neighborhood exit, he called Allen Boone.

The call was answered on the second ring. "Major Boone."

"Allen, we have a lead on Bishop's location." Kruger

gave him the address. "We're on our way, but won't be there for at least fifteen minutes."

"On it, I'll get the Columbia PD and Boone County Sheriff's department headed that way. I'll let them know you're coming in hot."

"Thanks, Allen."

As soon as the call was over, Kruger flipped the switch, and the Mustang's lights and siren lit up.

The neighborhood was east of the campus. The streets were narrow, the homes older, and cars were parked on the street and in yards. Kruger killed the siren, but kept the lights going as JR guided him to the address using Google Maps. As they approached, they noted several police cars with their light bars flashing. JR pointed. "The house is on a corner lot, looks to be a three-story colonial."

Kruger nodded as he parked behind a Highway Patrol car. Knoll parked behind the Mustang and left his emergency flashers on.

Turning to JR, Kruger's expression was grim. "I need to know what was said in the conversation with Thailand." His voice contained a sharpness JR had never heard before. Staring at the house, Kruger opened the Mustang's door. "Find it."

JR nodded, but remained quiet as Kruger walked toward the group of officers standing behind a SWAT van. Knoll followed.

Watching as both men shook hands with one of the officers, JR could not hear the conversation, but noticed Kruger stand a little straighter and put his hand to his eyes. Knoll stood behind him, stoic and unmoving.

***

"We've evacuated the house." Captain Matt Hughes stared up at the house. "The Bryant woman lives in a second-floor apartment. She doesn't have a land line, so we're using optics to look under the door. So far, we haven't seen any movement in the apartment. Door's locked, no response to our attempts at contact. We're now using optics to look through windows."

Kruger stared at the house. "He's gone."

An officer in a SWAT uniform walked up to Hughes and spoke in a low tone, "We have a body in a bedroom."

Kruger stood still and stared up at the house.

"Get an entry team and go in." Hughes took a deep breath. "Be prepared. This may be the second one tonight."

The SWAT member nodded and trotted back to his team. Hughes turned to Kruger. "Who is this guy?"

"Long story, Captain."

"Appears we have a few moments. Enlighten me."

***

Connecting with his servers in Springfield, JR isolated the call from the NSA computers and listened to Bishop's conversation with the man in Thailand. After his second time listening, he noticed Kruger walking toward the car.

When he reached it, he turned his back to the Mustang and leaned against the hood. He pressed his palms to his eyes and bent over until his elbows rested on his knees. JR wasn't sure, but he thought he saw his friend heave. Concerned, he exited the car and stood by Kruger.

"You okay?"

Kruger nodded, but then violently shook his head. "No. I'm not. This was the worst one yet. I just saw hardened, veteran law enforcement officers turn away from the scene in revulsion and puke."

JR just stood there. It was several minutes before Kruger spoke again.

"You have any luck with the phone call?"

"Yeah. I did."

"Let's hear it." Kruger's tone was clipped and matter-of-fact.

Reaching back into the car, he lifted his laptop from the

passenger seat and held it to play the recording.

"Yes."

"I need a new ID and money."

There was a sigh and a long pause before the conversation resumed.

"You are becoming, what you Americans call, a money pit. Where is the return on our investment?"

"You'll get it. Until then, the new ID and cash."

"Why should we continue to help you? I tire of your excuses and delays."

"I can always turn myself in and start telling them about your operation here. They'd like that and all your years of work and careful planning will be wiped out."

Another long pause.

"Call back in six hours."

"Four. Just be aware I know more about your operation than you think I do."

The call ended abruptly, and JR looked at Kruger. "I've confirmed it was Bishop's voice."

Kruger nodded. "He's desperate." He pushed off the car and stood looking at the house with his hands on his hips. Without addressing anyone in particular, he shook his head. "How did he get away?"

"I have a theory."

Turning to look at JR, he tilted his head to the side. "What?"

"I looked at the call record on Mandy Bryant's phone. There were a series of calls to and from one number just before the call to Thailand. The number belongs to a Sara Ferguson. A quick check on Facebook shows Bryant and Ferguson were close friends."

"Are you suggesting she might have been here when Bishop invaded the apartment?"

"It's a guess. I don't have any evidence she was."

"But what if she was? Do you have an alarm on the Ferguson phone?"

"Yeah, and I've pinged it a couple of times. It appears to

be turned off. No response."

Kruger was silent for a moment. "Women her age don't turn their phones off."

"I know." JR took a deep breath. "Sean, what did the voice from Thailand mean?"

Staring at JR, Kruger shook his head. "Sorry, what are you talking about?"

"The end of the call, when he said, 'all your years of work and careful planning will be wiped out.'"

"Guess I wasn't listening. Play it again."

JR replayed the recording and watched Kruger. His expression remained neutral as he listened. When it was finished, Kruger was silent.

It was several minutes before he spoke. "Does the Ferguson woman have a car?"

JR nodded.

"What about the Bryant woman?"

"Not that I can find."

"We have to assume Bishop has the Ferguson woman's car, maybe her too. Get this information to Boone." Kruger tuned back to stare at the house.

"What about the phone call?"

Kruger shook his head. "Not sure. We need to take Bishop alive."

"Uh… You might want to pass that on to Boone."

Without responding to JR, Kruger pulled his cell phone out of his pocket and dialed a number. The call was answered on the third ring. "Allen, we need to take Bishop alive." He paused listening to the response.

"Yes, I know, everyone has to defend themselves. But Bishop has information we need."

More silence.

"I don't know, but I need to question him. He needs to be taken alive if possible."

Another pause.

"Thanks, Allen. I'm going to give my phone to JR. He has information that will help with your search."

JR took the phone and passed on the information about Sara Ferguson along with the make and model of her car. He ended the call and handed the phone back to Kruger. "Now what?"

Taking a deep breath, Kruger closed his eyes and sighed. "Nothing we can do, but wait."

CHAPTER 37

Highway 63, North of Jefferson City

Sara Ferguson was a small woman, barely five–foot-two and slender. Her red hair and blocky glasses kept aggressive males away, but allowed the ones really interested to ask her for dates. One of those interested males was now her fiancé. Currently a senior with a major in business and a minor in accounting, her plans after graduation were already set. The previous summer, she interned at a large international beverage company in St. Louis and was slated to join it after graduation.

At this moment in time, her hands gripped the steering wheel of her ten-year-old Ford Focus so hard her knuckles were white. She stared at the SUV in front of her, not looking at the man in the passenger seat. As he cursed, she wondered if she would live to get married, have a career with the beverage company, and someday start a family. She felt tears forming in her eyes, but blinked hard to make them dissipate.

"Why the fuck is the traffic backed up so far?" Bishop was not asking Sara for the answer; he was just talking. She remained quiet.

The Focus was trapped between a large SUV and a

tractor trailer unit in unmoving traffic. Guard rails on both sides of the highway prevented any car or truck from steering out of the congestion. They were on the exit ramp of southbound Highway 63 as it merged onto Highway 54 and the bridge crossing the Missouri River. Traffic sat bumper to bumper for at least three quarters of a mile from the bridge crossing the Missouri River north of Jefferson City.

Sara could smell the sweat of the man next to her as he grew more agitated with each passing moment. Emergency lights on the bridge were visible from their location. A tear flowed down her cheek as she sat behind the steering wheel, her efforts to make them go away unsuccessful.

***

The growl of the Mustang GT's 5.0 liter V8 could be heard above the siren as it screamed south out of Columbia on Highway 63. JR glanced over at the speedometer and noted it was showing one hundred ten miles an hour. He looked in the side rear-view mirror and saw Knoll's Denali close behind. He turned to Kruger, who was concentrating on his driving. "How long before we get there?"

"Boone told me the car is trapped on an exit ramp. The Highway Patrol has the bridge blocked and is not letting traffic move until we get there. Sara Ferguson's Ford is between a United Movers semi and a large Cadillac Escapade. We'll have cover getting to it. We're about five minutes away."

JR nodded. "What do you want me to do?"

Kruger was silent for a few moments. "Under your seat is a metal box. It has my back-up weapon. If things go sideways and Bishop gets past Knoll and me, shoot the SOB."

"Won't there be other cops involved?"

"Yeah, but I trust you more than I trust them."

JR nodded. His feelings about Kruger were similar, an uncomplicated blind trust.

Kruger was silent for a few moments. "We have to get the girl out unharmed. I don't want another innocent woman to be a victim of this monster."

"How?"

"I'm working on it."

***

Kruger, Knoll and JR advanced slowly on foot next to the right side guardrail. They were several cars away from the United Mover semi and could not see the Ford Focus yet. Three members of the Highway Patrol SWAT team were on the other side of the ramp advancing at the same pace. They were dressed in full assault gear and would be Knoll and Kruger's back-up. JR held the small Glock 26 at his side. They stopped just behind the semi, and Kruger turned to Knoll.

"Sandy, as we planned, you handle Bishop, I'll get the girl."

Knoll nodded.

Kruger moved to the left side of the semi with Knoll moving toward the Civic on the right. He bent down low as he advanced toward his target.

***

Randolph Bishop was extremely agitated. He looked over at the girl and saw her staring at the Cadillac in front of them, she did not look at him. He took a breath and released the catch on his seat belt. "Don't move. I'm going to open my door and stand. Maybe I can see a way out of this mess."

Sara did not respond, but stared straight ahead.

He opened the door, leaned out and stood on his right leg, his left foot still on the car's floorboard. The sound of car horns, the semi behind them, and all the engines running around them hid the slight click of Sara undoing her seat belt.

Bishop looked around. Nothing was moving. The

guardrail next to him kept cars from careening down an embankment after an accident, but now trapped him. He removed his left foot from the floor board and now was fully out of the car. His CZ 9mm was in his right hand at his side, hidden from the surrounding drivers.

Suddenly, the driver's side door of the Focus flew open, and Sara ran toward the cover of the semi behind them. Bishop brought the CZ up and aimed the weapon at the fleeing woman. He did not see the large man behind him, nor was he aware of the massive elbow connecting with the side of his head.

The CZ hit the roof of the Focus as Bishop collapsed to the highway.

***

Sara watched as the man sitting next to her opened the door and stood up. The noise from the surrounding traffic was more prevalent with the passenger door open. She realized this might be her one chance to escape alive. She slowly released her seat belt and held it as it retracted. As quietly as possible, she pulled the handle to open her door as she watched the man's torso turn to the rear of the Focus. She stopped from opening the door, waiting for him to turn back to the front. When he did so, she pushed the door open and sprang from the car, running toward the semi as fast as she could.

The sound of a gunshot never materialized as she ran for her life to the safety of the massive semi parked two feet behind her car. As soon as she was past the front of the semi, she ran into a man who grabbed her, and swung her around. "You're okay now, Sara. You're safe. I'm with the FBI."

She gasped and stared up at the tall man who held her, his face illuminated by the headlights of the stalled traffic. It was a kind face smiling down at her. She placed her arms and forehead against his chest and started sobbing.

***

Knoll watched from the shadows of the semi's tractor as the passenger door of the Focus opened. Randolph Bishop stood up and looked around. Pressing himself against the truck, he kept an eye on his target. When Bishop turned away from his position and started looking forward, Knoll started moving toward the man.

His peripheral vision caught movement to his left, but he ignored it as he moved forward. Bishop's head twisted to his left and he brought a weapon up, aiming at something. Knoll sprinted the last two yards as he raised his right elbow. It made contact with the side of Bishops head and the man collapsed like a puppet with its strings cut. Knoll secured the dropped weapon and started binding Bishop's arms behind him with flex cuffs. Once completed, he did the same to Bishop's ankles.

Not a shot was fired.

***

It took thirty minutes for the Highway Patrol to open the bridge, clear traffic and block off the exit ramp. Sara Ferguson was in the back of an ambulance being attended by two EMTs. She was staring at the man who comforted her after running from the Ford. Kruger sat across from the gurney she lay on. "Sara, I have to ask you a few questions."

She nodded.

"Did he attack you or hurt you in any way?"

"No, he never really touched me except when I walked into Mandy's apartment, and he grabbed me. But that was the only time. How's Mandy? Is she okay?"

Kruger did not smile. "No, I'm afraid she isn't."

Sara closed her eyes and tears flowed from both. "I was afraid he hurt her."

"Sara, did Bishop say anything to you?"

"Was that his name? He never told me."

"Randolph Bishop."

She gasped. "The man in the news?"

Kruger nodded. "You were lucky. He needed you for something."

The tears flowed faster and she started breathing hard. One of the EMT's said very softly. "Agent, we really need to get her to a hospital. Can this wait?"

Nodding, Kruger stepped out of the back of the ambulance and helped close the door. He watched as it drove toward Jefferson City across the bridge.

JR walked up to Kruger. "I've got his laptop."

Turning, Kruger stared at his friend and for the first time in several days, felt relief.

CHAPTER 38

Jefferson City, MO

The Cole County Sheriff's Office building was located in downtown Jefferson City. Randolph Bishop sat alone in an interrogation room, shackled and chained to a ring embedded in the concrete floor. An hour passed while Kruger and Allen Boone observed him on a video monitor.

"Can you talk to him?" Boone asked as he stared at the figure on the video screen. "Without doing him physical harm."

Taking a breath, Kruger was silent for a moment. "I think so. My first impulse is to walk in there and shoot him. But we know that isn't an option."

Boone chuckled and nodded. "How long are you going to leave him in there?"

"A few more minutes. JR's searching his laptop. I need some information before I go in there."

"You haven't changed, Sean. Always know more than the person you're interrogating."

Kruger nodded his head once, but remained quiet as he stared at Bishop's image.

Twenty minutes later, Kruger unlocked the door to the

interrogation room and entered. Bishop could not see him, but Knoll was outside and could be in the room in seconds. Kruger sat across from Bishop, placing a manila file folder on the table between them.

Remaining quiet, Bishop stared at Kruger.

"Remember me, Randy?"

"I don't believe we've met."

"Sure we have. Parking lot of Harmon, Harmon, and Kinslow. It was a Thursday evening about six years ago."

"Don't know what you're talking about. I want a doctor and a lawyer, in that order."

Kruger smiled. "Well… we might have a problem with both. No, that's not correct. We don't have a problem. You have the problem."

"I've probably got a concussion from the brutal attack I suffered. So until I have a lawyer present, I'm not answering your questions."

Kruger chuckled. "At the moment, you'll get neither." He opened the folder and slid a photo of a man presenting his passport to a TSA agent in an airport terminal.

Bishop stared at it and shrugged. "So. It's a picture of a man in a hat."

Taking another picture from the folder, he laid it on top of the other one. This time the camera caught the image of the man's face. It was Bishop.

"Recognize the man in the picture?"

Bishop remained silent.

"It's you, but you already knew this. Records indicate the man in the picture presented a passport with the name of Everett Stewart." Kruger watched Bishop. There was a momentary tell of alarm on his face, but it was replaced with a neutral expression just as fast.

"Unfortunately, Randy, you entered the United States under a false ID. That's problem number one. Problem number two, Everett Stewart is the prime suspect in the disappearance of Malaysia Airlines Flight 24 this past March."

Bishop stared at Kruger, his eyes widened slightly.

"Randolph Bishop and Everett Stewart were on the manifest as a passengers. Bishop's boarding pass was used. Stewart's wasn't."

"People miss flights for a lot of reasons."

"True, but the real Everett Stewart never returned home. Then, we find you using his passport to enter the United States. Which means, you entered the United States under false pretense for the expressed purpose of terroristic acts. In other words, you've been classified as an enemy combatant. We can hold you forever without allowing you access to a lawyer."

Bishop directed his eyes to the photo in front of him, but remained quiet.

"Here's your third problem. We know Randolph Bishop murdered four women in St. Louis over the course of ten years."

"My brother confessed to those murders. I had nothing to do with them."

Kruger smiled again. "So you're admitting you're Randolph Bishop?"

"I'm not admitting anything."

"Your brother did leave a note at the scene of his suicide confessing to the murders. But there's a problem with this confession."

"There is no problem. My brother killed those women. You're throwing mud against the wall hoping something will stick. It won't because I didn't kill those women."

"Trace DNA was found on one of the victims."

Bishop remained silent.

"Apparently, the killer used a condom when he raped the women. But semen was found in one of the victims. Small amount, the condom had a leak, but it was enough to send to our FBI lab. The DNA was tested against Paul Bishop's profile. It was close, but not a match. In fact, it was so close, it could only be a sibling. You are Paul's only sibling."

Bishop laughed. "You're grasping at straws, you have no proof it was my DNA."

"Not yet."

"I'm done talking to you."

"Suit yourself. But the story gets better. I'll let you think about it some more."

"I have to piss."

Kruger nodded, stood, and opened the door. He said something as he stepped out and was replaced by Sandy Knoll. Knoll was accompanied by two of the largest men Bishop had ever seen. The two large men were dressed in sheriff deputy uniforms and stood behind Knoll.

Kruger spoke from outside the room loud enough for Bishop to hear. "These three gentlemen will escort you to a holding cell where you can relieve yourself and contemplate your future. Or the complete lack of one. They outweigh you by at least five hundred pounds, so try not to do anything stupid."

***

An hour later, Bishop was escorted back into the interrogation room. Kruger was already sitting at the table with three thick files next to him. He ignored Bishop as he sat down and one of the deputies secured his shackles to the ring on the floor.

Kruger continued to disregard Bishop as he sat reading the open file in front of him. Bishop cleared his throat several times, but Kruger remained silent. After ten minutes, he looked up from the file. "Tell me about the man you call in Thailand."

"Thailand? I don't know anyone in Thailand."

Kruger nodded and went back to reading the file.

Another ten minutes went by before he looked at Bishop again. "We haven't decided where to send you yet. Guantanamo Bay is out; it's going to close soon. The CIA has a few really special hell holes we're thinking about. There's one in Turkmenistan, or a particularly nasty one in Uzbekistan that would work. Do you have a preference?"

Bishop stared at Kruger, his eyes narrow and his brow furrowed.

"Probably best not to pick. We'd send you to the one you don't want."

Kruger went back to reading.

"Okay, Kruger, what do you want?"

Looking up he smiled. "So you do know who I am. Good. I want to know about your contact in Thailand."

"I told you I don't know anyone in Thailand."

Pulling his cell phone out of his jacket pocket, he touched an icon and sat it down. The recording of Bishop's conversation on the previous day played. After it concluded, Kruger picked up the phone, ended the app. "This phone call was intercepted by the NSA yesterday. The voice without an accent has been confirmed to be yours. The phone making the call is owned by Mandy Bryant. She was found brutally murdered last night. Care to make a comment?"

Bishop shook his head.

"Now, again, who is your contact in Thailand?"

Bishop's eyes narrowed and he leaned toward Kruger. "You can't prove anything."

"We know more than you think we do. Do the names Brenda Bishop, Judith Day, Thomas Zimmerman, Stephen Blair, Christine Daniels, Rosie Singleton and Anna Rhodes mean anything to you?"

Bishop continued to stare at Kruger, his expression defiant.

"The only one you probably don't recognize is Anna Rhodes. She was shot in the head with a CZ 9mm while sitting in a car in her driveway. She never knew what happened or why. I doubt you even knew her name."

Bishop snorted. "You can't prove anything."

"On the contrary. Ballistics indicate the bullet that killed Anna Rhodes was fired from the CZ found in your possession."

Bishop's expression softened and he studied the top of the table were they sat.

"The Attorney General of Missouri is already filing charges against you and wants to pursue the death penalty. Unless…"

Bishop looked up, his eyes narrow. "Unless what?"

"You tell me about the man in Thailand."

Bishop grinned and shook his head. "Not a chance."

Kruger's cell phone vibrated, he glanced at the sender, kept his expression neutral and stood up. "Think about it for a while. Consider this: if you don't answer, you might never see the sun again."

He returned Bishop's grin and walked out of the room.

***

JR smiled as Bishop's laptop spilled its secrets.

It had taken two hours to crack the log-in code, a long time by his standards, until he realized he was dealing with a professional, well-constructed firewall. Once this was established, he made rapid progress.

One of the files contained a list of addresses in a PDF file of scanned documents. As he worked through the documents, one address stood out.

Once he realized what it was, he picked up his cell phone and sent a text message.

JR sat in a small conference room down the hall from the Cole County Sheriff's Office. He was the only occupant of the room as he waited for his friend to join him.

When Kruger walked in he saw JR staring at his computer screen.

"What was the urgent summons about?" Kruger threw the files he held on the conference table, his tone unhappy about being interrupted.

"Found something of concern on Bishop's laptop."

Kruger exhaled and nodded slightly. "Sorry, what'd you find?"

"Take a look at this." JR pointed to the scanned page on his laptop screen.

Silence was his answer as Kruger looked at the information. "So? Looks like a bunch of addresses."

JR pointed to one particular address. "Recognize this?"

Kruger shook his head.

"It's the home address of the man who kidnapped Stephanie and Kristin."

Kruger's eyes widened and he straightened in his chair. "You're kidding?"

"Nope."

"What does it mean?"

"Think about it for a moment."

Kruger was silent for several minutes as pieces of the puzzle fell into place.

"Ahhh…. shit."

"Yeah, I would agree."

***

It took thirty minutes for everyone needed on the conference call to find a suitable location to talk unencumbered. In the sheriff's office conference room sat Knoll, JR, Allen Boone, with instructions to remain quiet, and Kruger. Joseph was at the safe house where Brian and Michelle were now located. Seltzer and Director Stumpf were at FBI headquarters and could connect the call to the President if needed.

Stumpf started the meeting. "Okay, Sean, what've you found?"

"Our friend found the information. I didn't."

"Fine, go on."

Kruger looked at JR and nodded. "We have a recording we need you to listen to." JR touched a key on his laptop and Bishop's phone call to Thailand was heard. After it was finished, Kruger continued.

"The call was intercepted yesterday by our friends over at NSA. It was from a phone in Columbia, Missouri to a phone in Thailand. The voice of the caller from the US was identified as Randolph Bishop. Voice print match."

"What are the plans mentioned in the call? Do you have details?" The question was asked with growing concern by Seltzer.

"No, but a document was found on Bishop's laptop. It's a handwritten document with numerous addresses all over the US. The document appears to have been scanned in a hurry, it's not centered. To me, this indicates it was scanned clandestinely. We have zero proof, but we think Bishop scanned it as insurance."

"Insurance against what?" It was Stumpf's voice.

"Bishop indicated on the phone call he was aware of a plan being organized by the man in Thailand." Kruger paused, but no one spoke. He continued. "The document found on Bishop's computer is a list of addresses in the United States. One of those addresses was the home of the man who kidnapped my wife and daughter."

"What kidnapping?" Stumpf tone was harsh.

"I kept it quiet; they're safe."

Joseph spoke up. "Paul, I'll explain later. It was deemed necessary to keep it out of the media."

Stumpf responded with silence. After several moments they heard, "Fine. Next time inform me."

Kruger smiled slightly. "The kidnapper was a known associate of the man in Thailand."

Seltzer spoke next. "Was?"

Joseph interjected, "Terminated."

The reaction was silence. Stumpf said, "Got it. Keep going."

Kruger took a deep breath and looked at JR, who smiled slightly. "It's our assumption the list of addresses may be locations of men who are waiting for a call to conduct a series of preplanned and coordinated terrorist attacks."

"What's your proof?" Stumpf voice was less confrontational.

"We don't have proof. We have a lot of data points, a lot of assumptions and conjecture, a list of addresses, and a gut feeling. That's all."

"How many addresses?"

Knoll spoke up, "Over twenty in different cities."

A slight whistle could be heard over the phone connection. Stumpf voice sounded concerned. "Any indication of when they might attack?"

"None." Kruger's voice was louder than he meant it to be.

Silence returned to the conference call. Finally, they heard Stumpf say, "Joseph, what do you suggest?"

"We have to check each address and see if our assessment is correct."

"Do you have enough manpower?"

"I'll defer the question to Major Knoll."

"Major, what are your suggestions?"

Knoll smiled, "We've been planning for this possibility."

"Meaning?"

"My team will assess a number of the locations. If we deem it necessary, we will use FBI Rapid Response Teams or local SWAT."

Everyone in the conference room heard Stumpf take a deep breath. After letting it out slowly, he spoke, "Gentlemen, if your suspicions about these addresses are correct, we have a potential crisis on our hands. Proceed with your assessment. I will brief the President." He paused briefly. "Next time anything of importance happens, Sean, inform me."

Kruger gave a slight smile. "Yes, sir."

The call ended, but no one stood. The silence was deafening as each man dealt with his own thoughts. After a minute, Kruger looked at the big man. "Sandy, where do you want to start?"

Knoll looked at a copy of the file JR had printed for him. He was quiet for several moments. He looked up. "Dallas."

CHAPTER 39

Jefferson City, MO

After the conference call, Kruger realized he was going on twenty-four hours without sleep or a meal. It was almost noon, and he left the sheriff's office to walk down the street to a small café. Knoll had left for the airport, and JR was busy with Bishop's laptop. They seated him at a two-top table, and the waitress left to get his iced tea. After she was gone, he placed his elbows on the table and pressed the palms of his hands against his weary eyes.

He felt someone sit down across from him.

"You look about as bad as I feel."

Kruger looked up and smiled. Allen Boone sat there, his eyes bloodshot with dark circles highlighting his weariness.

"Have you looked in a mirror lately?"

Boone chuckled. He kept quiet as the waitress placed Kruger's drink in front of him. Boone pointed to Kruger's tea. "I'll take one of those, too." He watched as she walked away. "What can I do to assist, Sean?"

Kruger shook his head. "I don't really know at this point. We need to see what Sandy finds in Dallas. There's an address in St. Louis; why don't you start there and put it under surveillance."

Boone nodded. "What about Bishop?"

Kruger took a sip of his tea. "I'm going to take one more shot at him and then turn him over to you. I don't trust myself around him. During my last interview, I struggled not to strangle him. I think it would be a good idea for you to be in the room with me. But I want to wait until we hear something from Sandy. Maybe tomorrow. Let Bishop cool his heels for a day."

Boone smiled. "Sounds good."

***

Bishop shuffled into the interrogation room and his shackles were secured before Kruger and Boone entered. After getting a good night's sleep and an update from Knoll in Dallas. He was ready to talk to Bishop.

They watched Bishop on the video monitor for five minutes before going in. Kruger entered first, holding a file folder. Boone closed the door and leaned against the door frame behind Kruger, his arms folded across his chest.

Bishop looked up. "Who's he?"

Kruger glared at Bishop. "I ask the questions. You don't."

"Fuck you, Kruger."

"Yeah, well, get used to it, Bishop. Where you're going, you may find someone doing it to you daily."

Snorting, Bishop sat back in his chair.

Kruger extracted the printed sheet of the PDF file from the file folder and slid it across the table for Bishop to see. He remained quiet as he watched Bishop's eyes momentarily grow wide and his lips pull back against his teeth. Then the expression went back to his normal scowl.

"What's that?"

"I'm surprised you don't recognize it. It's from your laptop." Kruger pointed at one address in particular. "Your friend who kidnapped my wife and daughter lived at this address."

"I have no idea what you're talking about."

Kruger took a deep breath as he thought of what Stephanie and Kristin endured because of this man. He took a few moments to calm himself. "Sure you do. These addresses are the reason you came back to the United States, Randy."

Bishop shook his head.

"I'm not stupid, Randy." Kruger watched Bishop tense when he said "Randy." "You, don't like being called Randy, do you, Randy? Not sophisticated enough for you?"

Glaring at Kruger, Bishop started breathing hard.

"Back to the piece of paper. We know what it is, and we're shutting it down as we speak."

"You have no idea of what this piece of paper means, Kruger. You're stumbling in the dark."

"Good, so you do know. Now we're getting somewhere."

"Do you think I'm stupid, Kruger? I know how the game is played."

"No, Randy, I don't think you're stupid. I think you're a manipulative psychopath who thinks he's invincible. You're not." Kruger pointed at the chains. "Your presence here proves it." He paused for a few seconds. "I thought you would have had a better escape plan than the one you tried. Really lame."

Bishop's face grew red as he tried to stand up. The shackles stopped him before he could rise three inches. Boone stopped leaning against the door frame and uncrossed his arms.

"Sit down, Randy." Kruger put the piece of paper back into the file. "Let me tell you what's going to happen next. With the knowledge of the addresses and information gleaned from various intercepted phone calls, the FBI is going to shut down the operations of the man from Thailand." Smiling, Kruger looked straight into Bishop's eyes. "I haven't forgot about the man from Thailand. Have you?"

Continuing to glare at Kruger, Bishop remained silent.

Kruger continued, "Once all the individuals on this list are compromised, your friends overseas will think you told us. How else would we have found all of the addresses?"

Bishop's confident smirk changed immediately. His brow furrowed, and his breath suddenly grew short.

"My guess is, once we have you in a state penitentiary, your friend in Thailand will find some way to get to you. We don't like it, but, you know, shit happens." He stared at Bishop.

"You have no idea what is going on, Kruger. There is no way you can stop it."

"Actually, there is." Kruger stood, smiled and turned toward the door. Just before exiting the interrogation room, he turned. "We've already shut it down in Dallas. Fortunately one of the suspects was taken alive, and he was more than happy to tell us what he knows."

***

The drive back to Springfield seemed longer than the trip to Columbia. JR's seat was tilted back and he was trying to sleep. It wasn't working. "Where do we go from here, Sean?"

"With the information you found on the laptop and what Sandy found in Dallas, the raids on the addresses will take place sometime early tomorrow morning. Probably around 3."

"You're not going to one of them?"

Kruger shook his head. "I'm not interested. Sandy can handle it."

JR straightened his seat and looked over at his friend. "That doesn't sound like you, Sean. You always want to be in the middle of things."

Watching the road in front of them, Kruger did not respond right away. After trying to understand his feelings, he exhaled. "Yeah, I know. Not this time. I need to get back to Stephanie and Kristin. I've been gone too long."

JR nodded as the conversation lagged. The comfortable silence of two old friends deep in thought ensued. Five minutes later, JR asked, "What's it like being a father?"

Kruger took a quick glance at his friend.

JR kept his gaze forward watching the road. "I've been trying to imagine being a dad, but so far I can't."

"It can be scary. Your concerns turn away from yourself and concentrate on your child. Even when they grow up and leave the house, you worry about them. But being a father has more wonderful moments than scary ones. Watching them grow, their first words, accomplishing new things, laughing, becoming a person you enjoy being around, your first deep conversation, the list goes on."

"I hope I can be a good father. I never really knew my parents. They died when I was six in a car wreck."

"You've never talked about them."

"Don't remember much. I don't even have a picture of them."

"Did you live with your grandparents?"

JR shook his head. "No, both pairs died before I was born. I was placed with foster parents. They adopted me within a year. I was lucky; they were good people." He paused briefly, a catch in his voice. "They died while I was in the service. I still miss them."

"How old were you when you joined the army?"

"On my eighteenth birthday. It was the only way I could afford college."

"Was that when you crossed paths with Joseph?"

"Yeah, I don't remember him, but he followed my career. Particularly the marksmanship awards I won."

"I remember him telling me about those. Long and short guns."

"Yeah, my dad taught me how to shoot." JR's eyes stared ahead. "A .22 long rifle and squirrels. We lived on ten acres of walnut and oak trees, far more squirrels than trees. During the fall my father and I gathered up walnuts and took them to a local huller. He let me keep the money." A smile came to his lips as he reminisced. "I haven't thought about that for a long time."

A long silence occurred. "You never mentioned where you went to college."

JR glanced over at his friend. "I didn't?"

Kruger shook his head.

"MIT, graduated summa cum laude. Lot of good it did me."

"MIT, really?"

"Yeah, that's where I met Stephen Blair. He was smarter, but I did better in classes neither one of us liked."

"Huh…"

The silence returned for ten more miles. Smiling, Kruger interrupted the quiet. "What do you want, boy or girl?"

"I think Mia would like a girl, but she's like me; she just wants the child to be healthy."

"That's every parent's wish."

"I've never been good at sports. Not sure I know how to be a father."

"None of us do until it happens. Some do it better than others. You'll do fine." Kruger watched the road for a while as the mile markers passed by. Finally, he turned to his friend. "Go by how your foster dad acted. He sounds like a good role model."

JR nodded, "He was."

"Thanks, JR. I needed something else to think about."

"Yeah, me too."

Another long silence transpired before Kruger asked, "Do you still shoot? You never talk about it?"

JR nodded. "Yeah, Sandy's been working with me. It's like riding a bicycle. You don't forget."

Kruger chuckled, "I've heard that."

PART 4

Two Months Later
Springfield, MO

Kruger sat at his home office desk finalizing a report to Paul Stumpf. The room was isolated on the west end of their house away from the living area where Kristin played. A mature white oak tree dominated the front yard and provided shade for his window during the heat of summer. His desk chair faced away from the window, preventing distractions of the busy neighborhood from gaining his attention.

It had taken six weeks for Sandy Knoll and his team, utilizing local law enforcement agencies throughout the country, to wrap up their take-down of the individuals on the list provided by Randolph Bishop's laptop. Only two were in the process of carrying out their part of the conspiracy, but were stopped prior to any actual attack occurring. His report summarized the operation.

Stephanie walked into the office, a big smile on her face. Kruger looked up and chuckled, "What?"

"Have you talked to JR in the past few days?"

"No, he's been tied up with a client. Why?"

"Mia called. They know the sex of the baby."

"Are you going to tell me or make me guess?"

"They're having a boy."

Kruger leaned back in his chair and nodded. "I think he secretly wanted a boy. He's never said one way or the other, but from comments he's made, you could tell."

Stephanie bent down and stared out of the window behind her husband. Her smile disappeared. "Why are two Highway Patrol cars parked in front of our house?"

Kruger turned in his swivel chair and watched as Allen Boone stepped out of a dark gray Ford Explorer with the Missouri Highway Patrol emblem on the front door. Kruger shook his head. "Don't know, but I assure you it's not good news."

As he spoke, two officers exited the vehicles and stood by the cars as Boone walked toward Kruger's front door.

Kruger opened it just as Boone stepped onto the porch. "Allen, I hope this is a social call."

"Wish it was. Can I come in?"

Kruger stood aside, and Boone entered.

***

One of Stephanie and Sean's favorite spots in their house was a breakfast nook next to the kitchen. It allowed a panoramic view of their treed backyard and deck. When possible, it was the place where the busy husband and wife caught up on each other's day. The small glass table with four chairs was perfect for a lazy Sunday brunch or early morning cup of coffee. Kruger and Boone sat across from each other with Stephanie between.

"When did he escape?" Kruger asked.

"Early this morning. I was conducting a budget meeting here at Troop D when I was told. Thought I'd better get over here to let you know."

"What happened?"

"He was being transferred to St. Louis County Court in

Clayton for arraignment on the four murders you investigated six years ago. We're guessing, but we think a truck ran the Boone County sheriff's car off the road. One of the deputies was found outside the car, and the other still in the driver's seat. Both were killed with a shotgun."

"Ah, boy." Kruger took a deep breath. "Why do they think it was a truck?"

"There was a 911 call received a little after 5 a.m. about a large pick-up and a sheriff's car stopped along I-70. The caller said it looked like an accident."

"I take it the pick-up wasn't there when first responders arrived."

Boone nodded and hesitated for a second. "Uh… One more thing."

Kruger frowned.

"A Ford F-250 was stolen from a lot in St. Louis yesterday. It was found forty miles south of I-70 on Highway 19, near Drake. Damage on the passenger side contained traces of paint the same color as the sheriff's car transporting Bishop. Our lab is analyzing to see if it matches. A shotgun was found in the back floorboard. In addition, two bodies were found, a male in the truck and a woman on the side of the road. Neither had identification."

"Tell me about the male." Kruger turned to look out the window.

"Short black hair, mid-twenties, small frame, and of Asian descent."

Kruger nodded. "The woman?"

"White, mid-to-late sixties, curly gray hair, overweight."

Everyone at the table was silent. They could hear birds chirping in the back yard. After a minute, Kruger returned his attention to his visitor. "Concentrate on identifying the woman. Bishop's got her car."

Boone nodded. "I'll see if we have any missing person's reports from the area." He stood and was about to walk out of the kitchen, but turned back to Kruger. "Something else."

"Yes."

"The weapon of the deputy killed outside the car is missing."

Kruger's expression did not change as he turned back toward the bay window. With a grim smile and a nod, Boone left the kitchen.

Stephanie reached for her husband's hand. "Do what you have to do. Stop him, Sean. Just don't lose your soul."

Kruger turned to his wife but remained quiet. Finally, he closed his eyes and nodded.

Boone returned to the kitchen several minutes later. "They have a possible ID on the woman. Her name was Janet Pratt, sixty-seven, lived in Hermann, Missouri."

Looking over his coffee cup at his friend, Kruger raised his eyebrows. "That was fast. How?"

"Gasconade County Sheriff's Office received a call from the woman's daughter. She didn't show up at her sister's house, and her cell phone isn't being answered. Description matches the female body found near the truck."

"Do you have the cell phone number?"

Boone nodded and handed Kruger a slip of paper. "It's there along with the make, model, and license plate of her car."

Silence returned as Kruger stared at a bird hopping around on the deck hand rails while he absorbed the news. Stephanie turned her attention to Boone, her hands intertwined in front of her. "Do you think he's headed here?"

"We have no proof, but, yes we do."

Kruger's gaze was still directed out the window. "If he follows his normal pattern, and I have no reason to believe he won't, he'll switch cars again."

"I agree with you." Boone paused, took a deep breath and continued, "You three need to take a vacation."

Kruger took out his cell phone and pressed a speed dial icon. "Damn, I'm tired of reacting to this guy. It's time to get aggressive."

The call was answered on the third ring. Kruger said, "We have a situation."

***

A white Ford Transit van arrived at the Kruger household thirty minutes later. It pulled into the driveway just as the garage door opened. Two men hustled out of the side door and went inside the Kruger home. Joseph stepped out of the passenger door and followed. The two Highway Patrol vehicles remained parked in front of the house with their drivers watching the street.

Joseph stepped aside as the two men returned, carrying several suitcases back to the van. Boone and Kruger stood in the breakfast nook when Joseph entered the kitchen. Turning his attention to Boone, he extended his hand. "Allen, good to see you again."

Boone smiled grimly as they shook. "You too, Joseph."

Kruger tilted his head slightly. "Is there anyone in this state you don't know, Joseph?"

"If they're in law enforcement, probably not. Sandy will be in town in an hour. Meanwhile we're going to get Stephanie and Kristin to my property in Christian County. We'll swing by JR's and pick up Mia before we head that way."

Kruger frowned, "Why Mia?"

"A precaution. You told us Brian and Michele are visiting her father in North Carolina, so we don't have to worry about them."

"Yeah, they left last Saturday."

Joseph lost his smile. "Sean, I think you should come, too."

"I will. I'm going to secure the house and head over to JR's. I'll finish my report to the director there."

"Joseph, I'll stay here with my guys until Sean leaves." Boone gave his old friend a mischievous grin. "You can stop worrying."

Clearing his throat Joseph muttered under his breath. "Someone has to worry about him." He walked out of the kitchen into the garage and disappeared.

Kruger's half-smile betrayed his true feelings. He walked back to his office and shut down his laptop. As he placed it in his back pack, Allen Boone appeared at the office door.

"I've seen that look before. What're you thinking?"

Looking up, Kruger stopped packing. "Running and hiding isn't going to end this. Bishop's out there, probably watching the house right now."

Boone stiffened.

"If he is out there, you wouldn't recognize him."

"What do you mean?"

"He's a psychopath with an uncanny ability for self-preservation. He's also a chameleon who will blend into his surroundings. He blames me for forcing him to flee the country six years ago. The fact he killed four women doesn't matter to him. Internally he justified the killing because it helped him gain the position of CEO at Harmon, Harmon, and Kinslow. He is psychologically incapable of feeling remorse. Nor does he feel guilt that his brother killed himself trying to take the blame for the murders. He just doesn't have the ability to feel emotions like you and me."

Boone listened, remaining quiet.

"Is he out there? Yes, he can't help it; he's driven. He will die trying to reap revenge on those who have crossed his path. I'm the one who started this, the root of all his problems. Pull the root out, and he believes his problems go away. This isn't going to end until one of us is dead." Taking a breath, he paused for a few moments. "I'd prefer it be him."

"I'd prefer that as well, Sean. What's next?"

Putting the remaining files he needed into his backpack, he looked at Boone again. "During my last interview with him I saw something in his eyes. It's hard to describe, but it was almost like he knew this would be over soon."

"Is he dumb enough to think he can get to you through all the security we'll throw around you?"

"I don't think dumb is the right description. More like

his ego won't let him believe otherwise." Kruger paused for a second, trying to put his thoughts into words. "Allen, he doesn't think like you and me. I made the mistake of not recognizing how strong his narcissism was six years ago. He thinks—no, that's not right. He knows he's smarter than the rest of us." He stopped talking and lifted the backpack onto his shoulders. "Right now I need to get to JR's and then I'm going to find this guy."

***

"Janet Pratt's cell phone was recognized by cell towers here, here, and here." JR was pointing to a Google Map of Missouri displayed on a twenty-two inch flat-screen monitor.

Kruger noticed the locations were all on Route 42 heading west toward Osage Beach. "Has he made any calls?"

JR shook his head. "No, it's almost like he didn't know it was in the car."

"What about now?"

"There aren't any sign of it past Osage Beach. The phone is dark, so he must've found it and taken the battery out."

Kruger stood and started to pace.

JR was sitting in his favorite cubicle on the second floor of his building watching his friend walk from the cubicle to a spot ten feet beyond and return. "Do you think he's ditched the car?"

"Yeah, probably."

"What now?"

Kruger stopped pacing and stared at the computer screen with the map. "He has no money and he's probably still in his prison jumpsuit. Since one of the dead Boone County deputy's service weapon wasn't found, we will assume he has a gun. So he has two problems to solve. Money and clothes. Plus his other problem is the Highway Patrol concentrating their search for him in the counties around the lake."

"That's a big area, Sean."

"I know."

Silence prevailed as both men stared at the computer screen, deep in their own thoughts. JR broke the silence. "Another victim."

"Yeah, another victim."

JR frowned. "Lots of places to hide around the lake."

Kruger nodded.

JR suddenly turned back to the computer and started typing. Kruger watched, as soon as JR stopped typing he frowned. "What was that all about?"

"Looking for robberies between here and Jeff City." He stared at the monitor, then back at the Google Map and pointed. "Bank of Mack's Creek was robbed at two this afternoon by a man wearing a ski mask. He shot the surveillance cameras out before forcing everyone in the bank into a storage room. He cleaned out all the cashier drawers but left the bundles with the dye packs behind."

"How much?"

"This report doesn't say."

"Lots of back roads in the area and few deputies. He wouldn't have trouble eluding a search."

"You think it was him?" JR looked at Kruger, who was staring at the computer monitor.

Kruger nodded. "I'd want to see the surveillance video of the robbery before I made a determination. But odds are, it was. I'll call Allen and see if we can get a look at it. After all, I'm with the FBI, I'm entitled."

***

Thirty minutes later, the video file arrived attached to an email from Boone. JR opened it, and they watched. The time stamp read 13:32 and the date. The customer count was low. Only three individuals entered the bank, completed their business, and left before a man wearing a ski mask entered at 13:57. He pointed a gun at an object out of visual range and fired. He then pointed the weapon at the camera making the recording. The image blacked out.

"JR, back it up to where he points the gun at the other camera."

They watched again until Kruger held a finger up. "Stop."

JR froze the image. Kruger got closer to the screen. "Blow up the image of the gun."

JR did so. When the pixel count was compromised, JR reduced the image in size.

Kruger touched the screen where the shooter and gun were frozen. "Looks like a Glock. The deputies at the Boone County jail in Columbia had Glocks in their holsters. Back it up to the beginning. I think I saw something."

During the next viewing, the second person entering the bank kept his head down as he went to a teller window. Kruger leaned closer to the screen. "Stop and enhance the man's profile."

JR did so. Kruger stared at the image. "Do you have a profile picture of Bishop you can compare this image to?"

JR nodded. "Yes, his booking photos in Jeff City."

"Compare the profiles using your facial recognition software."

Five minutes later, JR smiled. "It's him. Ninety percent match."

Kruger sat back in his chair. "Now we know he has money and a gun, and he's changed clothes. We just don't know what he's driving."

"But we know he's heading this way."

Taking his cell phone out of his pocket, Kruger made a call.

CHAPTER 41

Central Missouri
Earlier the Same Day

It was 5 a.m., and Bishop stared out the backseat of the sheriff's car. The only thing to keep his mind occupied was watching the value on the mile markers increase as they headed toward St. Louis. His hands and feet were shackled, with the ones on his hands too tight. The deputies in the front ignored his complaining so he stopped half an hour earlier.

He heard the rumble and saw the lights of a large pick-up truck trying to pass on the left of the patrol car. Out of pure boredom, he glanced over to watch it pass. As the truck pulled even with the patrol car, it suddenly veered to the right, crashing into the side of the car. The driver fought to keep control of the skidding car, and the deputy in the passenger seat started shouting at the driver.

"Get a grip on it Jim, keep it under control."

The pick-up slowed as the sheriff's car skidded to a halt on the side of the highway. The deputy in the passenger seat unbuckled his seatbelt, drew his service weapon, and opened the side door. Just as he did so, Bishop heard a loud roar as the driver's side window exploded inward and blood from the now-dead driver splattered the interior of the sheriff's car.

More gunfire could be heard as the deputy who exited the car fired his weapon at the truck. The fire fight was over after two more blasts from a shotgun ended the life of the remaining deputy.

Bishop sat still. He could feel the driver's blood sliding down his face. The door on the right side of the car flew open, and the barrel of a shotgun pointed at his head.

"You want to live?" Bishop could tell the man was Vietnamese from his accent, but the face was hidden by the roof of the vehicle.

"Yes."

"Get out and get in truck. No questions."

Bishop held his hands forward. "Get these off of me."

"No, do yourself."

Exiting the car, he bent down to search the deputy lying next to the patrol car. The man's face was missing. In the darkness, the Vietnamese man lowered the shotgun and stared back toward the highway as a series of headlights could be seen approaching.

In the light of the passing cars, Bishop saw the deputy's service weapon, a Glock. With his back to his would-be liberator, he secured the weapon in a side pocket of his jumpsuit.

"Give keys."

"Still looking. Here they are." He stood but hesitated until the shotgun barrel poked his chest. With a grim smile, he handed the keys to the smaller man and watched as he put them in his right jeans pocket. As he walked to the truck, the barrel of the shotgun pressed against his back.

"Hurry, before cars come again. Move."

The small man steered the F-250 back onto I-70 and headed east a mile before taking the exit for state road 19. Now traveling south, the man spoke for the first time since leaving the sheriff's car. "You pay debt now."

Rolling his eyes, Bishop shook his head slightly. "How? I'm shackled and in a moving vehicle."

"No, no, no. Not now. When we get to place we go. You pay debt or die."

Bishop did not answer. He just stared at the road as they passed through the rural Missouri countryside.

***

Janet Pratt was confused. The four-way intersection seemed unfamiliar to her. She knew the route, having driven it a hundred times to visit her sister in Owensville. But this morning she couldn't remember which direction to turn. Frustration and sadness were her emotions as she sat in her stopped car, trying to remember.

She was in her late sixties, overweight, with curly gray hair. Widowed for twenty years she lived alone and, unknown to everyone but her and her doctor, was suffering from early on-set dementia.

She was unaware of the large Ford F-250 pulling up behind her. She was also unaware of the flash visible in the front window of the truck and was unaware of the man racing up to her door with a gun in his hand. Confusion would be the last conscious thought she would ever have.

***

The Vietnamese man cursed in his native language at the old Chevrolet Impala stopped at the intersection. With the man's attention momentarily trained on the unmoving car, Bishop eased the Glock from his pocket and aimed it at the small man's head. A moment of realization appeared on the small man's face as he turned to look at his passenger.

"Who's in control now, dumbass."

Bishop smiled and pulled the trigger. He found the keys in the dead man's pocket and released the shackles. Amazed the Chevy was still stationary at the intersection, Bishop rushed to the driver's side door and saw an older woman staring up at him. He yanked the door open and grabbed her by the arm.

"Out," he yelled. His adrenalin surged as he pulled her from the car and pointed the Glock at her. She stared at him with a look of pure confusion. Pushing her around the rear of the car she fell into a ditch beside the road. Now on her knees and looking up at him, Bishop could see tears welling up in her eyes. The only emotion he experienced was disgust as he pulled the trigger and hurried back to the Chevy.

***

Traffic was light, and Bishop passed only a car and two pick-ups as he drove west on Route 42 in the woman's Impala. Keeping low in the driver's seat, he tried to keep the orange prison jumpsuit from being seen by passing motorists. The towns in this part of Missouri were no more than wide spots in the road and sparsely populated.

Traffic increased as he approached the town of Vienna, but he managed to drive through without attracting attention. Again, traffic diminished as he continued west.

Bishop looked at his face in the rearview mirror and saw dried blood in his hair and forehead. Realizing he needed to do something about his appearance, he started looking for isolated houses on the road. It was approaching eleven a.m. when he spotted an older gray Honda Accord pulling into a side road. He slowed and followed the car down a winding gravel road until it stopped at an old house with a falling down barn several hundred feet behind it.

Bishop watched as an elderly man with stooped shoulders exited the Honda and walked slowly toward the house. As he parked the Impala behind the Honda, the old man noticed and turned to stare. A puzzled expression appeared as he slowly walked toward the Impala.

Bishop opened the Chevy's door and stepped down. When the elderly man saw the orange jumpsuit, his eyes grew wide. Raising the Glock, Bishop smiled. "Don't say a word."

***

Two and half hours later, Bishop stood outside The Bank of Mack's Creek and pretended to be talking on a cell phone. His real purpose was determining where the surveillance cameras were located.

Once he spotted them, he took one of the checks he found at the old man's house and walked into the bank to a teller.

"Can I cash a check?"

The young teller appeared to be a recent high school graduate. She wore thick glasses, was slightly overweight, and in bad need of fashion advice. She looked at the check. "I can, but your check is from another bank. We'll have to charge a service fee. All I need is a driver's license or some form of ID." She smiled. Bishop could see her teeth needed straightening.

"How much is the service fee?"

"Five dollars."

Shaking his head, he turned and started walking out. "Thank you, but I'll pass."

The old man's gray Honda was parked several blocks from the bank in a deserted area of the small town, away from buildings and nosey neighbors. In the car, he changed out of the slacks and shirt appropriated from the late Mr. Addison and put on a pair of jeans and a dark brown hoodie purchased at a Walmart store in Camdenton an hour ago.

He returned to the bank, parked on the side of the building, slipped a ski mask over his head, pulled the hood over it, and walked into the bank. Saying nothing, he raised the Glock taken from the deputy and shot out the surveillance camera on the right side of the bank. Sweeping the gun to the left, he took out the camera on the opposite side. He then spoke in a gravelly voice, "Every one into the store room, and you won't get hurt."

It took less than thirty seconds to get everyone secured.

He then went to the teller drawers and grabbed all of the cash he could find not booby trapped with dye packs. It took less than a minute to secure all of the cash he could find quickly. Exiting the bank, he walked casually toward the parked Honda, slipped behind the wheel, and drove west on State Highway W.

Two hours later, Mr. Addison's dark gray Honda drove through Kruger's neighborhood. As Bishop passed the house, he saw two Highway Patrol cars parked in front with two uniformed Highway Patrol officers standing beside them watching the street. Not wanting to attract undue attention, he did not slow and proceeded to leave the neighborhood.

He found a fast food restaurant several miles from Kruger's home and stopped to eat while he waited for the Highway Patrol to leave. He made another pass on an adjacent street an hour later. Between two houses, he could see the Highway Patrol cars still parked and the addition of a Ford Transit van parked in the driveway. He stopped briefly, then drove back to Kruger's street and parked in front of a house several blocks from the Kruger home. Ten minutes later, a dark gray Mustang drove past him. The driver was Sean Kruger.

CHAPTER 42

Christian County, Missouri

Kruger and JR arrived at Joseph's property in Christian County just as the sun disappeared behind low clouds on the western horizon. He saw Sandy Knoll's GMC Denali parked in the circle drive and Joseph's Range Rover in front of it. Kruger parked the Mustang behind the Denali.

Joseph's property was a sprawling parcel of land five miles south of Sparta and a half mile west of Fairview Road. To the east, Fork Bull Creek ran through the front part of the property. Trees were the main feature of the twenty acres behind the house. Access to the home was by a dirt road barely accessible by anything other than an SUV. Kruger's Mustang struggled.

Few individuals outside of Joseph's immediate friends and colleagues knew about the house.

As he exited the car, Kruger could see Stephanie on the wrap-around front deck holding Kristin's hand. Kristin was jumping up and down and pointing at her daddy's car. Kruger marveled at the elegance and beauty of the structure and he never tired of their visits.

JR walked around the car and stood beside him. "Did

you notice the gray Honda Accord following us?"

Kruger nodded. "The same car was waiting at the end of my street when I left for your place."

"I ran the license plate just before we lost cell service a few miles back."

"And?"

"Registered to a Henry Addison." JR paused for a moment. "Blumley, Missouri."

"It's him. As soon as I get to the house, I'll use Joseph's satellite phone to call Allen and tell him."

"Not sure I like being without cell service out here."

"Relax, Joseph's got satellite phones and a dedicated T-1 line running underground. It's faster than your place."

"I should have known." JR chuckled. "I need to find Mia. I'll see you three inside later."

After Kruger climbed the eight steps to the front deck, he picked up Kristin and hugged her. He then kissed his wife and embraced the two women in his life. JR waved at Stephanie just before walking through the front door.

"I'm glad you're here," Stephanie smiled. "I was worried."

"No need to be."

She nodded but remained in his embrace. "I love this place. I wish we were here under different circumstances."

"Me, too." The hug lasted a few more moments. "Let's go in."

Stephanie took Kruger's hand and he kept Kristin in his other arm as they walked toward the front door.

***

Darkness was total in this part of Christian County. The lights of the nearest city were far enough away the Milky Way ribbon was clearly visible above the isolated house. Kruger stood on the back deck and stared up at the night sky. Joseph joined him on the deck and handed him a crystal highball glass.

Kruger accepted the glass and took a sip. "Damn, Joseph. When did you start keeping the good stuff out here?"

"Since I started spending more time here. The solitude is quite intoxicating."

"Sorry to intrude on it."

Smiling slightly, Joseph took a sip of the twenty-one-year-old Glenfiddich. "Not a problem. Sandy's team is out there." He nodded in the direction of the trees. "They haven't seen the gray Honda Accord yet."

"I spoke to Boone about ten minutes ago. They found the Pratt woman's Impala in a barn belonging to a Henry Addison. Henry was in his late eighties and a widower. From what neighbors told the Highway Patrol, they saw the Chevy turn down Henry's driveway sometime during the late morning. The only reason they noticed was because Henry doesn't get too many visitors anymore."

"Bad?"

"Bishop just broke his neck and put him in a chair with the TV on. If someone looked in, they would think he was napping."

All Joseph could do was nod.

"It has to end, Joseph. His killing has to stop."

"How?"

Kruger took a deep breath. "I haven't got that far yet."

***

The call came at midnight. Allen Boone was on the satellite phone and asked to speak to Kruger. Joseph went to get him. Five minutes later, Kruger took the phone.

"Yeah."

"Sorry to wake you, but we may have an issue."

Kruger was quiet for several seconds. "May have an issue, or do have an issue?"

"We found the gray Honda Accord registered to Henry Addison."

"Where?"

Boone took a deep breath and blew it out. "Abandoned."

"Again, where?"

"Two miles from your location."

"Damn."

"Yeah, that's our assessment."

"Any ideas where he might be?"

"We're going door to door along the corridor to Joseph's property. So far, no luck."

"It's midnight Allen. He's hiding somewhere. If you find a residence that doesn't answer, let me know."

"So far, we've only found one residence with no response."

"Where is it?"

"A mile north of the entrance to Joseph's property, west side of the highway."

"Who lives there?"

"A family named Owens. Husband and wife, teenage boy and girl, plus a baby."

"Do you have the house under observation?"

"Yes."

"Any signs of life?"

"As you said, it's midnight. Not too many signs of life anywhere."

"Keep me posted."

***

Three minutes after five the phone rang again. Kruger answered.

"Yeah."

"It's Boone. There's a male body on the front lawn of the Owen's home."

"When did it appear?"

"No one knows. A porch light came on ten minutes ago, the body was already in the lawn. Bishop appeared on the front porch and announced he would kill the husband and a baby if you didn't appear in front of the house at 8 a.m."

"Can they tell who the body is?"

"No, but it looks like a small male."

"One of the teenagers?"

"Probably."

"I'll be there."

***

JR held the rifle as Sandy Knoll pointed out several enhancements. JR nodded after the lesson concluded. "If he goes, I need to back him up, Sandy."

Knoll gave JR a grim smile. "I'll be there, too."

"He won't agree, trust me. He'll think it's too dangerous."

Knoll put his hand on JR's shoulder. "He won't know we're there."

***

Kruger sat at the breakfast bar in Joseph's kitchen loading magazines for his Glock with 147 grain 9mm hollow point bullets. Joseph was standing across from him sipping coffee.

"Want some coffee?" he asked.

Kruger shook his head.

"Does Stephanie know where you're going?"

"She does. She's not happy, but understands."

"I can't let you go alone."

"You have no choice. If Bishop suspects there's anyone besides me…"

"He won't."

"I can't take that chance, Joseph." He looked up as he spoke. His eyes were narrow and his brow furrowed. "Too many innocent people have lost their lives because I didn't put this maniac away a long time ago. It ends this morning. If I don't…" He paused briefly. "You'll have to."

Joseph did not answer right away. With a frown, he nodded. "I understand."

***

Kruger parked Joseph's Range Rover a quarter of a mile from the Owens house on Fairview Road. It was 6:30, and the sky was lightning in the east. The crisp morning air allowed Kruger to see his exhaled breath. He needed time to observe the home before he walked up to the front door. Taking his time, he circled the house keeping within the tree line. He saw no activity as he circled around the back. He stopped behind a large oak fifty feet from the rear door of the modest ranch style home and stood still, just observing.

Several vehicles were parked on the north side of the house. All were at least ten years old. The house appeared to have been built in the seventies, but looked well maintained. A small swing set could be seen halfway between Kruger's position and the house. It looked unused. Other than a barbecue grill and a little clutter around the yard, it looked like a typical rural home in Christian County. The family was like most folks around the area, coping with the injustices of life and just trying to survive. Bishop invading their home was just another slap in the face by the gods of chance. He started to move further north when his peripheral vision picked up movement on his right side.

Moving into the shadows of the early morning, he saw a figure dashing from the house into the woods to his right. More than likely it was Bishop moving into the grove of trees behind the Owens house, preparing to spring a trap. Smiling slightly, Kruger moved deeper into the brush and trees to hide his presence.

Minutes crept by as Kruger stayed perfectly still. His only thoughts were about Stephanie and staying silent. A rustling of leaves and a snapped tree limb were heard to his right. He did not turn his head, only his eyes tracked in the direction of the sound. The sound of dry leaves crushed under the weight of a man's step came to his ears as he tracked the movement. In the dim light of early day, Kruger saw a shadowy figure emerge from several small trees five yards to his right. The man stood with his back to Kruger and stared at the house in the clearing.

Timing his movements to when the man was facing away, Kruger crept forward in the darkness, raising his gun from pointing down to pointing up. His eyes did not deviate from the shadowy figure now only a few feet in front of him.

As the figure started to move, Kruger lunged forward and grabbed the man's neck with his left hand. He twisted the body around and shoved him hard against a tall oak tree only a foot from where he stood.

With his right hand, Kruger pushed his Glock into the soft tissue under the man's chin and demanded, "Where are they?"

Bishop's surprise only lasted a heartbeat. "Who?"

"The owners of the house."

Smiling, the imposter stared at Kruger. "Haven't got a clue what you're talking about."

Tilting his head to the left and then to the right, Kruger felt the muscles of his neck pop. Pressing Bishop harder against the tree, he placed his index finger inside the trigger guard. "You have five seconds to tell me where they are before I pull this trigger."

Chuckling, Bishop stared hard into Kruger's eyes. "You won't pull the trigger. You're like all the others. Weak. You won't kill me, your conscious won't let you."

Kruger could feel his heart racing, and sweat dripped from his forehead even in the cool morning temperatures. His finger started to apply pressure to the trigger. He stared into Bishop's cold eyes and took a deep breath to calm himself. Stephanie's words about not losing his soul echoed in his mind. He released the pressure, but kept his finger on the trigger.

"Why would my conscious bother me for ridding the earth of a creature such as you, Randy?"

The smile disappeared, Bishop narrowed his eyes. "You have no idea of who you're dealing with."

"Oh, I know."

Bishop suddenly relaxed and he chuckled. "Do you? You think just because you have a PhD in psychology you know who I am?"

Kruger's hand started to tremble as he fought to control his anger.

"You're trembling, Agent. Something wrong?"

Continuing to stare at Bishop, Kruger remained quiet.

"You should have seen your ex-wife beg for her life. It was pathetic…"

"Ahhhh…" Kruger screamed as he brought his knee up with as much force as possible to strike Bishop's groin. The air gushed out of the man's lungs like a deflating balloon, and his eyes rolled up. Kruger released him and watched as Bishop crumbled to the ground gasping for air and holding his genitals.

Kruger stood above him and kicked the man as hard as he could in the back. Immediately regretting his action, he back off and pulled his cell phone out of his pocket.

Just as he was ready to push an icon on the phone, he heard a blood curdling scream emanate from the house. Training and instinct caused him to start running toward the sound, but within seconds he stopped. Releasing his mistake, he turned back to where Bishop lay.

The man was gone.

Before he could react, an excruciating pain shot through his right arm. He dropped the Glock as he staggered to his left. Another savage blow struck him in the back, and he collapsed against a large oak tree.

Kruger's vision blurred as he turned and put his back against the large oak tree. Holding his right arm with his left hand, he looked up.

Randolph Bishop stood there, a Glock in his hand pointed at Kruger's head.

"You should have pulled the trigger when you had the

chance, Agent."

Kruger stared up at Bishop, but remained quiet.

"I don't think you appreciate the situation you're in, do you, Agent Kruger?"

"I guess I don't, Randy. What situation am I in?"

Bishop cocked his head to the left, then the right. Kruger could hear the joints in Bishop's neck cracking. "Actually, I really haven't thought about it. Sometimes the goal is just to capture. What to do next is more of an afterthought."

Kruger could tell his right arm was broken. He had no use of his right hand and could feel the swelling starting. "You won't get out of this alive, Bishop. The area is swarming with Highway Patrol and Christian County deputies."

"Doesn't matter really. My objective was to kill you. In my opinion, everything else is meaningless."

"I find that hard to believe."

Bishop suddenly got a far-away-look in his eyes, and he let the Glock fall to his side. "I've known all along I would die in a hail of bullets. Kind of a Bonnie and Clyde sort of thing. Did you see the movie with Warren Beatty and Faye Dunaway?"

Kruger did not answer the question. He just stared at Bishop.

"The way Warren Beatty died was very cinematic. Slow motion with bullets ripping through his body. That's how I imagine my death."

Kruger shook his head. "This isn't a movie, and you're not Clyde Barrow."

Bishop woke from his brief stupor and raised the Glock. "No, I'm not Clyde Barrow. But I've done something no one else has done."

"What's that, Randy?"

Bishop frowned, lowering the Glock again. "I've stopped the great Sean Kruger."

"You haven't done shit. All you've done is terrorize and murder innocent people. People who did nothing to you."

"Well, at least I get to pay you back for all the headaches you've given me over the last six years. I had to live in squalor for a year in Bangkok because of you. You owe me."

"I owe you nothing."

Kruger's thoughts turned to Stephanie as he stared at Bishop. The Glock was rising slowly. Time stood still as he waited for the bullet that would end his life.

Bishop's wild smile returned. "No, I don't suppose you think you do. But it's time to pay up. Say good bye, Agen…"

As the Glock rose even with Kruger's eyes, Bishop's head disappeared in a mist of red, gray and white matter. The arm holding the Glock twisted to Bishop's right as muscles in the now dead body constricted, pulling the trigger. A bullet struck a tree to Kruger's left. The headless body collapsed backward into the morning dew. The echo of a high-power rifle shot reverberated off trees in the crisp morning air, masking its location.

Kruger could feel moisture on his face and realized it was probably splatter from Bishop's demise. He felt a spasm in his back as he struggled to stand. He leaned against the tree and looked down at the lifeless body. Fearing he would not be able bend over and stand again, he kicked the Glock out of Bishop's hand. When he looked up, he saw JR and Sandy Knoll running toward his position. Both held Remington 700s with sniper scopes.

When they arrived, Knoll asked, "You okay?"

Kruger nodded. "Arm's broke, but other than that, yeah, thanks to you."

"I couldn't make the shot, didn't have the angle. JR took it."

Kruger looked at his friend.

JR stared down at Bishop's body. "Not sure what it says about me, but I don't feel anything except relief."

Placing his left hand on JR's shoulder, Kruger's smile was grim. "It says you're more interested in life than death. Bishop was death."

JR looked at Kruger, who was holding his right arm

again. "You're hurt. Let's get you back to Joseph's."

CHAPTER 43

Springfield, MO

"Your arm has a comminuted fracture." The ER doctor pointed to the x-ray on a light screen in the emergency room occupied by Kruger and Stephanie. "I'm not an orthopedic specialist, but I believe you'll need surgery."

Kruger winced, took a deep breath, and asked, "How long to recover?"

"Like I said, I'm not a specialist, but experience tells me it will be awhile."

"And that means?"

The doctor just smiled. "They'll be down in a few minutes to take you to surgery. Do you have a specialist you prefer?"

"No, this is my first broken bone."

"Lucky you. The one on-call is excellent."

With those words, the doctor parted the curtain and walked out of the room. Kruger sat on the bed, and Stephanie stood next to him. She asked, "How's your back?"

"Just bruised. I was lucky; he could have shattered my spine."

"What did he hit you with?"

"Fallen tree limb. Apparently it struck something before it hit me."

She rubbed his left arm, but remained quiet.

Joseph moved the curtain back and asked, "What's the verdict?"

Stephanie tightened her grip on Kruger's good arm. "Shattered humorous. He's going to surgery in a bit."

Joseph grimaced, entered, and let the curtain fall behind him to close off the room.

Kruger asked, "What'd I miss?"

Taking a deep breath, Joseph shook his head. "Bishop executed everyone in the Owens' house except the daughter. She was spending the night with a friend, she came home early and slipped past a couple of patrol cars watching the place. You probably heard her scream when she got home."

Looking down at the floor, Kruger nodded. "Yeah, I heard it. I started to react to it, but realized I would be leaving Bishop alone. I wasn't going to make that mistake again."

"Bishop's body was turned over to the Highway Patrol. Allen Boone told me it will be cremated, and the case closed." Joseph paused for a few moments. "Sean, I know you don't want to hear this, but one good thing resulted from this affair."

Kruger looked at his friend. "What the hell could be good about all the people he murdered?"

"Sandy's team stopped a lot of terrorists. You and JR's discovery prevented a lot of carnage and destruction. Some of the attacks could have left hundreds dead."

"I wish I shared your enthusiasm." Kruger reached for Stephanie with his still-functioning left hand. She took it and squeezed.

A commotion in the hall stopped their conversation. A young nurse slid the curtain aside, a cheery smile on her face. She looked at Kruger. "Are you Sean Kruger?"

"Yes."

"I'm Brenda, I'll be taking you to surgery. You'll be assigned a room after that." She turned to Stephanie. "Are you Mrs. Kruger?"

"Yes."

"If you'll follow me, I'll show you the waiting room."

***

Stephanie flipped through the magazine for the fourth time. She did not see or remember any of the words or pictures. Joseph sat next to her quietly watching the door leading to the surgery rooms. They were the only ones left in the waiting area, others having come and gone.

She dropped the magazine on the empty chair next to her. "What is taking so long?"

Joseph placed his hand on her arm. "It's only been ten minutes since I checked."

Standing, Stephanie started pacing. She looked at a wall clock. "It's been four hours, Joseph. How long does it take?"

He was about to respond when a slender man in his mid-forties dressed in blue scrubs walked through the door next to the waiting room. He looked at Stephanie and asked, "Are you Stephanie Kruger?"

She nodded.

"I'm Doctor Morgan. Your husband's in recovery now. He'll be transferred to a room in about an hour. You can see him then."

"How is he?"

The doctor did not smile. "There was substantial damage to his right humorous, and I had to rebuild it. What took the most time was finding all the bone fragments."

Joseph stood. "What about recovery?"

"He should regain full use of his arm, but it will take time." He smiled slightly. "He'll probably be able to tell you when a change of weather is coming."

Stephanie just stared at him.

The doctor finally smiled. "Go get something to eat, and by the time you return, he'll be in a room. When you get back, ask at the nurse's station."

Without another word, the doctor turned and hurried back through the door behind him.

Stephanie turned to Joseph. "I'm not hungry."

Joseph nodded.

She crossed her arms. "This is the second time Sean's been seriously hurt on the job. The last time I almost lost him. It's time he quit."

Joseph did not respond.

"I'm serious, Joseph."

"I know."

"He has a daughter and will soon have another son. I don't want to raise them without him."

With a gentle smile, Joseph placed his hand on Stephanie's shoulder. "The current President won't be in office after this coming January. Sean may not have to worry about making the decision. It could be made for all of us."

She stared at him for a long moment, her brow furrowed. "What do you mean?"

"I don't know the two candidates running, never met them, and the current President doesn't like either one. It could mean our program goes away."

"What if it doesn't?"

"Then you and Sean will have to make a decision."

CHAPTER 44

Washington, D.C.
Two Months Later

Joseph and Kruger were shown into the Oval Office by the President's Chief of Staff. President Osborne was seated at his desk looking through a file. He glanced up, smiled, stood, and walked around the desk to greet them. "Gentlemen, good to see you."

"Thank you, Mr. President, it's good to see you as well." Joseph shook the offered hand and stepped aside.

The President looked at Kruger. "Your country is very grateful for your service again, Agent Kruger. You have saved more lives than any of us can imagine." He offered his hand, and Kruger shook it with his left, his right arm still immobilized with a cast and sling.

"Thank you, sir."

"When does that come off?" The President pointed to the cast.

"Sometime in the next few weeks. Depends on the x-rays."

"Good. Would either of you like coffee?"

Joseph nodded. Kruger shook his head, still not

comfortable drinking coffee in the Oval Office, especially with his left hand. The President went to his desk and touched a button on his phone. Almost immediately, a steward with a tray of coffee entered the room.

After a few more pleasantries, they sat across from the President. "The candidate I least wanted to win the election won, even though we're in the same party. He won on a platform of taking secrets out of government. Everything has to be out in the open, no special projects, nothing in the shadows." Osborne paused for a moment. "He's a naïve fool."

Joseph took a sip of his coffee. "So what does that mean for our little endeavor?"

"I don't know, Joseph. The government has numerous projects the public doesn't know exist. Projects, I might add, that keep us safe. I hope when he takes office he will understand the need."

Kruger spoke up. "Have you discussed any of them with him?"

"Not personally. We've reached out to his appointed Chief of Staff, but the reception was not… Let's just say the response wasn't encouraging."

"Most disappointing." Joseph frowned. "So, what do you want us to do?"

"I have three weeks left in office. There is a little housekeeping we need to do before then."

Joseph remained quiet as the President paused.

"Has the man in Thailand been identified?"

Joseph gave the president a slight nod.

"Good." The President sat back in the sofa and smoothed his tie with his hand. Looking at Joseph, he asked, "Do you have contingency plans for this individual, Joseph?"

"We have several."

The President nodded again, but remained quiet as he looked out the window behind his desk. After several moments of silence, he turned his attention back to Joseph. "Do you remember the words I used the day the Imam from

San Francisco had his fortunate accident?"

"Yes, sir. You told me, and I quote, 'Find them, Joseph. Find them and make them go away.'"

The President nodded. "I believe this individual in Thailand is one of them."

Joseph's only response was a slight smile.

Kruger asked, "When you leave office, what then, sir?"

The President sighed. "For your own protection, shut it down."

Both Joseph and Kruger did not speak.

"We can justify Agent Kruger's activities because he's an FBI agent. But your involvement, Joseph, could lead to embarrassing questions neither of us want to answer due to your previous employer's identity. You've done too much good work. I don't want that to happen."

"What about Major Knoll and his men?"

"Once the individual in Thailand is dealt with, they will be retroactively assigned to the FBI. Director Stumpf signed the document this morning."

"Can Sean direct their activities under FBI jurisdiction?" Joseph was sitting on the edge of his seat, leaning toward the President.

"As long as Director Stumpf is the head of the FBI."

Joseph sat back and smiled. "He's only been in his position for two years; he still has eight more."

The President nodded. "Unless he does something illegal, which he won't. There is one other problem, and the real reason I asked to see you both."

Kruger frowned. He didn't like the direction the conversation was going.

"Using JR and his skills, after the new president takes office, could put him in jeopardy of being arrested."

"How?" Kruger stiffened, his anger growing.

The President sighed. "The new administration will appoint a new director of National Security. If that person is as pragmatic as the incoming president, they will cut off JR's access to the NSA computers and possibly prosecute him."

Kruger thought for a few moments. "Who knows about JR's arrangement with the NSA?"

"Just myself, Director Stumpf, the director of the NSA, you two, and the person who set up the link."

This answer was better than he expected. "Have them shut down the link. Today."

The President frowned and sat a little straighter. "Are you sure? You don't want to wait for the new president to make that decision?"

"No, I don't want JR put in a position to be arrested for doing something he did for the country, not personal gains." Kruger paused for a second. "The reason the president-elect wants these secret programs eliminated is his belief others are profiting from them. While there may be a few who are, far more good than bad has been the results of these activities. Unfortunately, the American public believed him and he won the election."

The President nodded. "I hadn't thought of it that way, Sean. You may be right."

Kruger shook his head. "We may find that the president-elect is using his rhetoric as a shield to hide his own intentions."

Joseph stared at Kruger. "That's a cynical point of view."

"But more than likely the correct one." The statement from the President caused both Sean and Joseph pause. They looked at the man as he stared out the window behind his desk. The President continued, "I fear we're entering a dark and dangerous period for our country, gentlemen. We all need to be vigilant."

The room was silent after the President spoke. He returned his attention to Kruger. "Paul Stumpf asked me to apologize for is absence this morning."

Kruger smiled. "No need."

"He's uhh…" The president chuckled slightly. "He's taking care of a personnel problem today. It seems the recording you made of Franklin Dollar's attempt to compromise you was reviewed by the FBI Office of

Professional Responsibility, which in turn handed it over to the Office of the Inspector General. A more thorough investigation was conducted into Dollar's career. The Department of Justice has reviewed numerous convictions where he was the lead investigator. They found proof he tampered with and in some cases, made up evidence. Dollar is facing time in a Federal prison."

Kruger shook his head. "To this day, I don't know how he made it through the academy."

"This too is being investigated."

"Figures."

The President's demeanor turned serious. "I don't know what the next few years hold for our country gentlemen, but I would be honored if both of you would keep counsel with me after I leave office. There is still a lot of work needed to keep all of us safe. I'm afraid the good citizens of this country have just made it more difficult."

CHAPTER 45

Springfield, MO
Two Weeks Later

JR and Kruger were alone in JR's conference room. The cast was off, but Kruger was instructed to keep the arm in a sling except during therapy sessions.

"How long do you have to keep that thing on?"

"The therapist says another two weeks, maybe more. She seems pleased with my progress."

JR nodded.

"Did you check the original NSA access link?"

"Yeah, it was shut down the day you got back from Washington, D.C."

"Does your work-around still function?"

Nodding again, JR chuckled. "I closed those down and made new ones. I'll keep repeating the process every week or so until we don't need them."

"They won't notice?"

"No, Sean, they won't."

Kruger gave him a half-smile. "I don't want any of this to blow back on you."

"I appreciate it."

Standing, JR walked out of the conference room to the Keurig he kept outside the room on a table. He made a cup of coffee and returned. "Did they ever find Stephen Blair's body?"

Nodding, Kruger took a deep breath. "Yes. I received an email from Tom Stark several days ago. The family who purchased Blair's estate raises Carin Terriers."

"Uh, oh."

"You see where this is going don't you?"

JR nodded. "I had one when I was a kid. Great dogs, but they love to dig."

"Yeah, about two weeks ago, one of them was seen playing with what appeared to be a human foot."

"Hope one of the kids didn't find it."

"No, it was the nanny." Kruger stood and walked to the Keurig. "I'm going to buy you a drip coffee maker one of these days." When his coffee was ready, he returned to the conference table. "The body was found in a shallow grave in a remote section of the estate."

"Cause of death?"

Kruger rubbed his face with his free hand. "Dehydration."

JR closed his eyes. "Did they find anything else?"

"No trace of his regular meds. Bishop probably didn't let him take them. The ME suspects Blair's mental state deteriorated to the point he didn't realize he wasn't taking in water."

JR was quiet for several moments as he studied his coffee mug. "Stephen didn't deserve to go that way."

"None of Bishop's victims deserved it."

The room was quiet as both men were lost in their own thoughts.

Finally JR asked, "Did you make a decision about your involvement?"

"If I stay, I'll have to take a promotion. Which, in effect, will keep me out of the field. Something Stephanie would like." He stopped and turned toward the windows in the room. "Not sure I can do that and still feel effective."

"Well, if you leave, I'm out too. I won't work for anyone but you."

"I appreciate that, JR," Kruger smiled. "Maybe it's time we both got out."

Both men were quiet and lost in their own thoughts.

JR broke the silence. "You've expressed doubt about the new president's intentions."

"I can't put my finger on it yet. There just seems to be something phony about his holier-than-thou attitude."

"You told me you didn't vote for him. Sour grapes?"

Shaking his head, Kruger put his coffee mug down after a sip. "No, nothing like that. I've seen the pattern before. He exhibits all the traits of a narcissist. While a president needs to have a strong ego, they also need some humility. He doesn't, his ego will get him in trouble and possibly the country. I have a bad feeling he thinks he can do no wrong. Dangerous for a President of the United States. Did you vote for him?"

"I didn't vote. I don't exist, remember?"

Kruger smiled. "Got it. So, what do you want to do?"

"If you go back to teaching, we won't be running around the country chasing bad guys anymore. Right?"

Kruger nodded. "No, we won't. I don't want to stick my head in the ground, but Stephanie wants me to go back to the university. She's never mentioned it, but I can tell it's the direction she would prefer."

"Yeah, Mia's making noise about me following your lead. The baby is due in a month, and she thinks I need to be around to help." He paused briefly. "I tend to agree with her."

"Did you tell Mia everything?"

JR shook his head. "No, I didn't. I told her most of it, but left out the part about who fired the shot. I just told her he was no longer a problem."

"It'll be our secret."

"So, what are we going to do?" JR sipped on his coffee

again.

Silence was his answer as Kruger stared out the windows of the conference room. After taking a deep breath, he let it out slowly. "I'm going back to the university for the spring semester. Stephanie is right; I need to concentrate on our family."

"You'll be bored."

"Probably. What about you?"

"Like I told you earlier, I won't work for anyone but you. Guess that means I get to concentrate on my family and company again."

"So, you'll be bored as well."

JR nodded.

***

Stephanie glanced out the breakfast nook window and saw her husband sitting in a chair on the back deck. It was after nine and dark with a cold wind blowing in from the northwest. She opened the door and stepped out. "Aren't you getting cold?"

The light from the kitchen window barely illuminated his frame. Kruger shook his head without saying anything.

She walked up behind him and put her arms around him. He did not respond.

"What's wrong, Sean?"

He shook his head, again.

Stephanie frowned and sat down in the chair beside him. "Something is up. Tell me."

He handed her his cell phone. "I received a call from Allen Boone a few minutes ago. He sent that after we finished talking."

She looked at the phone. On the screen was a picture and an obituary. "Did you know her?"

"No, the only time I saw her was after Randolph Bishop invaded her home and assaulted her. Her name was Rosie Singleton. She was unconscious when we found her."

Stephanie handed the phone back to him. He took it and stared at the screen for a few moments. "Allen told me she passed away in a skilled nursing facility two days ago. She was sent there due to being in a catatonic state from the time the EMT's got her to the hospital until she died."

Stephanie remained quiet and started to shiver.

He looked over at her. "You're cold, go on in. I'll be there in a minute."

"I'm fine. I'm worried about you."

"I'll be fine, too." He stared out into the darkness of the back yard. "She was married twice and divorced twice. The Boone County Sheriff's department told Allen there are records of domestic violence against her by the two ex-husbands."

Stephanie remained still and let him talk.

"Apparently, she got rid of the husbands and was getting her life together. Then Bishop followed her home." He took a deep breath and let it out slowly. "We found a plane ticket in her house. She was supposed to leave for a week long cruise. Friends told the sheriff's department she had been saving several years for it."

The cold wind ruffled his hair as he continued to stare into the night sky.

"Bishop followed her home the night before she was to leave."

With the dim light from the kitchen window Stephanie wasn't sure, but she thought she saw moisture in the corner of her husband's eye. She remained silent.

Kruger shook his head slightly. "I thought we were in time to rescue one of Bishop's victims." He sighed and returned his attention back to her. "Guess I was wrong."

EPILOGUE

Bangkok, Thailand
Two days before the Inauguration of a new United States President

He was a small framed man, skinny, and barely five feet tall. Originally from the southern part of the Socialist Republic of Vietnam, Trinh Huy was an important man in this isolated neighborhood of Bangkok. Known for giving money to the poor and homeless children who occupied the back alleys, he commanded respect from everyone who dealt with him. If anyone showed disrespect they simply vanished. Officially an exporter of silk, his real money was earned from the illicit sex and drug trade of Thailand. In addition to giving to the poor, he was an enormous financial supporter of Islamic militants in Malaysia. He also retained a fifty-year loathing of the United States.

The identification of Huy as Randolph Bishop's contact was made by JR from his computer tap of the NSA computer servers. Huy used only one cell phone to conduct his regular business. It was registered to a shell company in Bangkok, and Huy's name was not associated with the phone or the company. By monitoring the cell number and the use of well-placed resources in Bangkok, JR and Joseph had narrowed the possible suspects to two individuals.

With this information, Knoll's team was dispatched to Bangkok to place both suspects under observation. The identification of Bishop's contact was soon confirmed, and afterwards, placed under constant surveillance by the team.

Huy's moves and activities were monitored. While the team already knew his cell phone protocol was sloppy, they discovered he frequented the same restaurants on a routine basis. By the third week, the team had a plan.

***

In a sixth-floor room of an older hotel several blocks from one of the cafés frequented by Huy, a large man with closely cropped blond hair stood at the left side of a triple wide window, a pair of binoculars in front of his eyes.

"You smell like garlic and cloves." Sandy Knoll did not divert his eyes from the binoculars as he spoke.

Jimmy Gibbs was prone behind the scope of a Remington MSR sniper rifle. He smiled but did not remove his eye from the scope. "I like Thai food. You should try it sometimes, Major."

"Gives me gas."

Gibbs wore baggy cargo pants and an ivory linen shirt. His long hair was pulled back in a ponytail and secured with an elastic hair tie. "Any sign of him yet?"

"No. Is there a back entrance?"

"Yeah, but the owner keeps it locked because beggars wander in from the alley."

"Good." Knoll kept his eyes on the restaurant.

Silence filled the room as both men waited for their target to arrive. Fifteen minutes later, their patience was rewarded. "Got him. One hundred meters to your right, heading toward the café."

Gibbs moved the aim of the suppressed rifle to his right

and found Huy walking with two bodyguards, one in front and the other behind. He was surrounded by little kids, their hands out begging for money. Frowning, Gibbs took his eye off the scope. "Don't like it. What do you think?"

"I don't either. Too many kids." Knoll was quiet for a few moments as he thought. "If he follows his habit, he'll pause after he walks out of the restaurant to light a cigarette."

Nodding, Gibbs remained quiet.

After Huy entered the café, Knoll lowered the binoculars. "Stand down for a few. He'll be in there for at least an hour."

"I'm good. Don't want to miss him."

After a few quiet moments, Knoll shook his head. "I don't understand. There are jihadists in the mountains of Afghanistan who practice better phone security than this clown. When they use cell phones, they use burners, but this moron has used the same phone for a year. He doesn't even rotate where he eats or sleeps."

"Guess he feels safe," Gibbs replied. "Who knows? Makes our job easier." His right eye was still behind the scope of the rifle. "Tell me the distance again."

"Five hundred and eleven meters."

Nodding, Gibbs looked at the dials on the scope. Satisfied they were set correctly, he settled back behind it to wait.

The hour passed slowly. Knoll kept his binoculars on a beggar with long stringy hair and soiled clothing sitting next to the window of the café. The beggar stood, started to shuffle away and nodded once.

Knoll stiffened. "Show time. Bobby just signaled Huy is coming out. Get ready."

"Got him. Bodyguards are behind him."

"Sloppy. They should be in front."

Gibbs did not comment. His concentration was total as he fell into his zone. His breathing slowed and became rhythmic.

"He's walking out."

Taking an easy breath, his finger moved to the trigger of the MSR and he started to squeeze. When Huy stopped to light a cigarette, his forehead was in the crosshairs as the trigger broke. The .338 Lapua 250 grain round left the rifle with a velocity of 2,970 feet per second and a sound no louder than a book falling on a desk. The din of street traffic below masked the sound as the bullet struck its target half a second later.

Huy stumbled backward from the force of the bullet as blood and brain tissue sprayed the men behind. The body crumpled to the sidewalk as surprised diners watched him fall.

Knoll kept his eyes on the man until he was on the ground and the astonished body guards started looking for the source of the shot. A broad smile appeared. "Bingo, target down."

Gibbs' latex gloved hand patted the MSR as he stood. "I'll miss this one. Too bad we have to leave it."

Minutes later, both men were seated in a rental car heading east toward the airport.

About the Author

J.C. Fields is an award winning writer living in Battlefield, MO. He enjoys creating short stories and novels in the mystery/thriller genre, with an occasional foray into science fiction. He is a member of the Springfield Writers' Guild, and Missouri Writer's Guild. He has written and published numerous short stories and three full length novels: *The Fugitive's Trail*, published in 2015, *The Assassin's Trail* released summer of 2016, and his third novel, *The Impostor's Trail*, in July 2017.

All three are available on Amazon.com, with audio versions available on Audible.com. Visit his website at www.jcfieldsbooks.com. Follow him on Facebook at www.facebook.com/jcfieldsbooks/

Made in the USA
Coppell, TX
27 January 2023

11803971R00184